# DUELING HEARTS

"Don't you see what we are doing?" Olivia asked. "We're fighting over the countess, you and I. It's really very senseless of us to be in competition with each other, for I think we each love the countess so very much."

Antony ran one distracted hand through his hair and muttered, not quite to himself, "You're the most unpredictable young woman!"

"Does that mean you agree with me?" she asked, brightening.

She received no answer to her question, and to gain his attention, she slipped her small hand confidingly in his.

The responding pressure of his long fingers tightening about hers made her hopeful. "You *do* agree with me!"

He gave a short laugh that held little humor. "Yes, you atrocious young woman! I agree with you!"

She looked up at his handsome face, and her heart went out to him. His was not the face of a callous, unfeeling son, as she had once supposed. In his eyes she saw gentleness and affection and devotion—and she was filled with a sudden and keen desire to see his face reflect those same emotions whenever he looked upon her.

from SWEET COMPANION, by Nancy Lawrence

# WATCH FOR THESE REGENCY ROMANCES

# A MOTHER'S LOVE

*Violet Hamilton*
*Valerie King*
*Nancy Lawrence*
*Jeanne Savery*

Zebra Books
Kensington Publishing Corp.

http://www.zebrabooks.com

# CONTENTS

# CHANGE OF HEART

## Violet Hamilton

# One

"I fear your mother has taken me in dislike, Susan. I wish I knew what I have done to offend her." Lieutenant Denzil Capehart sighed, looking at his companion with admiration as they stood on the steps.

Susan was well worth admiring, her cheeks flushed and her blue eyes sparkling with indignation. Errant wisps of blond hair blew across her cheek, and she raised a hand to brush them away, unheeding of the enticing picture she created.

"I can't understand Mother. It's so unlike her to be discourteous, and in her own home, too," Susan complained. "It's not as if you haven't been polite to her or treated me with anything but the most careful propriety."

She smiled up at the young man, thinking how handsome he looked in his regimentals. Denzil Capehart was an unusually attractive young man, tall, with the narrow hips and lean muscular strength of the cavalryman, deep, dark eyes, bronzed skin and carefully styled brown hair worn in the fashionable Brutus cut. He had raised flutters in every girl of Susan's acquaintance, and she was flattered that he had singled her out for attention. He had ridden out today to secure her promise of the first and supper dances at Saturday evening's assembly in Bath, some six miles from the Woodhall manor house. Despite Mrs. Woodhall's cool reception, he had made his request, and to Susan's astonishment Mrs. Woodhall had refused on her behalf. And she had made no explanation of this strange action, causing an awkwardness that forced Denzil to cut short his visit. He had been hoping to be invited for luncheon.

"Well, I suppose I had better be on my way. I would not like your mother to have any cause for further objections to me," he offered a little wryly.

Susan waved him off with a smile, but his amiable acceptance of his rebuff did not temper her anger. She watched as he rode down the long, tree-lined drive, admiring his straight back and confident posture. Really, Denzil was the very beau ideal, whom every girl dreamt of courting. He had perfect manners and an easy, entertaining manner. She could not find a fault in him. Why her mother was behaving so abominably toward this paragon not only puzzled her, but it angered her. She determined to challenge her and find out the reason. Her chin set, Susan marched into the house, just refraining from slamming the door in a fit of temper, and crossed the hall.

Her mother could usually be found in the morning room doing her sums and correspondence at this hour. She had received Denzil in the drawing room, with great formality, an untypical action, for she was the most hospitable and welcoming of creatures, enjoying the company of most young people. Without knocking, Susan burst into the pleasant, sunny retreat, where she found her mother sitting at her desk.

Mrs. Woodhall turned, and sighed upon seeing her daughter and recognizing the defiant stance. She had been unwise to show her animosity toward that young officer so blatantly; but she could not help herself, and now she would have to explain her reason, a task she had been dreading. Susan had inherited her beauty from her mother, who still retained her trim figure and creamy complexion. Mrs. Woodhall was not much above forty years old and possessed a mature charm that had attracted many an interested eye during her years of widowhood.

"Really, Mother, you behaved hatefully to Denzil, and I want to know why," Susan charged, standing with her arms akimbo over her mother.

Oh dear, thought Margaret Woodhall. She had hoped to postpone this confrontation. She doubted that Susan was seriously interested in Lieutenant Capehart, merely one among the many officers who flocked to Susan's side at Bath's assemblies and her frequent visits to the Pump Room. Susan had a penchant for underdogs, and her mother suspected that she had acted unwisely in showing her distrust of Denzil. In time Susan would have discovered the young man's character, but Margaret had been concerned about her daughter's preference for the young officer and had behaved coolly toward him.

"I do not believe I was anything but cool, Susan, and certainly hateful could not describe my behavior," Mrs. Woodhall claimed.

"You as much as ordered him out of the house, and inferred that his attentions to me were not acceptable." Susan had calmed considerably. She was fond of her mother and, looking at her now with a grudging affection, reflected she had, perhaps, been too quick to criticize.

"Sit down, Susan, and listen to me. As you must admit I rarely interfere in your friendships. I want you to enjoy yourself, and I welcome your friends, and beaux, when they call. But my feelings about Lieutenant Capehart are not based on unreasonable fancies."

Susan sat down, still angry, but willing to entertain her mother's attempt to explain. "You are not a snob, Mother, I know. What is it about Denzil that you object to. He's certainly charming, handsome and well mannered," Susan countered.

"Yes, he is all of those things, but I believe he is also

an opportunist and incapable of fidelity and loyalty. I greatly fear he is courting you for your dowry. You are quite a catch to put it vulgarly."

"Really, Mother, I had no idea you could talk cant." Susan was amused despite herself. But she was not to be swayed from her purpose. "What reason do you have to suspect him of such devious designs. Could he not just be attracted to me?"

"Of course. You are a lovely girl, but I had a disturbing conversation with Colonel Bushnell about the young man. You must agree that his commanding officer would be in a good position to judge him," Mrs. Woodhall insisted in a quiet tone of voice.

"And what did Colonel Bushnell have to say, a prosy, stiff man if ever I met one," Susan complained, shifting uncertainly under her mother's gaze.

"He told me that Lieutenant Capehart had caused considerable trouble at the regiment's last post in Tunbridge. A merchant's daughter was involved, and also a girl of dubious reputation who worked in a local tavern. He was not specific about Lieutenant Capehart's transgressions, but he warned me that the young man was not a suitable companion for you."

"And you believed him. Really, Mother, the colonel is probably jealous of Denzil's popularity and good looks, being deficient of such attributes himself."

"Colonel Bushnell is a very worthy gentleman, if a bit dull, I agree, but I don't believe he would distort the truth."

"No, I suppose not. But perhaps the women in question were reading more into Denzil's attentions than they warranted. Girls can be so silly about men," said Susan from her vast experience.

Margaret Woodhall barely suppressed a smile. Susan liked to think of herself as experienced and adult, but she was barely nineteen and had led a most protected life. Margaret hoped she would make a sensible choice for a husband, and she was inclined not to interfere with Susan's exposure to the young men who paid her assiduous attentions; but Denzil Capehart had cleverly positioned himself as a leading contender for Susan's hand, discouraging others from entering the lists. He was charming, even to her, when he had sensed her disapproval and had adopted a puzzled air, as if he could not understand her objections to him. Still, she could not forgive him for trying to alienate her daughter. She remembered only too well another young man who had used just such tactics with her own parents.

"There is some other reason you object to Denzil, isn't there, Mother?" Susan asked, sensing that her usually tolerant mother would not be so adamant without cause. Margaret Woodhall, a widow for some twelve years, had guided her children wisely. Susan's brother, Alan, now a midshipman in the navy, had never given her a moment's worry and was an estimable young man. Susan had to concede that she and Alan were fortunate in their parent, which was why she had to take Mrs. Woodhall's objections to Denzil seriously.

"Well, yes, there is, but I had hoped not to use this argument," Mrs. Woodhall conceded, looking suddenly very sad.

"Well, what is it?"

"You don't remember your father, do you, Susan?"

"Not very well. I was only six when he died. Alan never talks about him, although he remembers more, I think."

"Gerald was charming, very attractive and persuasive. He also was in possession of a fine income. Like you with Lieutenant Capehart, I could see nothing but happiness ahead with such a man, although my parents were not as enthusiastic. I would not listen when my father insisted he was a gambler, a drunkard and a womanizer. I saw no such signs. He was too clever for that. And I talked my parents around to approving of the match. I was a stupid, credulous child who thought Gerald was a knight in shining armor. I soon learned differently. On our honeymoon I caught him in bed with a chambermaid, and worse was to follow."

Susan gasped. She had no idea. "Why have you never told me of this?"

"I wanted your memory of your father to be a happy one."

"Did Alan know?" Her brother, five years her senior, would have protected her from any distasteful picture of the father she had loved, although her memory of him was dim. As she recalled, he had not been around much, but when she had been in his company, he had entertained and charmed her.

"Yes, he did. But fortunately he was away at school during the worst of your father's excesses. We never told you how he died. In a drunken tavern brawl over a girl."

Susan could see this recollection of her marriage was painful to her mother, and Susan's warm heart was touched. She saw why her mother was so alarmed, fearing that Denzil was also a rake who would bring tragedy to whatever woman he married. But Susan was not about to judge him so harshly. She lacked her mother's insight and experience.

"But what makes you think Denzil is like Father?"

"He is the same type, my dear. There is no mistaking these rogues for all their charm, a lesson I learned to my distress. I don't like telling you tales about your father. I had hoped you would always be able to hold a fond memory of him, but I cannot let you walk the same path I did. Believe me, the young man is not what he seems. What do you know about his background?"

"Not much, except that he is an officer and a gentleman, of course."

"Does he speak of his parents?"

"No, I assume they are dead." She paused, frowning. "And I know he is pressed for money. One of his fellows told me so, but I discounted Richard's tales, thinking him jealous."

"Richard White. Yes, a zealous and rather undistinguished young man, but sensible, I think."

"A total bore, Mother, you mean." Susan laughed at her telling description of Lieutenant White.

"But not a liar or so jealous that he would traduce an innocent man, I think."

"I suppose you're right. Oh dear, I will never look upon Denzil the same way again, but he is entertaining and handsome." Susan sighed, regretting that her feelings for the young man would now be tinged with her mother's judgment.

"That's all I can ask of you, my dear. And you are so young, with many young men to choose from. I want you to be happy." Margaret was not prepared to go into any detail of the sordid and unhappy times in her own married life, but hoped that Susan's good sense and trust in her mother would lead her to the proper decision.

"Well, I can't promise to drop Denzil entirely, but you have given me a great deal to think about, not much of it reassuring. I am sorry, Mother, that you were forced to confide the story of your own wretched experience with father. It cannot have been easy for you." Susan went over to her mother and gave her a hug, hating the look of wary despair that etched Margaret's usually calm features.

"I'm sorry you are so upset, Mother, but I think you may be mistaken about Denzil. Nevertheless, I will respect your confidences about father. I've often wondered why you never married again, but I suppose you are wary of committing yourself to another man under the circumstances." Much of her anger at her mother's treatment of Denzil had vanished, although a lingering regret remained. Susan suspected her mother was suspicious of all men she had not known for years, and was only doing her duty in protecting Susan from making a disastrous choice. She should have more faith in her daughter's judgment, Susan insisted with all the arrogant self-confidence of the young.

"Perhaps I am, Susan, but please consider my objections. It was difficult for me to destroy your faith in your father, but I can only plead my concern for your future." Mrs. Woodhall looked anxiously at her daughter. She loathed giving Susan any reason to resent her or defy her. They had always enjoyed the most comfortable relationship.

"Well, you have given me a great deal to think about. And I am going for a nice brisk ride to dispel all this gloom. I will see you at luncheon." Susan dashed from the room, eager to put all unhappy thoughts behind her, leaving Margaret to sit down exhaustedly in her chair, wondering if she had been wise or fair to have told Susan her opinion of young Denzil Capehart.

Susan had been both touched and embarrassed by her mother's story, and she needed time to consider how she would deal with the sordid revelations about her father. A ride on her favorite mare, Betsy, would be a temporary distraction. She must decide what to do about Denzil. As she galloped out of the stables, without the groom who should have accompanied her, she hoped she could come to some decision. But Denzil was so attractive. How could she ignore him.

# Two

As Susan rode down the long entrance to the road bordering the Woodhall acres, she looked with lifting spirits at the green fields and meadows that stretched as far as her eye could see. She wondered how her mother had managed to hold their land so securely with a spendthrift, feckless husband. As she turned Betsy, she looked back at her home, a red brick manor house, built in Queen Anne's time, crowning a small rise, a pleasing situation which had always delighted her. Her mother's family had lived here for three hundred years, the current house built on the site after the original Tudor house had been destroyed by fire. Margaret Woodhall, an only child, had inherited it from her father a few years before her husband died. Her provident father had tied up the house and land tightly so that Gerald Woodhall had not been able to benefit from the wealth these acres had brought and continued to bring. Susan loved her home and knew she would leave it only for a man whose love and respect could insure her future happiness.

On she galloped, the stark story of her father's transgressions marring her delight in the balmy April day, unclouded by any depression except her own thoughts. In a meadow to her left, workers were planting the spring crop of grain, but their distant figures were the only sin of life in the bucolic scene. As she neared the boundaries of the Woodhall property, she entered a small copse that bordered the road to Bath, the old Roman road, which marked the edge of their land. It was dark in the woods, the sunlight not penetrating through the heavy canopy of trees now wearing their spring greenery.

Suddenly Betsy shied as a covey of birds flew from a huge fir to the right of her path. Susan pulled on the reins tightly and brought Betsy to a standstill. What had disturbed her? Then she saw the boots protruding from a clump of bushes beneath the fir tree. Jumping from her mare, she stood hesitantly, wishing now that she had allowed Jem, the groom, to accompany her. She could not ignore the boots, attached to a man who might be dead or injured. But what was he doing in this copse? How had he managed to stray from the road on the other side of the small wood? Well, she could not just leave him there. She must investigate, although she dreaded what she might find.

After tying Betsy to a nearby tree, she approached the recumbent man gingerly. He was stretched out, seemingly unconscious, dressed in smart kersey britches and a black riding coat with several capes, a youngish man with dark hair and a pale face. Then she noticed blood pouring from a wound in his shoulder. She knelt beside him and took his flaccid hand. He showed no sign that he was aware of her. Should she leave him and ride for help? She must, for she had no means of reviving him and she doubted he would be able to help himself. She had no recourse but to ride back to the stables and find some assistance. How long had he been here? He felt quite damp and cold. Susan was frightened. What if he should die while she was gone? She had no idea how severe his wound was or how he had come by it. It looked more serious than a fall. And where was his horse? She laid her hand on his forehead. It felt clammy.

Susan was not a timid girl, and believed she could manage most situations, but this was beyond her capabilities.

She must leave him and find someone to carry him up to the house. She took off her jacket and carefully bundled it under his head to protect him from the wet ground and, giving one more worried look at the unconscious stranger, mounted Betsy and rode off. She had not gone far when she met Jem, trotting along on an old hunter and looking anxiously around him.

"There you are, Miss Susan. You know you shouldn't be riding off by yourself. Your mother would rake me up and down allowing you to cavort around without me," he complained as she came up to him.

"Never mind that, Jem," Susan dismissed his complaints. "There is a strange injured man in the copse, under the big fir. I think he is badly hurt, and we must get him up to the house and send for Dr. Warden immediately."

"Lawks, who could it be?" Jem, slow-witted and far from young, looked alarmed, but he knew his duty. "Show me, Miss Susan, and then you must get Tom Evans and Bill Shore; they're planting in the forty-acre field."

Reassured now that she was not alone, Susan nodded, and led Jem back to the injured man. His situation seemed unchanged. He made no sign of awareness when Jem and Susan bent over him.

"He's a gent, he is. Wonder what he was doing here?" Jem said, his countryman's stoicism shaken by the sight. "And you shouldn't have taken off your jacket, Miss Susan. You'll catch your death, and your mother will blame me." Jem's priorities were bound up in the estate. The fate of strangers foolish enough to get themselves injured was not his business, but Miss Susan was. No nice-minded, respectable young woman should be a seein' sights like this, he thought.

"Never mind that. You stay with him, and I will get the men. And don't frighten him if he should recover his senses," she warned, feeling that if the stranger awoke and saw a man bending over him, he might try to struggle. Without another word she was back astride Betsy and galloping toward the field where she had glimpsed the farm workers.

It seemed forever before the men had marshaled their wits, secured a wagon and followed Susan back to the copse where Jem squatted patiently by the unstirring figure. But in reality they had been quite quick to answer Susan's summons. She stood over them while they gently lifted the man onto the cart lined with straw and some burlap sacks, and under Susan's admonishing eye, they carefully trundled back along the path toward the house, chivvied by Jem, who kept shaking his head at this untoward occurrence.

Finally to Susan's impatient concern they arrived, and sending Jem to fetch the doctor, Susan rushed into the house, calling for her mother. The Woodhall butler, Jennings, hearing the disturbance, came from the servants' quarters, alarmed to see Miss Susan, jacketless and disheveled, trying to explain what had happened to Mrs. Woodhall, who had emerged from the morning room, aghast that Susan might have suffered some mishap.

However, Margaret Woodhall quickly restored order. Maids were summoned to ready a room, and the stranger was carried up the broad stairs to the upper floor, attended by Margaret and Susan.

Once the injured man was settled on the bed, Margaret took charge, banishing Susan from the room. "We must undress him and get him ready for the doctor. This is no sight for you, Susan," her mother ordered in a voice that brooked no refusal. "Poor boy, I wonder what happened to him."

Susan, much as she wanted to stay, realized she had no experience in nursing and would only be a hindrance. She was dispatched to wait for Dr. Warden. The minutes ticked slowly by. Several times she crept upstairs and waited outside the door of the stranger's room, but could hear no sounds. She was quite unnerved to see Millie, one of the maids, scurrying away with a bowl of bloody water.

Finally Dr. Warden arrived, puffing slightly as he hurried into the hall to be greeted by Susan. Susan had known him all her life, although she had been spared any serious illness. But he had set her brother's broken collarbone when Alan had fallen from a tree, and treated her during a bout of influenza.

"What's all this, my dear? A mysterious, wounded man found on the estate? I couldn't get much sense from the groom you sent," he queried as they walked upstairs.

"I found him, Dr. Warden, in the copse near the Bath road. He was unconscious with blood coming from his shoulder. I think he's in a grave condition," she reported somberly.

"Horrid for you, but I know you acted promptly and did not give way to hysterics." Dr. Warden looked at her with approval. He was a kindly, portly man, who made an effort to gain his patients' confidence and reassured them as much by his manner as by his treatment.

"I hope so. Go right in. Mother says I cannot stay."

"Quite rightly. We will soon put the man to rights, I hope."

Dr. Warden always behaved as if death was unthinkable, although he had presided over many tragic victims of disease and accidents. Somewhat comforted by his presence, Susan drifted down the hall to her own bedchambers, hoping her mother would soon come with news. The disaster had driven all thoughts of Denzil from her mind. A compassionate girl, Susan had rarely met with tragedy, and she was apprehensive as well as puzzled by what had happened to the stranger.

It seemed a long time until she heard her mother and

Dr. Warden coming from the patient's room. She met them in the hall.

"What is happening, Mother, Dr. Warden? Please tell me."

Mrs. Woodhall looked worried and signaled to the doctor.

"The young man was shot," he explained. "I removed a bullet from his shoulder. It could have been a poacher, but it seems unlikely in the middle of the day on a well-traveled highway. He stood the removal of the bullet well, recovered consciousness, and muttered a bit, but then fell asleep from the laudanum I gave him for the pain. With rest and good nursing, which I know he will receive at your mother's hands, he should make a good recovery. But this incident will have to be reported to the authorities. And we must discover who he is and notify his family."

"I removed some papers from his coat. No doubt they will give us the necessary information," Mrs. Woodhall said. "Now, Dr. Warden, you must have some refreshment. Or can you stay for luncheon?"

"I will not say no to a glass, but I must be off shortly and check on Tom Evans' wife. She is expecting a new baby any hour."

Mrs. Woodhall and Susan waved off the doctor after his brief respite and then went into luncheon.

"I don't feel much like eating, Mother."

"No, neither do I, but we must keep up our strength. This is a dreadful affair. Who could have shot the gentleman as he went about his business on a well-traveled road?" Mrs. Woodhall wondered as she resolutely cut a lamb cutlet. Then, seeing Susan's pale, distressed face, she continued gently. "You were very brave, Susan. I am proud of you."

"Jem and the men did all that was necessary. I just stood there dithering."

"At least you did not go into a faint or have hysterics. Many girls would have."

"Will he recover, Mother?"

"I think so. He's young and healthy, seems to have been in a tropical clime recently. He's quite tanned and fit. I wonder where he was going. I suppose into Bath. We will have to go through those papers and find out the direction of his family. They must be notified as soon as possible. I know how I would feel if some mischance happened to Alan."

"Yes, fortunately Alan seems merry as a gig from his last letter. He's in Jamaica now, isn't he?" Susan was eager to bring the conversation around to safe, everyday topics.

"Yes, and I fear it will be a long time until we see him again." Mrs. Woodhall worried about her scapegrace son, although she knew he was enjoying his naval duties, and there was no longer the threat from French warships. Waterloo was two years behind them, thank goodness.

"Is someone watching over the stranger now?"

"Yes, Millie, who has had plenty of experience, what with her large brood of sisters and brothers and a father who always gets the worst of it in some brawl. She will call me if the young man's condition changes."

After the meal the mother and daughter adjourned to the morning room, where Mrs. Woodhall gingerly went through the papers she had extracted from his clothes. She disliked prying into his personal business, but she must find his name and an address where his family could be contacted. Susan watched impatiently as her mother deciphered some letters and then gave a gasp of surprise.

"There is a letter here from the Earl of Edgebury. It appears he had invited the young man to visit him. Our stranger is Stephen Venner, and has recently landed in England from several years in India."

"The Earl of Edgebury? Doesn't he live on the other side of Bath?" Susan asked, agog.

"Yes, Edgebury Hall is about ten miles from Bath to the north I believe, I have never met the earl. I believe my father knew his father years ago. He was Lord Lieutenant of the county, and father was a magistrate. But we have never been on calling terms. The current earl was an officer in the army, and fought with Wellington, I heard."

Susan, feeling she was in the midst of an exciting drama, wanted to know more. Here was a mystery disturbing the even tenor of her everyday life, and the young man upstairs was the key to the whole affair.

"Do you think he is a relative of the earl, Mother?"

"He may be. He appears to be a gentleman. Well, I will write directly and send one of the men with a message to the earl. There is no mention in these papers of any family, poor boy. And there is a considerable sum of money, which I will keep safe for him. I can't understand what he was doing riding alone without luggage or a man. Very odd."

"Yes, I wondered about that, too. And where is his horse?"

Mrs. Woodhall smiled. Susan, a passionate rider, was always concerned about horses. "Perhaps the horse will turn up. Anyway, I must send off a message to the earl right away. He will be expecting the young man and concerned, I know."

Susan agreed and left her mother to the unhappy task of apprising the earl of Stephen Venner's accident and whereabouts. Wandering into the garden for a breath of air, she felt restless and on edge. The thought of rogues waiting to ambush some innocent traveler so near their grounds worried her. There had never been any incident of robbery or mayhem so close to home. The worst trouble she had seen had come from farm hands fighting in taverns after too many ales. People she knew did not get shot as they were attending to their affairs. Could this have been a vagrant rogue, hoping to waylay an innocent rider, or some highwayman. If so, why hadn't the thief stopped to rob Stephen Venner? It was not only terrifying but mysterious, Susan thought. She looked about the well-tended garden, filled with daffodils waving brightly in the sunshine. She had always felt so safe and secure here. Now a man had been attacked almost on her doorstep, a sobering thought.

Huddling in her shawl against the light wind that had risen, she realized she was shivering, and not from the elements, but from the thought of the heinous crime committed so near to her beloved home. But Susan reminded herself she was not a timid, vaporing miss and soon gathered herself together. Whoever had attacked Stephen Venner would be caught and punished. The Earl of Edgebury, a man of substance and importance, would see to it. In the meantime, she would go out to the stables and see if there was any news of Mr. Venner's horse or if Jem had any other information that might shed some light on this peculiar accident.

# *Three*

Under Margaret Woodhall's careful nursing, aided by the estimable Millie, Stephen Venner slowly recovered from his wound. Upon regaining consciousness, he had seemed puzzled and then restless, not understanding what had happened to him. Margaret soothed him by giving a brief explanation as to his whereabouts. She did not want to excite him with questions that would bring on a fever. Within two days of the accident—if that was what it was, and Margaret had doubts—he was sitting up and able to take some nourishment. Seeing his healthy color, and after consulting with Dr. Warden, who had called several times to check on the invalid, she felt she must find some answers to this mystery.

"Mr. Venner, I do not wish to pry into your affairs, but I feel I must ask you a bit about your accident," she said, watching him carefully as he spooned up some broth.

"Not at all, Mrs. Woodhall. You have been so kind, to take in a stranger, and nurse him so carefully. I will always be indebted to you." Stephen Venner smiled at her, approving of her calm and gentle demeanor. She was obviously a woman of character and compassion. Having been orphaned at an early age, he responded gratefully to her motherly concern.

"Well, we have been wondering what you were doing alone on that road where you were attacked. Before you explain, let me tell you that I found some papers in your jacket that told me your name and of your connection with the Earl of Edgebury. I assume you were on your way to visit him. I have sent a message to the earl, letting him know of your whereabouts and accident. I do hope that was not presumptuous of me."

"Of course not. I have been worried about that, for my absence must have appeared most cavalier to the earl. And I would crave your further indulgence. My man is at the Royal York in Bath awaiting my arrival. He must have given me up for dead. Coats has been with me for some months and serves as a valet and factotum. Could you possibly send word to him, too, if that is not too much trouble?"

"Certainly. I rather thought you must have had some servant with you. But why did he not come to your aid?" Margaret realized she was behaving like a busybody and her patient might take offense, but the nature of his attack had aroused not only her curiosity, but her suspicions. If there was some deranged or vindictive rogue lingering around the estate, she had a right to know. She had Susan's safety to think of, her daughter roaming daily about their land on her mare.

"I behaved foolishly. I suppose I shall have to admit my carelessness, and after years in India, I should have known better. Somehow I thought England was a tranquil spot, with no danger threatening. After landing at Portsmouth, I spent some time in London, and then when the earl invited me down here in response to a letter I sent him, I packed up and started off. It was a relief to be in the country after the confusion of the city, where I felt a bit at sea, having been abroad so long, and with no acquaintances in the city."

"Yes, I understand," Margaret encouraged him. She was beginning to see that the young man felt isolated and eager to meet friends and whatever family remained to him.

"Once out on the road, I disliked being cooped up in the coach, so I sent Coats on ahead to secure rooms in Bath aboard the coach with my luggage, and I decided to ride. I wanted a chance to enjoy the spring. It's so wonderful to be away from the torrid heat of India, out in this English spring that I have only dreamt about," he confided. "Foolish, I suppose."

"Not at all. Were you in India long?"

"Seven years. My parents died there not long after I arrived from school to join them. My father was with the East India Company, and I stayed on with it, to make my fortune." He looked a bit abashed at this confession.

Yearning to know if he had accomplished this, Margaret bit her tongue. Obviously he had done well or he would not be journeying with man and carriage to stay at the Royal York, Bath's most elegant hostelry.

"And I was trotting along enjoying the sunshine, the trees and green meadows when suddenly this shot came from a clump of trees to the right of the road. My horse swerved and bolted from the road. I managed to hang on for a bit, but must have fallen off finally and landed where your daughter found me."

Margaret had told him a little of the circumstances that had brought him to her home, Combe Manor.

"Has my horse turned up?" Stephen asked. "I would not like to lose him."

"Yes, Susan was most concerned and sent the men out to look for him. He was grazing in the Long acre field some miles from the house. He is now being safely quartered in our stable."

"That's a relief. I certainly owe you a huge debt for all you have done, taking in a stranger and treating him with such kindness. Have you heard from the Earl of Edgebury? He's my cousin." Stephen Venner gave this information shyly, almost as if he were ashamed to claim any relationship with such an august personage.

"Yes, he wrote a very fulsome reply to my message. He seems to be laid up with some minor ailment, but asked if he could visit you as soon as he was well. I wrote back and told him you were recovering well and we would take the best possible care of you until his arrival."

Margaret had a great deal more she wanted to ask the young man, but could see he was tiring. She whisked away his tray and placed it on a nearby table. Then she straightened his coverlet and plumped up his pillows.

"Now, you must get some rest, and later I will send in my daughter Susan to keep you company. She will be most interested to meet you. She feels she has an investment in your health, having been your rescuer."

"Yes, I must thank her," he said and smiled weakly, ashamed to admit that Margaret's questions and his attempt to answer them had tired him. Also he had a great deal to puzzle and worry him. Mrs. Woodhall had offered no explanation of why he had been attacked or asked him what he thought of the wretched business. He was grateful for that as he felt tired and unable to cope with the mystery of it. His eyelids drooped, and he barely heard her tiptoe from the room.

Susan shared her mother's curiosity about their unexpected guest. She had seen nothing of him during the two days of his convalescence, but her mother suggested she pay him a visit when he recovered from his afternoon rest. Then Margaret remembered that today was Saturday, the date of the Bath assembly that had caused the difficulty with her daughter over Denzil Capehart's visit. She hesitated to broach the subject, but felt that Susan was due some explanation.

"I won't be able to accompany you to the assembly this evening, Susan. I don't like to leave Mr. Venner alone with Millie. Not that she isn't competent, but it would worry me."

"I quite understand, Mother." In truth, with all the excitement of Stephen Venner's accident, Susan had forgotten the assembly.

"I suppose I could prevail on Sir Edmund and Lady French to take you. They will certainly be attending with Matilda."

"Don't bother. There will be other assemblies. I would much rather quiz Mr. Venner."

A bit surprised at Susan's reaction, Mrs. Woodhall hesitated. But she was too relieved by Susan's indifference at missing the chance to see Denzil Capehart again that she did not pursue the matter. She only warned Susan not to tire their patient, and then told her a bit about his circumstances.

"Quite a mystery man. Do you think he is the earl's long-lost heir?" Susan asked.

"I don't know about that, but the earl seemed very concerned about him and will be calling here after he recovers from some slight indisposition."

"Who is the earl's heir?"

"I have no idea. I only know he is not married. I really know little about him, except that he fought in the late war, had quite an admirable record, I believe. But that's all gossip. He must be in his late forties, still time to marry and have a son. At least that is what the local on dit is. I'm afraid I don't pay much heed to the tea table rumor mongering."

"Well, I am full of unseemly curiosity about Mr. Venner and intend to get him to reveal all his secrets," Susan explained merrily, finding the current state of affairs an exciting departure from her usually routine days. She had enjoyed her year at home after her school days in Cheltenham, but occasionally found the county society dull. Despite her popularity with the local beaux, Susan had no wish to give up her comfortable home for an establishment of her own yet.

"Well, don't badger the young man or weary him with unwelcome questions." Margaret Woodhall smiled. She often worried that Susan might find life at Combe Manor monotonous, although her daughter appeared to enjoy country affairs and was content with their rather mundane existence. Margaret had not felt able to take her to London for her come-out, pleading the expense and the time away from her estate duties, although she had an efficient agent. She felt a bit guilty about her lapse. Susan deserved a season and an opportunity to meet eligible young men. She might then not be so attracted to dubious types like that young officer. But Margaret confided none of her doubts to her daughter. They had been within a whisker of arguing over Lieutenant Capehart, a situation Margaret hoped to avoid in the future.

"I promise to behave with every consideration, Mother. And now I will take some exercise, for the afternoon promises to be fair," Susan said and left for one of her interminable rides.

"Do be careful, Susan, and take Jem, for whoever attacked Mr. Venner might still be loitering in the neighborhood."

"If he's not a frightened poacher, he would have had the sense to flee from the scene, I should think. Somehow I don't think it was a poacher, and I wonder who wishes the mysterious Mr. Venner harm," Susan informed her mother, who only nodded and held her tongue. The whole affair worried her, for like her daughter, she did not believe in the convenient poacher solution.

Susan, neatly dressed in a tight fitting blue linen riding habit, and a dashing hussar's hat, trotted sedately from the stable yard trailed by a grumbling Jem, who had hoped to put his feet up and have a little kip during the warm afternoon.

Determined to take another look at the scene of the crime, as she put it, Susan galloped off toward the copse to Jem's dismay. Drat it, he thought, Miss Susan was up to some monkeyshines.

As they approached the path leading to the small woods where Susan had discovered the wounded Mr. Venner, she was surprised to see a horseman approaching from the road and riding rapidly through the trees. She pulled up when she recognized Denzil Capehart.

"Well met, Susan. I was hoping to see you and was hesitant about calling at the manor," Denzil greeted her, thinking what a delightful picture she made, her cheeks tinged with pink and her blue eyes aglow from her exercise. It really wasn't fair that she was so beautiful and so well dowered. She fancied him, too, and he was prepared to take advantage of that. It was time he found a well-to-do wife. His affairs were quite precarious, and if he could become engaged to Susan, prosy Colonel Bushnell might look upon him with more favor.

Susan reined in her mare, cocking her head and looking at Denzil in a friendly manner.

"That might not have been a good idea," she agreed. "Here, let us dismount. Jem can tie the horses and I will explain."

Denzil nodded and jumped from his horse smoothly, coming to Susan's side to assist her. If his clasp verged on the familiar, Susan ignored it. Jem, securing both horses, stood stubbornly by, keeping an eye on the proceedings. He was impressed with Denzil's regimentals, and conceded that the young buck had a good seat on a horse, but he was a mingy tipper and had an off-hand manner which did not endear him to the stable hands. Jem hoped Miss Susan was not considering him as a husband. The officer had a shifty eye, and Jem had heard down at the Two Bulls that he was quite a man for the ladies, and not just the respectable ones. Jem had put Susan up on her first pony and was very fond of her. He stood just out of earshot, but with a wary eye on the pair.

Susan indicated a fallen tree as a convenient perch, and Denzil sat as close to her as possible.

"Well, what is this occurrence that would make it inconvenient for me to call? I had hoped your mother would have recovered from her ill temper."

Susan, quick to rise to her mother's defense, did not take kindly to this criticism. "It was not ill temper, Denzil. Mother naturally is concerned about my choice of companions." Susan looked quite severe, and Denzil hurried to retrieve his mistake.

"And quite right, too. I only wish she had not taken me in dislike."

"You remind her of an unfortunate experience in her own girlhood, but enough of that. I have quite a budget of news."

Though Denzil wondered what he had to do with Mrs. Woodhall's past, he wisely kept his surmising to himself. "And what is that?"

"After you left the other day, I rode out in this direction and found a wounded man in the copse. Some intruder had shot him. He is recovering now, but he was badly hurt, lost a lot of blood."

"And you took him in?" Denzil sounded disturbed.

"Of course. It turns out he was on his way to Bath, had sent his man and coach on to the Royal York. He has just returned from India. He was on his way to visit his cousin, the Earl of Edgebury," Susan reported.

Denzil barely suppressed a curse. He didn't like the sound of this stranger who was allied to the eminent earl. He could be a dangerous rival. And girls were so credulous and foolish; Susan had probably dreamed up all sorts of romantic fancies about the chap.

"What's he like?"

"Aside from being an obvious gentleman, I don't know. He has been too ill for me to meet him yet, although I have been asked to visit him later today. At first glance he appeared very passable."

Denzil was not happy over this sudden arrival of a possible obstacle to his plans. However, he was not so stupid as to admit it. Still, a little show of jealousy should not come amiss.

"I hope he's an ugly fellow with no address," he countered, implying a certain possessiveness that Susan found not to her taste.

"Mother says he is quite nice, rather shy, and very grateful for all her attention and care."

Noting the reproof in her voice, Denzil decided he had gone far enough. "What I really came to see you about was tonight's assembly. You have not forgotten I asked you for two dances, I hope," he said avoiding the fact that her mother had already refused him those dances.

"Oh, Denzil, I will not be attending the assembly. Mother feels she cannot leave Mr. Venner to her maid's care."

"Well, surely you could prevail on someone to chaperone you. I will be devastated to miss you." He adopted a crestfallen air.

"Don't be silly. There will be lots of attractive girls at the assembly. You will hardly notice my absence." Susan was not sure she welcomed Denzil's concentration on her. He was attractive and entertaining, but she was far from ready to commit herself to the young officer.

"But not like you, Susan," he whispered. Damn it, if that surly groom were not hovering, he would give some token of his regard, a resounding kiss.

As if Jem sensed that matters were approaching an undesirable climax, he spoke up. "It's getting late, Miss Susan. Your mother will be worried."

"Of course, Jem. I must say goodbye, Denzil. I am sorry about tonight, but there will be other assemblies." And Susan rose, rather relieved. Denzil was becoming demanding.

"I will prop myself against the wall and regard all possible partners with disfavor, mourning my loss," Denzil quipped, determined not to lose ground with this maddening female. "I will call later in the week and hope to meet this mystery man. Do you think your mother will receive me?" he asked with real concern.

"Of course. Just be on your best behavior. And I will enjoy a visit. For now goodbye." Susan allowed Denzil to help her mount and trotted off, leaving her disconsolate suitor, if that was what he was, behind. He stared after her, an angry scowl darkening his face. He had lost some influence with the delectable Miss Woodhall, and that would not be countenanced. Somehow he must regain her interest, and smugly he reminded himself that few females could withstand his cajolery when he put his mind to it.

# *Four*

While she was dressing in a crisp, new sprigged muslin gown after her ride and bath, Susan wondered what she would find to say to Stephen Venner. Her mother approved of him, that was obvious. Susan herself was inclined to view him as a man of mystery, intriguing but possibly an opportunist. Then she laughed. He could hardly have arranged to have himself shot just to gain entree into Combe Manor. And there was his connection with the Earl of Edgebury. This seemed to guarantee his bona fides with her mother, but Susan was not convinced. She knew he had spent seven years in India, and she viewed that dark continent with suspicion. Well, she would play the inquisitor.

But when she knocked for admittance and entered the patient's chamber, she was surprised to find a tanned young man with a shock of brown hair and kind eyes who greeted her with a shy smile. He looked amazingly healthy despite the sling around his neck.

"How do you do, Mr. Venner. I am Susan Woodhall."

"The young lady who rescued me, I understand. Do sit down. Your mother insists I spend another day or so in bed, but I feel quite well."

Susan drew up a chair to the side of the bed and looked at him with interest. "You had better do what she says. She's usually right, I have discovered to my chagrin."

"She's a lovely woman, so kind-hearted and hospitable."

"She has been very concerned that you suffered this attack just yards from our property."

"You must have been appalled to discover me laid out in your woods."

"I was, although all I really saw of you was your boots. I am happy to have a better view now," she said with a cheeky grin.

He raised his eyebrows but made no answer. Susan was at somewhat of a loss. She wanted to quiz him about the attack and his presence on the road, but somehow she felt he would not welcome questions of a personal nature.

"I understand you have just recently arrived in England?" she offered, hoping to learn more.

"Yes, and if I had not wanted to sample an English spring, I might have avoided being shot. I should probably have stayed in the coach and ridden into Bath."

"Mother told me you were on your way to visit the Earl of Edgebury." Susan introduced the topic that fascinated her.

"Yes. He is my only relative. My parents died in India, and I have no brothers, sisters or other kin, as far as I know."

"You will be anxious to see him. I heard that he was not feeling well and wondered when he would appear."

"Mrs. Woodhall tells me she had a very cordial letter from him. I hate imposing on you all until I can remove to the Royal York, but your mother was quite fierce when I suggested leaving. I hope she has notified my man, who must be concerned at my absence."

"I am sure she has, but she will not want you to leave until you are quite recovered. How remiss of me. I have not asked you how you feel."

"Restless and eager to be about my business." Then feeling that perhaps he was being ungracious, Stephen hurried to reassure her. "Of course, I am being thoroughly spoiled. I was fortunate to land in such pleasant surroundings and with such a devoted nurse."

Susan waved away this compliment as of no importance. "Tell me about India. It sounds so strange and romantic."

"Sorry to disillusion you, but mostly it's hot, dirty and disease-ridden. I was most happy to leave it."

"Will you return?" Susan asked, and then blushed. She was being much too inquisitive. "Not that it is any of my business."

"I certainly hope to stay in England, but it all depends on my future."

"Are you one of those nabobs, richer than Croesus?" Susan looked guileless, but felt she was really behaving in an outrageous manner. "Pardon me. I have an insatiable curiosity. We so rarely have visitors and none from abroad."

He smiled and looked at her kindly. "Not at all. You deserve some answers. No, I don't want to return to India, and I have enough funds to keep me in comfort."

"I suppose you made a fortune with the East India Company. And you lived in a palace, comported with rajahs and had rafts of servants. It must have been thrilling."

"Not quite. Mostly a lot of hard work and traveling about to secure the tea and spices."

"Were you there when the Duke of Wellington was?" Susan found the hero of Waterloo a fascinating figure and would have loved to have met the Iron Duke.

"Yes. Of course, he was not the duke then, just a competent military commander named Wellesley." Stephen appeared perfectly content to answer all her questions, but Susan felt she had stayed long enough, mindful of her mother's warning not to tire him.

"Is there anything I can get you? A glass of barley water, perhaps?" She indicated the jug standing on the dresser.

"I'd really like some Madeira, but my careful nurse refuses. I'm not too fond of barley water."

"I will use my influence. And I do hope you will be up and about soon. But I must leave you now."

"Oh, don't go. It's so boring lying here, and I am not a bit tired. If you will stay, I will tell you all about the Maharajah of Jaipur and his carved pink city," he coaxed.

Susan, intrigued and quite relaxed now, agreed, and Stephen entertained her for quite another half an hour with tales of India. She would have stayed much longer, her suspicions about this strange young man lulled, if her mother had not interrupted.

Margaret Woodhall slipped into the room and smiled at the two chatting away as if they were old friends, pleased to see that Susan was getting along famously with her patient.

"Well, Stephen, you seem to be in good form. I hope Susan has not been exhausting you with questions. She can be quite tiring."

"Not at all. I feel wonderful, much better for her visit. And I want to get up. Surely it would not hurt me to get outside for a bit. It looks a lovely day," he cajoled. Then, remembering. "Has my man arrived?"

"Yes, he just came with your luggage and the coach and horses. He will be up shortly when he has seen to them."

"Good. He can help me dress and shave me. I feel very bristly," Stephen insisted, running a hand over his raspy cheeks.

"Maybe tomorrow, if Dr. Warden agrees." Mrs. Woodhall nodded. She was not eager to let Stephen out of her hands.

"If I remain here like a docile patient today and Miss Susan promises to visit me again, I promise not to fuss. You have been so good to me." Stephen obviously enjoyed Margaret Woodhall's ministrations, and Susan thought he yearned for some maternal attention. She rose reluctantly before her mother could chide her, but promised to return.

"Thank you for relieving the tedium of my convalescence. I am sure you have much more interesting affairs to see to," Stephen said, watching her rather anxiously.

"Not at all. It was great fun hearing about India and your adventures. I will return for a further installment," she promised and slipped from the room.

She had found her interview with the mysterious Stephen Venner intriguing, not at all what she had expected. He had not tried to flirt with her or pay her extravagant compliments, quite a change from most young men who pursued her. Whether she found this disappointing or not, she could not decide, but it was a novel experience. What Susan did not understand was Stephen's maturity. He had none of the callow bumptiousness of most of the officers she had met or the self-absorption and conceit of her country beaux. Not that he was a beau, of course, just a young man who had suffered an unwarranted attack and fallen into her mother's kind hands, for which he seemed very grateful. And she had not had the opportunity to ask him what puzzled her. Did he have any enemies? Because Susan did not believe it was a highwayman's or poacher's shot that had wounded him. Just why she was so sure of that, she did not know, but she sensed there was a real mystery here and one she determined to solve.

She retired to her bedroom, her brow furrowed in thought. Perhaps when the earl arrived she would learn some of the answers to the puzzle of Stephen Venner. But on first acquaintance she decided she liked him. He was so different from the young men who formed her circle. He had none of the assurance or address of Denzil Capehart, for example, but Susan felt instinctively he had much more character than that young man, even if he lacked Denzil's practiced charm. She took up her book, wondering idly if Denzil would indeed be propping up the wall at tonight's assembly. Somehow his flattering assurances that he would be pining for her company lacked sincerity. Men were a bother, both Stephen and Denzil, and she would forget them both for the moment and enjoy instead the trials of Elizabeth Bennett in Miss Austen's latest novel, a heroine who had her own problems in reading the character of the men in her life.

On her way down to dinner, Susan thought she might just pay a brief visit to their patient, but as she neared his door at the end of the hall, she saw a sober, suited man with a tray in his hands about to enter Stephen Venner's room. He did not see her, and she decided she would postpone her call. As she and her mother ate their roast chicken, Susan asked about the newly arrived manservant.

"What is Mr. Venner's valet like? I just glimpsed him in the hall, taking in dinner, I presume. I do wish Mr. Venner could join us for meals."

"Yes, it would be quite agreeable for you to have a nice young man to entertain you at the table. I'm afraid I have no romantic tales of foreign parts to amuse you," her mother answered, feeling again that Susan must find life at Combe Manor rather dull with only her mother for company.

"Don't be a pea goose, Mother. I love being home with you, and believe me your conversation is much more entertaining than Miss Prody's." She was referring to the estimable if overly proper headmistress of the seminary at which she had received her education.

"Well, that's a relief. On the few occasions I talked with Miss Prody, I found her worthy but lacking in any sense of humor, probably a necessary quality in a schoolmistress. But about Stephen's man, he appears to be also proper and worthy, if not very forthcoming. Coats did say that be had not been in India with Stephen, but had entered his employ in London."

"Oh dear, how unfortunate. I intended to ply him with questions about Mr. Venner's past on the dark continent. How much more exciting if his servant had been a turbaned Sikh with a dagger at his waist."

"Really, Susan. I suspect that Miss Prody was delinquent in teaching you geography."

"Not at all, we had daily sessions with the globe, as she called it. Though I admit that many of my ideas about India come from rather lurid novels."

"My father would never allow me to read novels, said they gave me unwholesome ideas. I have been too indulgent with you, I suspect," Margaret Woodhall teased. "Who knows what maggots you have in your mind."

"Not maggots but a passionate desire to learn more about our patient. I am convinced Stephen Venner was attacked by some unknown enemy. And the villain might try again," Susan explained.

"What a horrid idea. I hope you are wrong, but I have had my doubts about this troubling incident and hope that the earl when he appears may be able to tell us more."

"I confess I find the idea of the earl intimidating, but I promise to behave with all circumspection. I wonder what he is like?"

"We will find out soon. I had a letter today informing me he expects to arrive in Bath on Monday, two days from now, and that he will put up at the Royal York, not wanting to impose on us. I imagine he will ride out soon after to inquire about Stephen.

"That gives me forty-eight hours to solve the mystery of Mr. Venner's assailant," Susan said with a blithe air that her mother found worrying. Who knew what her reckless daughter would discover and if it could be dangerous? She tried to dissuade her from taking any foolish action, but although Susan reassured her, Margaret was not convinced.

At least, she comforted herself, the startling arrival of Stephen Venner had distracted Susan from Denzil Capehart, unless Susan was masking her real interest in the officer because she knew her mother disapproved. Margaret had feared her objections to Lieutenant Capehart might have caused a rift between them, but Susan was not a girl to sulk or brood. Neither was she very adept at hiding her feelings. There had always been trust and respect as well as affection between them, and Margaret dreaded the meretricious lieutenant spoiling their relationship. If Stephen Venner's opportune arrival kept Susan from seeing much of Denzil Capehart, she would keep him here as long as possible. Certainly his wound would offer a good excuse. And Margaret liked the young man who was modest, respectful and well-connected. Mothers had to consider these factors when the future happiness of a loved daughter was at stake. Margaret had been genuinely concerned by Colonel Bushnell's warning about his young officer, and her own reactions, tempered by her experience, had forced her to confide the tawdry tale of her marriage to her daughter. Much as she had loathed exposing her late husband's flawed character and wounding behavior to his daughter, she had felt it the only way to make Susan take another look at her admirer.

After Susan left her to pay another visit to Mr. Venner, Margaret Woodhall again wondered if she had been right to lay the burden of her own unhappy married life on Susan's shoulders. Wanting to protect her daughter, she had antagonized her. Fortunately, Stephen Venner had distracted her. Obviously her interest in Denzil Capehart had not gone too deep. For that Margaret could only hope the risk she had taken would not prove damaging.

# *Five*

The Earl of Edgebury arrived at the Royal York in Bath late on Sunday evening accompanied by a crested coach, two outriders, a manservant and his agent, Nigel Thorndyke. He was received with obsequious attention by the inn's host and bowed into a private parlor. The landlord reported that he had also reserved two of his best bedchambers for the earl.

It had not been an arduous journey, for Edgebury Hall lay just ten miles from Bath. However, the earl seldom visited the popular spa, preferring his own ten thousand acres. He had spent the major part of his life in the army, which included postings to the West Indies, Canada and the Peninsula during the late war against Napoleon. Travel held little appeal for him, and he rarely left his home except for brief visits to London.

He was very anxious to meet Stephen Venner. The young man was descended from his grandfather's favorite sister, and he had heard commendable reports of Stephen's career in India. Unfortunately, due to his cousin's absence in India and his own army career, he had never met the young man. He did not know what to expect, and this troubling business of the attack on Stephen added to his anxieties. Well, he knew there was no point in worrying until he had seen the fellow, but a great deal rested on this meeting.

A lavish supper of roasted pigeon, rare beef, several

removes and an exceptional claret raised his spirits. He was joined in this meal by his agent, Nigel Thorndyke, who had insisted upon accompanying him. He had seen no need for this, but recognizing Nigel's purpose and being an obliging employer, he had agreed. Naturally, Nigel was concerned. He understood the agent would be interested in a young man who might inherit the earl's estate. Not that the earl had informed Nigel that Stephen Venner was his heir, but he might have divined the situation. Godfrey St. John Montgomery, the Earl of Edgebury, was neither a snob nor a peer who liked flattery. He only demanded that those who served him were capable and honest. He rarely suspected his fellows of devious or self-serving actions, and if proved wrong, he was competent to deal with the situation. On the whole he had found Nigel diligent and trustworthy, and the earl was not often mistaken in his judgments.

He looked across the table at Nigel, a pleasant-appearing man of some thirty years with fair hair, pale blue eyes and a bland, smooth face that showed little emotion. Nigel had been of great assistance to the earl. Although the earl took an avid interest in his estate, he had little experience of agricultural matters. But his long and distinguished army career had taught him how to deal with people. He only wished Nigel was more forthcoming. He was well paid, worked hard and was respectful. The earl expected service, and he received it from Nigel.

If Nigel was curious about what Stephen Venner's arrival meant to him and his position, he was too astute to show it. But he did wonder about the strange accident that had prevented the young man's arrival at Edgebury Hall.

"What do you think, sir, about the attack on your relative?" Nigel asked, toying with his wineglass as the two sat over dinner in the private parlor.

"Most peculiar. I suppose it could have been a stray

bullet from a poacher who, frightened, ran away, or perhaps an attack by a highwayman. But this is a quiet county on the whole. It's very mysterious."

"Would he have been carrying a great deal of money?"

"Perhaps. I think he did quite well in India. Worked for John Company, and those chaps usually manage to amass a comfortable income. But I don't think he was robbed. This Mrs. Woodhall, who took him in, made no mention of robbery. No good surmising until I meet the young man."

With difficulty Nigel did not pursue the question. Much as he wanted to learn more about this Venner and the earl's intentions, he was wise enough to know his employer would not welcome an inquisition. Nigel knew he was fortunate to have secured this lucrative post and had no intentions of irritating the earl. He was a tolerant employer, but Nigel sensed he was a man who would not take kindly to any interference in his personal affairs.

The earl, having a good idea of Nigel's thoughts, smiled at him. "You needn't worry, Nigel. His arrival will not affect your situation. I intend to remain at the helm for some years yet."

"Of course, sir. I mean no disrespect." Nigel hastened to reassure the earl.

Indeed, his employer, still a relatively young man, would be in control for many years, and if Nigel played his cards well, so would he. Certainly the earl looked in his prime. Tall, with a cavalryman's lean strength and narrow hips, he was the picture of health. The earl did not indulge in heavy drinking or any of the other vices enjoyed by so many aristocrats. His dark hair showed only a trace of gray which added to his distinction, and his brown eyes were bright. Nigel had often wondered why the earl was not married. Surely he would prefer to leave his wealth and estate to a son rather than to some unknown relation. Certainly he would have no difficulty in finding an eligible wife. His assets and his demeanor were both considerable. But Nigel did not probe. They did not have that kind of a relationship.

"Well, it's getting late, and I need some sleep. Tomorrow we will visit this Combe Manor and meet Stephen Venner. It should be an interesting session. I know very little about the young man." The earl rose, signifying that there was no more to be said, and Nigel had no recourse but to seek his own bed. But first he thought he would visit the private bar. The landlord might be able to answer some of his questions.

Soon after breakfast the next morning, the earl ordered his coach and, signaling that Nigel might accompany him, set off for the Woodhalls's, a journey of less than an hour. He said little on the trip besides making some flattering comments on the countryside. He had a great deal to think about.

At Combe Manor Stephen summoned his valet and requested that he assist him to dress. He was not going to receive the earl in his bed. He felt uncommonly well, his wound barely troubling him. Dressed neatly in Hessians, cream britches and a fine-fitting coat of black superfine, he joined Mrs. Woodhall and Susan in the morning room, where he was received with remonstrances.

"You really should not be up yet, Stephen," Margaret said, turning from her desk when he entered the room.

"I feel very fit. This sling is a nuisance, but I know you will insist on my wearing it. That's all the concession I intend to make." He smiled at her, but was obviously determined to have his way.

"Stubborn, that's what you are. But I can understand why you would not want to meet the earl in your sick bed, such a disadvantage. I have some accounts to do, but Susan would like to accompany you on a gentle stroll around the garden if that is to your taste, wouldn't you, my dear?" she asked, turning to her daughter, who was sitting by the window working on a tapestry.

"Of course. Such a relief. It's much too fine a day to sulk indoors, and it will get me away from this tapestry. I am not an accomplished needle woman," Susan confessed with a little moue.

"That sounds marvelous. I am yearning for some air." Although Stephen found Mrs. Woodhall comforting and kind, he was not quite sure how he felt about Susan. She was a charming girl, and quite without affection, but rather awe-inspiring. Stephen had no great experience with well-bred young ladies. Most of the types he had met in India had preferred officers and had little time to waste on hard-working businessmen. They had considered him little better than a clerk and had treated him with disdain. Since most of the females he had met were on the look-out for husbands, and he did not appear to qualify, his encounters had been brief and somewhat humiliating. It did not encourage him to try his manners on well-placed young women.

But Susan, sensing his shyness, was determined to set him at ease. She chatted away as they walked around the garden, pointing out the beauties of her home, which she obviously loved.

"You see, Mr. Venner, I have only been home a year from school, and it is so heavenly to have this freedom from lessons and strictures on my deportment."

"I fancy that deportment might have been a problem," he agreed, thinking she must have been a torment to her teachers. She was not a girl who took orders well, he surmised.

"Yes, I barely escaped expulsion. But mother is much wiser, and I would never do anything to cause her pain." She paused by a wooden seat. "Let us sit down. I don't want to tire you, and it's sheltered here."

"I suppose you want to ask me more questions. And please call me Stephen. I cannot be on formal terms with my rescuer."

"Then you must call me Susan, and I do want to ask you some questions. Impolite, I suppose, but you represent a challenge."

"In what way? I am a most innocuous fellow."

"Innocuous fellows do not get attacked on my doorstep. Really, Stephen, you must have some enemy, for I don't believe that shot came from a poacher or a stray highwayman. Do you?"

"But who could want to harm me? And I was not robbed. Surely any villain with such intentions would have attempted to see what valuables I was carrying."

"It might have something to do with the earl," Susan suggested, rather surprised at her effrontery, but she had been giving the matter a great deal of thought.

"You mean I might be the long-lost heir, and whoever thinks he is entitled to the earl's estate would want to remove me before my cousin dies? You have been reading too many novels, I suspect."

"I know. That's what Mother says," Susan admitted with engaging candor. "But what else could it be. Do satisfy my curiosity. Are you the earl's heir?"

"Not as far as I know. I only want to meet him because I have no other relatives, at least as far as I have discovered. You have a brother, have you not?"

Realizing that Stephen found the subject of his expectations distasteful, Susan launched into an account of her brother Alan's naval career. It was no hardship, for she loved talking about Alan. If only he were here, it would be much easier to discover who had attacked Stephen, she felt.

"You are fortunate to have a brother and such a wonderful mother," Stephen said wistfully after Susan had finished her tale.

"Yes, I know." Susan wondered if she should mention her father, but then decided that would serve no purpose. The problem with Stephen was he was so easy to talk to, no need to play a part or resort to the usual inanities.

They sat in companionable silence for some moments, and Stephen could not help but think how unusual it was to be comfortable with a female who did not feel she must fill every moment with chatter. He looked about him with appreciation. Often had he imagined an English spring, and this was what he had hoped to find, a cloudless, azure sky with the slightest of breezes and green meadows and gardens. Such a change from the enervating heat and dirt of India. He had fallen on pleasant days and a welcome he did not expect. For this he was almost grateful to his unknown assailant.

Susan looked at him with appreciation. What a calm, easy man he was, so comfortable, so unaffected. She had to admit he possessed none of the excitement of Denzil Capehart, nor did he appear to find her worthy of a flirtation; but, she thought, he had probably had little experience with the practiced address of fashionable chat. In a way his manner was a relief, but she wished vaguely that he would respond to her in a different way than the brotherly attitude he had adopted. Then she chided herself. Was she so conceited that she thought every man should be impressed with her charms? Before she could pursue the question of his attacker further, they were interrupted by Jennings making his stately approach across the garden.

"The Earl of Edgebury's coach has just drawn up to the door, Miss Susan, and your mother requests your presence and that of Mr. Venner," he announced.

"Thank you, Jennings." Somehow Susan was disappointed that this interlude was ending. With the earl's arrival she sensed that a new element would be introduced into their mundane household. Stephen Venner might even leave. She might not see him again, and she knew that she would miss him. She noticed he seemed quite cheerful at the prospect of meeting his relative, and as they walked back to the house, she regretted the coming change in their relationship.

In the drawing room Margaret Woodhall was entertaining the earl and his agent. She was somewhat surprised by both her visitors. She had expected a pompous peer, very much on his dignity, and the earl definitely did not behave as she had believed he would. He was both courteous and appreciative of the care she had given his unknown relative. And he was both younger and more compelling than she had assumed from her preconceived notions.

"You have been more than kind to take in Stephen after this peculiar attack on him. How fortunate that your daughter discovered him. He might have lain in your woods for some time and suffered even more serious injury," the earl said. He, too, was impressed, not realizing that the hospitable Mrs. Woodhall would be such an engaging woman. From her letter, he had pictured a matronly older woman, and she might have been a girl, he thought, looking at her trim figure and creamy complexion.

"We have become fond of Stephen. He seems an estimable young man, and I was happy to do what I could for him. But this unusual attack worries me, so close to our home. We have never had cause to think we entertained violence in our neighborhood."

"It must have been some villain looking for an easy mark," Nigel said. He was not unaware of his employer's obvious interest in Mrs. Woodhall, and he did not think it boded well. The earl was at a vulnerable age, prey for a designing woman, although he had no reason to think Mrs. Woodhall was of that company.

"Ah, here is Stephen and my daughter, Susan," Margaret said as the young pair entered the room. She made the introductions, watching the earl to see his first reaction to the young man.

"How do you do, sir. I have long looked forward to this meeting. I am only sorry that it should occur under such circumstances," Stephen said, extending his hand, which the earl grasped firmly.

"Not your fault, my boy. Most distressing." Then the earl turned to Susan and gave her a smiling bow. "And I am to thank Miss Woodhall for Stephen's rescue, I understand."

"It was mere chance that I discovered him lying in our copse and was able to summon help," Susan said demurely. She liked what she saw of the earl. He appeared far from the starchy, self-important aristocrat she had thought.

"I think, Susan, the earl and Mr. Venner have a great deal to discuss. Perhaps, sir, you would be more comfortable in the library," Margaret suggested. She then remembered Nigel Thorndyke, and hurriedly made the introductions. And what was she to do about him? Surely, he would not intrude on this reunion.

"That's most obliging, ma'am," the earl welcomed her thoughtfulness. He had forgotten about Nigel.

"Perhaps Mr. Thorndyke would like to meet my bailiff. Andrew Baird might show him about. I suppose they would have a good deal in common." Margaret was puzzled by the man. He seemed on very intimate terms with his employer, and she wondered at his influence.

"Fine idea, heh, Nigel," the earl said.

"Yes, indeed, sir." If Nigel Thorndyke was disappointed at being shunted off this way, he showed no signs of it. Margaret rang the bell for Jennings, who appeared very promptly. Susan suspected he had been hovering just outside the door, eager to learn what he could about their visitors.

"We hope you and Mr. Thorndyke will join us for luncheon," Margaret invited as she made her dispositions.

Jennings was dispatched to fetch Andrew Baird, and she shepherded Stephen and the earl into the library, closing the door firmly on them, as if to say she had no intention of intruding further on their reunion. The earl had accepted her invitation with pleasure, and now she had only to deal with Mr. Thorndyke, who stood stolidly awaiting her pleasure. Jennings returned smartly and informed his mistress that Mr. Baird was in the estate office and he would lead Mr. Thorndyke there. Nigel bowed a bit formally and followed the butler, his back rigid. He found his position demeaning, but he was well used to masking his feelings. Susan and her mother adjourned to the morning room to discuss the earl and what his arrival meant to their guest.

# *Six*

"Nice woman and lovely daughter, eh, Stephen," the earl said as they settled into leather chairs in the paneled library. He looked about with appreciation, admiring the room's appointments, a solid, workmanlike walnut desk, deep green velvet draperies and a fine collection of tooled-leather books behind glass cases fronting two walls.

"The Woodhalls have been more than kind to me, sir," Stephen agreed.

"Yes, well, about this attack. I want to hear more about it." The earl's expression was stern, and Stephen had no recourse but to go through the whole sorry tale again.

As he talked, the earl listened carefully, made no interruptions, and appeared to be weighing up his relative. He liked what he saw. The young man had a modest, unassuming air, looked competent, and made no effort to impress his cousin with his abilities or success.

When he had finished, the earl looked thoughtful. "This man of yours that you sent ahead to the Royal York with the coach and baggage, has he been in your employ long?"

A bit taken aback by the earl's inquiry, Stephen wondered if the earl suspected Coats of some chicanery, an idea that had never crossed his mind.

"No, sir. I hired him in London through an agency. I had a bearer in India who had been with me since before my parents' death, but he would not have been happy in

England, and I regretfully let him stay behind. A mistake perhaps."

"Yes, it's always best to have people in your service that you have known and learned to trust. How do you feel about this Coats? Could he have been in collusion with some rogue to rob you?"

"I suppose so, but I think it's unlikely." Stephen frowned, unlikely but not impossible.

"He knew of your plans, that you were coming on a visit to me?"

"Yes, sir, but he could not have known I would send him ahead to Bath because I wanted a solitary ramble in the countryside"

"He might have improvised when the occasion arose. That presupposes a confederate willing to abet him in the crime." The earl could not be deterred from suspecting the man.

"Yes, of course. I really know little of Coats. He had exceptional references, one from Sir Edmund Finnes, and he does his work well."

"Did you take up the reference before you hired him?"

"I tried, but Sir Edmund had left the country for the West Indies, I was informed."

"Unfortunate." The earl paused, thinking. "We must quiz this Coats more closely. But if robbery was his motif, why were your pocketbook and papers left untouched?"

"Perhaps Miss Woodhall's opportune arrival prevented whoever shot me from carrying out the rest of his mission," Stephen suggested. He had difficulty in taking this idea of the earl's seriously, but did not want to offend his cousin by saying so.

The earl read his reluctance easily. "Well, we cannot leave the matter there. I don't think it bodes well for your future, and I would feel it most deeply if I were robbed of one of my few relatives before we had strengthened our acquaintance. Now, tell me more of your parents."

Stephen was happy to oblige, and no further words were said about his attack, for which he was grateful. They exchanged news about their family, of which there was all too little, and the earl commented, "It's a regret to me that we are so bereft of close relations. I believe there was another cousin, brother of my grandmother, a bad hat, who absconded with some family money and fled the country, but as I have never heard from him, I must assume be died, and without issue."

"Regrettable," agreed Stephen. He could not help but wonder if he was, as Susan suggested, his cousin's heir, but was too polite to ask, a distinction the earl noticed and appreciated. Now was not the time to discuss his testamentary decisions.

"And you have never married, have no sons or daughters, sir?" Stephen could not resist asking.

"No, my army career was all-consuming and kept me on the move. I had no time for courtship. My father, before he died, made it quite plain that I had failed in my duty. And now, I believe it is too late to remedy that lack of foresight," the earl confessed with a grin. "I haven't had much experience with the ladies."

"Nor have I, sir. John Company kept sending me to odd parts of India where there were no suitable females."

The earl, having formed his opinion of Stephen by now, realized that here was a young man who had not succumbed to the temptations India offered so many well-bred young men: drink, native mistresses, gambling, and the self-indulgent leisure that led many into infamous conduct. Yes, he approved of Stephen, and he was not easily gulled. In battle men's character was quickly revealed, and the earl had learned to make life and death decisions on that judgment. He decided Stephen would have made a good junior officer.

He smiled and said, "Well, now that you are back in England, you will have to rectify that omission."

Stephen neither agreed nor demurred. He had his own ideas about what kind of wife he preferred, if he were fortunate enough to find her. His cousin seemed a decent, upright man of vast experience, but he would make his own choice.

While the earl and Stephen were strengthening their acquaintance and Andrew Baird drove Nigel Thorndyke around the Combe Manor land, Denzil Capehart was riding toward the Woodhall estate. He had debated for some time as to whether he should chance his luck and call again, despite Mrs. Woodhall's obvious reluctance to receive him. Events since his previous meeting with Susan had forced him to make the decision. When she had not appeared at the assembly, Denzil had endured some ribald teasing from his fellow officers as to her defection. Denzil, arrogant, conceited and a opportunist, was not popular in the mess. His fellows enjoyed seeing him thwarted for once in his conquest of the most eligible girl in the neighborhood. But he would have bided his time, secure in his feeling that Susan preferred him to any other claimant for her hand, if he had not heard of the earl's arrival in Bath. A complaisant bar maid at the Royal York had been only too eager to oblige the beguiling young man with tales of the hostelry's distinguished visitor and his plan to call on Combe Manor. She was on intimate terms with the earl's valet. Denzil felt he could not risk Susan developing an interest in this unknown relative of the earl. He assumed she would be impressed by the stranger's connection with the earl, for his own reaction would have been to cultivate anyone who could improve his own situation. Here was this victim of an attack on her doorstep, an object of romantic interest, wounded, probably wealthy and related to an aristocrat, a formidable rival. So he was riding off to remind her of his own attractions, which had rarely failed him when it came to gullible young women.

Margaret Woodhall and her daughter were having a comfortable cose about recent events when Jennings announced the arrival of Lieutenant Capehart.

Margaret eyed her daughter cautiously. She did not want to antagonize her again by refusing to receive the officer, and she entertained a faint hope that Denzil's deficiencies would be apparent when he was compared to Stephen.

Denzil, on his best behavior, entered the room, bowed to Mrs. Woodhall warily and then gave Susan his most bewitching smile.

"What a surprise, Denzil," Susan said, not entirely easy in his presence before her mother. He could not have chosen a more inauspicious time to call, she thought.

"Well, I missed you Saturday evening, and thought I must inquire as to your welfare," he announced smoothly.

"Do sit down, Lieutenant," Mrs. Woodhall invited. She was somewhat at a loss. It was almost time for luncheon, and she might be forced to invite the officer to join them, an invitation she was reluctant to give.

"I was too busy to come. As I told you, we have an unexpected guest, the young man from India who was attacked at our very gates," Susan explained, turning to look at her mother, trying to sense her reaction. Mrs. Woodhall wondered when Susan had given the officer the news. Had she been meeting him in secret?

"Has he recovered? The news is all over Bath, causing quite a bit of talk."

"Such a hotbed of gossip, Bath." Mrs. Woodhall frowned. She did not like her affairs bandied about the town.

"Well, the old tabbies must have some relief from

drinking the waters and going to dull tea parties," Denzil said irrelevantly.

"Stephen Venner is regaining his strength and appears to be in good spirits." Susan was finding this conversation a trial. Of course it was flattering that Denzil had missed her and exerted himself to call. She was not immune to his admiring gaze and his preference for her company.

"I understand his august relative, the Earl of Edgebury, has arrived in Bath to make inquiries about his relative, if that is what this stranger is." Denzil could not keep a certain sneering doubt from his tone. It was a mistake.

Margaret Woodhall looked at him with disapproval. What a cad the man was. "He is definitely the earl's young cousin. They are having a reunion this minute in our library. Perhaps you would like to meet him. We are about to have luncheon. Won't you join us?" Margaret had decided her best tactic would be to expose Susan to both young men. She could not help but contrast Stephen's modest and sensible character to Denzil's meretricious charm.

"Yes, do stay," Susan urged. Despite herself, the officer fascinated her, and she wondered what Stephen would think of him.

"I would be delighted. Thank you, Mrs. Woodhall." He was careful to pay obsequious attention to his hostess, sensing her reluctance, but determined to win her over. Susan might champion him, but he knew she would hesitate to oppose her mother. His self-assurance insisted that when the time came he might persuade her to go against her mother's wishes and accept him, but it would be much more convenient if he could convince Mrs. Woodhall of his suitability as a husband for her daughter. A rather daunting task, but Denzil had rarely failed to win a woman's approval whatever her age.

"Ring for Jennings, Susan, please. We must ask him to lay another place."

\* \* \*

Later, looking around her luncheon table, Margaret had reason to be grateful to the earl. It might have proved an awkward affair. She had to include the ubiquitous Nigel Thorndyke at the meal and had also invited Andrew Baird to join them to lighten the proceedings. For a Scot, he was unusually outgoing, cheerful and polite. A stocky man, about Nigel's age, with a shock of red hair and a freckled face, he was not only competent at his job, but an easy companion. Margaret had employed him five years ago and never regretted her decision.

The earl welcomed him kindly and asked him about his job. He also thanked him for escorting Nigel around the property. "You chaps should have found much to talk about. Where would we be without our loyal bailiffs, Mrs. Woodhall? Difficult for a woman to come to grips with estate matters, I think."

"Not at all, my lord. I grew up here. It is my family home, and I know every tenant on the place, as does Susan. But I am very fortunate to have Andrew's assistance."

The young man smiled gratefully. Only Nigel looked a bit grim. He found all this interest in a minor estate a bit much. Why, you could put the whole place in two of the earl's fields. He conceded that the man knew his job. He had noted the neat appearance of the three farmhouses he had seen and the prosperous condition of the stock and the efficient planting; but compared to the earl's acres, it was pitiable. In his own way Nigel was somewhat of a snob and found the Woodhalls beneath the earl's touch.

If the earl noticed Nigel's unwillingness to join in the conversation, he ignored it. He quizzed Denzil about his service, but found the young man, although all politeness, disappointing. He had never served abroad. Most of his duty seemed to have taken him to pleasant watering spots like Bath and Tunbridge, no post for a soldier. The earl was apt to look with scorn on a serving officer who had never faced an enemy's bullet, but be realized that was unfair. Since Waterloo there had been no dangerous assignments for young men to win their spurs. Possibly this lieutenant would behave creditably on the battlefield, but he had not been tried. Still, Denzil Capehart did not compare favorably with Stephen in the earl's judgment. His cousin had by his own efforts won success and respect in a hard field. India had spelled the doom of many young men in Stephen's position. As a final accolade, the earl decided Stephen would also have behaved well in battle, made a brave and resourceful officer. He hoped the attractive Susan was not seriously interested in this popinjay in his shining uniform seated beside Stephen. He decided the officer would make an indifferent husband.

Stephen Venner had come to somewhat the same assessment about Denzil, but reproved himself for his harsh opinion. He could not help but notice Denzil's interest in Susan. And certainly she was worthy of any man's interest. As well as her beauty, she had a kind heart and none of the simpering, silly chatter that he had met with many girls in her enviable position. However, Stephen was as adept as Nigel Thorndyke in hiding his feelings and conversed amicably with Denzil.

"We will leave you gentlemen to your port now. Susan?" Mrs. Woodhall, conscious of her duties as a hostess, rose after the savory and signified her daughter should accompany her. But the earl surprised her.

"I'm not too fond of port, especially after this excellent luncheon. Perhaps we could have a little chat, Mrs. Woodhall," the earl suggested.

"Of course, my lord." Margaret wondered what he had to say. Susan excused herself, to be quickly followed by the young men, who disclaimed any interest in port.

She took them out into the garden, leaving her mother alone with the earl. She supposed he wanted to make arrangements to remove Stephen to his own home. Looking at her patient, Susan decided he looked tired, and well he might be with all this excitement so soon after his wound. And he was not completely over the effects of that business, she thought. Gentlemen did not like being reminded of their weaknesses, but she suggested gently he might like a rest. She and Andrew would entertain Mr. Thorndyke.

Stephen, loath to leave Susan with the three men, especially Denzil, was reluctant to agree, but he did as she suggested, realizing she was concerned for his welfare, which gave him a warm glow. And he had a great deal to think about. He allowed himself to be dismissed without too much argument.

Denzil, hoping to get Susan alone, looked smug. He feared no trouble with the agents, but was happy to see his rival leave the field. To his surprise, Susan showed no sign of wanting a tête-à-tête. In fact, she appeared to expect him to take his leave. She watched Stephen mount the stairs slowly and then turned to Denzil.

"It was very nice of you to call, Denzil, and I was glad to see that Mother appears to have accepted you. But I have a number of chores to see to this afternoon, so I am sure you will excuse me."

Taken aback by this desire to rid herself of him, Denzil was about to protest, but then thought better of it. Best to leave while he was still in both the Woodhalls' good graces, but he was determined to make a date for a future meeting.

"Of course, Susan. I can quite understand that that business of an unwanted guest creates domestic problems. I must return to duty anyway. But when will I see you again?"

"Soon, Denzil. I will probably be coming into Bath before too long."

"Drop me a note and I will arrange to meet you. Until then, and I await our meeting with impatience, goodbye." He bowed in a theatrical manner that made Susan repress a giggle. Really, at times Denzil appeared overly dramatic. She waved him off from the front steps and then returned to the hall where Nigel and Andrew Baird were waiting a bit uncertainly.

"I have to ride out to see Mrs. Evans and her new baby, Andrew. Perhaps you could keep Mr. Thorndyke company until the earl is ready for him."

Andrew Baird agreed cheerfully. He found Thorndyke heavy going, but appeared always eager to oblige Miss Susan.

With a sigh of relief Susan left them and went off on her errand. She had found the luncheon a bit awkward and had sensed that Stephen had also found it a trial. She was eager to get him alone and discover how the interview with the earl had gone and what his plans were. She hoped he would not leave them yet, and wondered why she was so anxious to keep him. Just that she had not yet solved the mystery of his attacker. What other reason could there be?

# *Seven*

If Margaret Woodhall was surprised by the earl's intent to talk with her alone, she was too well-bred to show her astonishment. Perhaps he wanted to know more about the progress of Stephen's recovery and was reluctant to discuss it with the young man, who Margaret suspected would tend to dismiss any inquires out of hand.

Avoiding the drawing room, which the Woodhall women rarely used except for formal entertaining, Margaret ushered the earl into the morning room, her favorite retreat.

"Do sit down, my lord."

"I wish you would not call me that. It's so intimidating. You know, I have never completely come to terms with it."

"But you must have always known you would inherit from your father," Margaret said, puzzled.

"No, I had an elder brother, Robert, who died in a hunting accident when I was twenty and was already well established in my army career. Father wanted me to give up my commission and come home to run the estate, but I refused. I disliked thwarting him, but the war with Napoleon was at its height, and I didn't want to miss the action. Selfish of me, no doubt. I never expected to become the earl and hoped, after Robert's death, that father would live for ages; but he succumbed to pneumonia at sixty-two, and here I am."

Fascinated by this tale, Margaret still wondered why he was being so forthcoming. She found herself admiring his blunt, unassuming manner, not at all what she had expected from a peer of the realm.

"So you see," he added, "why I dislike being my lorded. My name is Godfrey, dreadful I think, but I would be most happy if you would call me that." He smiled shyly.

"Of course, and you must return the favor and call me Margaret." Still rather mystified by his request for this interview, she waited calmly for his questions.

"Stephen gave me a rather brief account of his accident, if that was what it was, but I wanted to ask you what you thought of the affair. It seems odd to me that he would be shot on a country road, not the usual haunt of highwaymen, I suspect."

"Yes, you're correct. We have never had any such incursions before, and the few poachers which roam about would not be apt to be shooting at that spot, especially in the daytime."

"So that leads me to think that Stephen was the target of some villain who had marked him out in particular."

"Oh dear, that's rather horrible, Godfrey," Margaret said, appalled at the suggestion.

"The only person who actually knew of his destination, knew he would be on that road, traveling alone, is his man, this Coats he hired in London. What is your impression of the fellow?"

"It's hard to say. He's very taciturn, keeps out of the way. But Jennings would be a better judge. And he appears not to object to the man."

"Well, he bears watching. Someone has it in for Stephen, I fear. It could be an enemy he made in India, but Stephen does not strike me as the kind of young man to attract enemies, do you think?"

"Not at all. I have grown very fond of him. He's modest, considerate and patient under the trying conditions of his convalescence. And I imagine he is also intelligent and shrewd. From what I can gather, for he talks very little of it, he must have had a struggle in India and worked hard for his success. He yearned to return to England, and it's a shame his homecoming should be scarred by this brutal attack."

"I quite agree, Margaret. I am very grateful for your care of him, but naturally I want to carry him off to Edgebury Hall as soon as possible. How is he coming along?"

"Very well. Dr. Warden is pleased with his progress, but I don't think he is ready to travel yet, even a short distance. I understand your impatience, but I really think he must remain here for a week or so more. Do you agree?"

"I have to be guided by you and the doctor, and I envy Stephen his comfortable circumstances here. I intend to remain in Bath for some days yet and ride out every day to visit with him if that meets with your approval," he said politely.

"Of course, you will be welcome any time, Godfrey." Margaret was impressed with the earl's consideration, his judgment and his courtesy.

"I will send Nigel back to the Hall, and he can keep an eye on matters. He's very competent. I think he wanted to meet Stephen because he believes him to be my heir."

"And is he?" Margaret could not resist asking, although she knew it was outrageously presumptuous of her.

"Possibly. I have no other relatives that I know of and the Hall is not entailed, rather unusual, but there it is." He did not seem offended by her curiosity.

He stood up. "Well, I must not presume on your time any further, but if you don't mind, I will call again tomorrow to check on our invalid and perhaps talk to the doctor."

"Certainly. Do come whenever you wish. It would be

more convenient if you stayed here, but the very proper ladies who preside over Bath would tear my reputation to shreds if I allowed it. I am sorry."

The earl laughed. "Yes, protocol must be observed, although as you can see I am a harmless chap."

Margaret smiled, but she was not so sure that this was a true assessment of the earl. She thought he could be quite formidable if the occasion arose. They parted on the best of terms, and she rang for Jennings to find Nigel Thorndyke and order the earl's carriage.

When the butler arrived she asked him about Susan.

"Miss Susan has ridden out to visit Mrs. Evans and her new baby. The other gentleman is in the garden with Mr. Baird."

"I will collect him and be on my way. Until tomorrow then, Margaret," the earl said and took his leave. He had a great deal to think about and was silent on the ride back to Bath, a silence Nigel thought ominous, but was unwilling to interrupt.

After Margaret had waved off her visitors, she returned to the morning room and rang for Jennings again. He appeared promptly.

"Jennings, the earl is concerned about this man Coats, whom Mr. Venner employed in London. What is your opinion of him?"

Jennings, who had his own suspicions about the man, was not reluctant to confide in his mistress. He had been in her service since her girlhood and felt quite protective about her, remembering what she had endured from her late husband, and he admired the way she had handled that libertine and demanding man.

"Well, ma'am, he is very quiet, says very little about his past or present circumstances. But the rest of the servants don't take to him, if you know what I mean."

"Yes, I do, Jennings." Margaret found this description of Coats daunting. Usually servants were quite loyal to one of their own, allied against their employers, although her staff always appeared devoted and, on the whole, friendly. She had a great opinion of Jennings' good sense, and if he found Coats puzzling, it worried her.

"We must keep an eye on him," she added.

"Do you suspect him of some involvement with Mr. Venner's attack?" Jennings asked shrewdly.

"I don't know. I hate the idea of entertaining suspicions of the man, but the alternatives seem most unlikely."

"Quite so, madam. I will keep my eye on him," Jennings promised and took his stately leave.

Margaret smiled, knowing that her butler enjoyed sharing this conspiracy with her. But the earl had aroused her uneasiness. If Coats was involved, it posed several problems. She was relieved that the earl was nearby, to be called on if needed. It had been a long time since she had been able to rely on a man when in difficulty or danger. Stephen Venner had stirred up more than he realized when he was carried, wounded, into her house.


The earl, true to his promise, called every day to check on Stephen's progress and spent a great deal of time talking with the young man. On further acquaintance, his first assessment of Stephen as a capable, unassuming and pleasant young man deepened. He was becoming fond of him and also of his hostess and her daughter, a feeling he thought Stephen more than shared, although he did not quiz him on the matter. The atmosphere of Combe Manor was a warm and friendly one, and the earl, accustomed to his bachelor quarters and rarely exposed to female companionship, responded gratefully to the welcome he received. But he was not so bemused as to forget to keep a close eye on Coats, who tried to be unobtrusive, but must have been aware of the earl's searching gaze as he revealed very little of his background under questioning.

It was no surprise to the earl when after a few days of his interrogations he arrived to discover that the man had vanished. He heard the news from Jennings upon entering the hall and asking for Mrs. Woodhall.

"I feel you should be informed, my lord, that the creature Coats, in whom you took some interest, has left," Jennings announced in his most impressive tones.

"Left, left, what do you mean left? Was he dismissed by Mr. Venner?" the earl asked impatiently. But before Jennings could reply Margaret Woodhall came into the hall.

"Oh, good morning, Godfrey. I suppose Jennings has told you about Coats' disappearance."

"Good morning, Margaret." Despite his eagerness to learn about Coats, the earl observed the courtesies. But Margaret paid little attention, taking him by the arm and almost dragging him to the morning room, regarded by Jennings with frustration He had a great deal more to tell the earl, and now madam would spoil his revelations. Shaking his head sadly he departed to the servants' hall, where speculation was rife.

"Now, what's this Jennings is saying, that Coats has decamped?" he inquired, waiting politely for Margaret to invite him to sit, which she did with little ceremony, pushing him down on the divan, to his amusement, and settling beside him.

"Stephen rang for him this morning as usual, and he didn't appear. After a bit Jennings went up to see why the bell kept ringing. Stephen asked for his man, and Jennings knew no reason why he should not have responded. But then he checked the man's room, and all his gear was gone. He must have stolen away in the night, for Jennings says he joined the servants for supper and no one has seen him since. What does it mean?"

"It means that Coats has the wind up, and is frightened his role in Stephen's attack might be discovered. Where is Stephen?"

"He and Susan have ridden out to see if any of the farm workers or tenants saw him, although I think it's very doubtful because he must have left in the night, don't you think?"

"Yes, but is Stephen well enough to ride?"

"He insisted, and when I objected he accused me of coddling him; so I had no choice but to let him go. Susan will keep a watchful eye on him. But does Coats' fleeing in the night mean he was the villain that shot Stephen. And then turned up here all concerned. Who knows what he would have tried next, poison or some other horrid ploy. And why would he attempt such a crime?"

The earl could see that Margaret was quite distraught, and thought his first responsibility was to soothe her.

"I'm sure he did not actually shoot Stephen himself, but was involved in some way. Probably as an informer. Which means, I think, that he met his coconspirator in Bath, as arranged, and informed him that Stephen was riding alone into town and might be an unprotected target."

Margaret looked at him with admiration. "How clever of you, Godfrey," she said, but then another possibility occurred to her. "That must mean that Stephen's enemy is someone in the neighborhood. Who could it be, and why would he want to kill Stephen?"

"Yes, that's the puzzle. I doubt it was simple robbery because he did not rifle Stephen's pockets. It might have something to do with India." Another possibility had struck Godfrey, but he was loath to mention it, the idea was so startling. He retreated to the obvious explanation of Coats' infamy.

"Coats must have been sent by Stephen's attacker to keep an eye on Stephen and inform him of his movements. That means he had to have gone to London and hired him. It must be someone who lives in this area or in Bath. Can you tell me about your neighbors?"

"Oh, no. They are all very proper, would never initiate such a dreadful deed." Margaret was shocked by his suggestion.

"Who are your closest neighbors," the earl persisted.

"Well, there are not too many. Sir Edmund and Lady French. He's a magistrate. You might have met him on the bench. The French land adjoins ours to the south. They are the only other large landowners in the vicinity. Of course, there are some gentlefolk in the village, the vicar; the doctor, whom you have met; the solicitor, who also has an office in Bath. The rest are farmers, worthy men on the whole. We have few resident villains."

"I know French slightly. Seems a prosaic chap, not too bright, and exceptionally vehement against poachers. Wants them transported on the first offense."

"Oh, Sir Edmund is mostly bluster and noise. I doubt he would harm a soul, and why would he want to kill Stephen? No, that's ridiculous."

"I'd like to talk to him, but that's a little dodgy. I can hardly go up to him and say, 'What were you doing on April twentieth? I think you may have shot my cousin.'"

"Don't be ridiculous, of course you can't." Margaret brooded for a moment. "I know. I can invite the Frenches to dinner. Their daughter, Matilda, is a friend of Susan's; they were schoolmates. And I will gather a few others so it won't seem so obvious. The vicar and his wife, and they have a daughter, a rather drab little girl, but presentable. Then there's Colonel Bushnell, commander of the regiment. Yes, I could gather a group."

"A fine idea," Godfrey approved, looking at Margaret with a fond eye. What an intelligent woman, able to grasp the nuances of the situation and not wail and wring her hands or offer inane suggestions. Really, she was an exceptional woman. He wondered why she had never married again, pretty, too, with her girlish figure and soft brown hair. And so easy and comfortable to be with, he decided. He realized that she had come to mean a great deal to him, but he put that dangerous emotion aside. Now was not the time to wonder about Margaret, but to take some action.

Before he could pursue either her plan or examine his own emotions, now in confusion, Jennings entered.

"Miss Susan and Mr. Venner have just returned, madam. They don't seem to have had much success."

On Jennings' heels came the pair, Susan looking flushed and disappointed while Stephen seemed to have suffered no ill effects from his ride.

"No luck, I'm afraid," Stephen said after greeting his cousin. "We asked everyone we met in the village, including the tavern keeper, and then we visited the farms. Of course, he must have escaped in the night when all respectable folk were abed."

"Yes," agreed the earl. "But it does prove he was some kind of rogue or why would he have crept away so secretly?"

Susan, Stephen and Margaret all agreed, and there was a heated exchange of views as to their next move. Despite the serious nature of their discussion, the earl found he was enjoying this business, and he determined not to leave Bath until he had solved the mystery, insured Stephen's safety, and perhaps chanced his own future.

# *Eight*

After leaving their elders Susan and Stephen retreated to the library, where they discussed her mother's plan for the dinner party and what it might reveal. Stephen appeared to take the whole business lightly. He was not really convinced that his life was in danger. Even Coats' strange disappearance had not unduly upset him.

"I was not too happy with the man. His dour face and manner was quite off-putting. But, of course, he fulfilled his duties well enough. And he came from a very reputable agency."

"He may have, but you were never able to take up his references. That's very suspicious."

"If I did not know that in reality you had a kind heart, I would suspect you were enjoying all this mystery," Stephen chided, a smile robbing his words of any criticism. He found there was little in either Susan's manner or appearance that he could fault. What a smashing girl she was.

Susan looked a bit shame-faced. "Of course I don't want you to come to any harm, Stephen, but this whole affair is intriguing. You must have some enemy you have not recalled. Why would someone want to shoot you?"

"I have no idea. I can think of a few chaps I bested in business in India, but none of them were the type to be vindictive." He looked puzzled.

"Then there must be someone here who has a motive

to want you dead, I still think it has something to do with the earl and the possibility of you being his heir."

"I can hardly quiz him as to his intentions. And I don't need the money. He mentioned giving me an allowance, and I refused. I have more than enough for my needs."

Susan nodded approvingly. She had never suspected Stephen of cultivating the earl for his possessions or his title.

"Mother tells me that the earl informed her that his estate is not entailed. Very unusual. I naturally thought that as his only relative you would inherit." Susan paused. "It's not very nice to be discussing his eventual demise; he's such a dear. I would hate anything to happen to him."

"Yes, he's a great fellow, and still young, only in his forties. I would think if some stranger had designs on the estate, his would be the life in danger, not mine." Stephen had given the matter a great deal of thought and remembered that the earl had told him of the family black sheep. But that had been well in the past. Even if there was some unknown claimant, he could not insure inheriting since there was no entailment."

"I wonder why the estate is left to the discretion of the earl to dispose of," Susan said.

"His father told him the entailment had been broken due to a black sheep in the family. He wanted to be paid off, and the price of that was to break the entailment, preventing him from any further claim on the estate."

"That was two generations ago. Perhaps this shadowy figure did not realize that even if you died, and then the earl, he still would not be able to take up the fruits of his crime."

"You're right. I hadn't thought of that. You have a clever head on your shoulders, Susan." He looked at her with approval and thought, not for the first time, what a wonderful wife she would make for some fortunate fellow.

"Thank you, Stephen. But what we must do now is consider all the possible villains among our acquaintances. That is the reason Mother is going to gather them all together for this dinner. But they seem an unlikely group to me, none of them capable of attacking you."

"Yes, I cannot imagine Dr. Warden or the vicar, for example, with fell designs," Stephen agreed.

"Or Mr. Pecksmith, the solicitor, although I think he is the right age. And there is Sir Edmund French. When he married Lady French he took over her family's manor and lands, for her father had no sons. I really know little about him, but he is not a man of great intelligence or ability, rather prosy and pompous but harmless, except to the poachers."

"The whole idea is ridiculous. From what you tell me, Sir Edmund is a man of substance. He would not risk his position by committing murder, do you think?"

"Probably not, but someone wants to dispatch you, Stephen, and we must discover who it is." She wrinkled her brow as she considered the possible culprits, and then her eyes widened as a thought struck her. "What about Nigel Thorndyke, your cousin's agent. I didn't take to the man, I must admit."

"My cousin respects him, and relies on him. I cannot think he would be mistaken in his judgment."

"But what does he really know about him. The earl took him on when he inherited after his father died. He's just the type to bide his time and then make a move."

Stephen disagreed. He was finding his alliance with Susan over the whole business more appealing than any real idea of unmasking a would-be murderer. Stephen had survived several sticky situations in India and did not believe he was in danger from some shadowy villain. If he were, he had his own candidate for the role, but not one he wanted to reveal to Susan. She might suspect his motives.

After some amicable arguing about the various suspects, they abandoned the discussion as fruitless for the moment and settled down to play piquet, a rivalry they thoroughly enjoyed.

Later that evening, after dinner at which the earl had also been a guest, Stephen was sent to his room. Margaret believed he needed more rest, although his wound was practically healed and he felt little effects from it. He agreed because he wanted to think. His cousin had spoken to him, after the ladies had left the dining room, about his plans for the future. Stephen had told him he planned to buy a small manor and farm, and the earl had nodded with approval. Then the earl had made his suggestion. Why not spend some months at Edgebury Hall before making up his mind?

"Thorndyke could introduce you to the business, and I would like your company. I have my own ideas about your future and want to discuss them with you once we have cleared up all this trouble about your attack."

"Thank you, sir. But I fear we may never find the answer to this matter. Susan is all for investigating every possibility. I think she suspects everyone from the vicar to Thorndyke with a passing interest in Sir Edmund French. She's such a darling, I hate to disabuse her." Stephen laughed as if the whole affair was incidental.

"Yes, her mother seems equally determined, an unusual pair, the Woodhalls."

Stephen, recalling this conversation and the earl's opinion of Margaret Woodhall, which he had shared with Stephen at some length, wondered if his cousin was attracted to his hostess. He thoroughly approved, and he wished he could be as fortunate. Those musings brought him around again to Susan and his own interest. On the boat coming home from India he had made a decision to look for a wife. That temperate and prosaic plan now appeared ridiculous. He had been fairly caught in Susan's toils, and all vague ideas of examining various candidates for the position of Mrs. Venner had been dispelled on meeting the charming Miss Woodhall.

A modest man and rather shy in the company of women, Stephen did not rate his chances very high. He wasn't sure how to proceed with his courtship. But more important he felt he had a serious rival. That handsome, sophisticated officer who had entered the list of suspects. Denzil Capehart was courting Susan, he had no doubt, which made it difficult for Stephen to suggest that of all the contenders for the inimical enemy, Denzil was the most obvious to his mind. If he mentioned his suspicions of the young man to Susan, he realized it would avail him nothing but her scorn and dislike. She would realize his motive was jealousy, and all the hard-won friendship between them would vanish. He could not chance it. Usually Stephen did not worry about events he could not control. His was an easy and optimistic nature, but Denzil Capehart threatened that peace of mind. To a young woman, the officer must seem a far more enticing parti. If he was also a villain and a cad, Susan did not view him that way, Stephen was convinced. He could only continue to play the brotherly role and hope that eventually the officer would betray his true nature. On that unsatisfactory note, Stephen doused his candle and settled down to sleep.

On the following morning Margaret Woodhall made up her guest list for the dinner party. Having completed it, she showed it to Susan. "Is there anyone else you think we should invite?"

Susan looked at her mother tentatively. Could she suggest Denzil?

"Come, Susan, you look as if you want to add a name and fear I will reject it."

"I thought since Matilda French and Prudence Coville

will be coming, we might need another young man. What about Denzil? Do you still take him in dislike?"

If she were surprised and unwilling, Margaret did not show it. She had hoped that Stephen's company had proved a distraction and that Susan had abandoned her interest in the unsuitable young officer, but she would not pursue the matter. Much better to treat his inclusion with indifference.

"Not dislike so much, Susan, as wariness, but I could be mistaken in his character. If you wish, we will invite him."

"Thank you." Susan thought it better not to engage in any more discussion with her mother about Denzil. It would only lead to an argument between them, and Susan wanted to avoid that at all costs. She wasn't quite sure why she had asked for an invitation for Denzil. Her own feelings about the young man were confused. Without realizing it, her exposure to Stephen in the familiar atmosphere of her home had made an impact. Her mother's tactful avoidance of Denzil's unsuitability, and her assessment of the officer's character, had also influenced her. Although she did not completely agree with her mother, believing her to be biased by her unfortunate experience with Susan's father, she valued her mother's judgment. She must see some trait in Denzil that rebounded against him. Susan decided that she would ask Stephen's opinion of Denzil after the dinner party. She never once considered him in the role of the villain who had attacked their guest.

While the Woodhalls were planning their party and discussing who among their guests would bear examination, another pair of plotters were hatching their own deviltry. The suspect valet, Coats, had not been seen in the neighborhood because he had taken refuge with the man who had employed him to spy on Stephen.

It was Coats who had met his master in Bath and relayed the news that Stephen was riding alone into the city. Coats himself had been unwilling to make the attack, but his coconspirator had no such scruples. He had planned too long to remove any impediment from his torturous path to the earl's estate. His grandfather was the scapegrace who had been banned because of his transgressions from sharing in the Edgebury wealth, but he saw no reason why he should suffer such a fate. He knew nothing of the breaking of the entailment and believed if he could remove this last possible claimant to the earl's title and estate, he could produce his bona fides and inherit the lucrative lands. He had spent several years carefully researching the family. And he had cultivated a disgruntled employee from Edgebury Hall who had heard the tale of his disgraced grandfather and learned of the existence of Stephen. As long as his cousin had remained in India, he had not worried, expecting the young man to die there. India was not a salubrious climate or a safe billet for young men aspiring to make their way in the world. But Stephen had confounded his hopes and represented a real threat to him. He must be removed.

His first attempt had failed. His shot had missed a vital organ, and he would have followed it up; but by the time he tracked down the injured man whose horse had carried him away, he glimpsed Susan riding in the direction of the copse where Stephen lay. Now he would have to make another effort. He had not come this far to accept failure. It was unfortunate that Coats had incurred the suspicion of the inmates of Combe Manor, but he had another string to his bow and was about to play it. Coats might still be of some use. He would be the instrument of luring Stephen to a rendezvous that would remove that young man from any hope of becoming the Earl of Edgebury. Ruthless and determined, he entertained no idea that Coats might himself represent a threat, for he had

plans for dealing with the valet once his mission was accomplished. If Coats had any expectation of profiting
from his association with the would-be heir, he would
shortly be deceived. But in the meantime, the man had
his uses. He set the valet to composing a note that would
draw Stephen to his death.

# Nine

The dinner party, despite the disparate guests, proved a great success. Sir Edmund French was quite impressed with the invitation and on his best behavior. The vicar, an amiable soul, was always happy to oblige Mrs. Woodhall and enjoyed her hospitality whenever it was offered as did his meek little wife and daughter Prudence, who admired Susan and considered her a bosom bow. Lady French was quite intrigued with Stephen Venner, hoping that he might represent a possible husband for her daughter, Matilda. A vain hope considering the vapid Matilda's lack of charm. She was a nice enough girl, but devoid of conversation or looks, having protruding teeth and a decided squint. Susan was fond of her, having known her all her life, and overlooked her inadequacies.

Prudence, dressed demurely in a plain white muslin gown, was quite accustomed to being outshone by Susan, who looked radiant that evening in a cerulean blue silk dress accented with alençon lace. Although Prudence thought Stephen acceptable, even quite attractive, she could see that he had eyes only for Susan. She had met Denzil Capehart at the same assemblies where he had been so attentive to Susan, but she thought shrewdly that the young officer had been supplanted in her friend's heart by the romantic and dramatic arrival of the young man from India. Perhaps there was a chance for her with Denzil. Prudence had no illusions about Denzil. She rec-

ognized that he was looking for a well-dowered wife; and
although her funds could not rival Susan's, the vicar was
not dependent on his pay, and as his only child she could
expect a generous settlement when she wed. Both Prudence and Matilda, unlike Susan, were thoroughly occupied in getting married. But they were realistic and knew
they could not rival Susan's attributes.

Lady French was fascinated by the earl and archly sim-
pered at him, trying to discover if he had any interest in
Margaret Woodhall, as all the Bath gossips inferred. She
thought Margaret looked a little pale and drawn that evening, although she admired her garnet silk gown and en-
vied her pearls. But Lady French was not a very perceptive
woman, inclined to make up her mind and not allow
events to disturb any judgment she had previously made.
No, the earl was not attracted to Margaret, she decided
thankfully. She would not have liked her widowed neighbor to become a countess.

If Margaret Woodhall looked a bit pale, it was not to
be wondered. Having offered to give this dinner to examine her friends and neighbors as possible enemies of
Stephen Venner had seemed clever in the abstract, but
now that the company was assembled, she had doubts as
to the efficacy of her plan. By nature charitable, she did
not like to think of any in her intimate circle capable of
such infamy, and looking over the guests, she decided
she had been foolish, grasping at straws. Also she was
concerned about Denzil Capehart's attentions to Susan.

While Margaret thought she was behaving in a distracted manner, the earl marveled at her composure and
her competent grasp of her hostess duties. He had a good
idea of what was passing through her mind. In meeting
these neighbors for the first time, he also found it incon-
ceivable that any of them—the vicar, the solicitor, the
colonel, the doctor or Sir Edmund French—could possibly be the perpetrator of such a crime. He was not so

sure of Denzil Capehart, however. He recognized in that young man the traits he had always decried in his own junior officers. He thought Denzil opportunistic, overly ambitious, self-indulgent, and conceited. He considered whether the officer might be their villain. He also noticed that Stephen was eyeing the young man and might share his suspicions. Denzil was on his best behavior, attentive to Susan but paying his respects to the older ladies, charming Lady French and the vicar's wife, while still implying he had a special claim on Susan's time.

After the dinner, a simple but tasteful meal of salmon, lamb, spring peas and new potatoes followed by a compote of sugared pears, the ladies adjourned, leaving the gentlemen to their port. Colonel Bushnell, knowing of the earl's experience on the Peninsula in the late war, quizzed him on the various battles, having served at Salamanca himself, which left the professional men to discuss local news. Thus, Denzil and Stephen were forced together, as the youngest of the assembly and supposed to have much in common. Stephen tried to discover a bit about the officer's past, but Denzil was skilled at avoiding any questions about his background and family. He treated Stephen with a careless bonhomie that implied he did not consider him a threat to his attentions toward Susan. With his conceit, Denzil would always find it difficult to think any female could prefer another young man, especially one who did not wear a uniform, to his own obvious good looks and practiced address. He found Stephen rather prosy and quiet, little attraction to a girl of spirit and beauty such as Susan. He hid his concern that Stephen living in close proximity to her might have managed to attract Susan in the role of a stranger who had arrived so dramatically on her doorstep. He made his own prior claim quite evident.

"You can tell me, Venner, how you find Mrs. Woodhall. She seems to dominate Susan, wants to choose her friends and dictate her life," he confided after the port had gone around twice.

"Mrs. Woodhall is a kind and gracious lady, a hospitable hostess. I have become very fond of her and believe she approves of me, thankfully." It was as he feared, Denzil had designs on Susan and thought she returned his interest.

"Widows can be demanding, expecting their children to dance attendance on them. Very annoying." Denzil did not understand that any criticism of Mrs. Woodhall would not be well received by Stephen.

"I don't think Mrs. Woodhall is that type. My cousin believes her to be both a sensible and charming woman." Stephen spoke dismissively. He did not like the tenor of the conversation.

"I wonder if she controls Susan's dowry," Denzil said, incurring further scorn. He assumed that any young man hanging out for a wife would be interested in how well fixed she was.

"I have no idea. How long will your regiment be in Bath, Capehart?" Stephen turned the talk away from these unpleasant speculations on the Woodhall finances.

"Some time yet, I hope. I find the environs and the company very pleasant, much improved from the Shropshire posting we had previously."

Before Stephen could probe further, the earl, acting as host, suggested the gentlemen join the ladies, so Stephen could not learn more, to both his chagrin and relief.

On entering the drawing room Denzil went straight to Susan. He had no intention of wasting any more time on Prudence or the horsy French girl.

"I haven't had a word with you alone in ages, Susan. Can we not walk in the garden? It's a lovely night," he coaxed.

Susan, who had her own questions to put to Denzil,

was not averse, but was also conscious that her mother would not be pleased at such forward behavior.

"I believe Mother wants some music, but we might take a short stroll." She went across to her mother to learn her wishes while Denzil waited impatiently by the door to the gardens which led from the drawing room.

"Mother, if it is all right with you, I want to take a stroll with Denzil. I find the air in here quite close," Susan said. Then seeing they were not overheard, she added, "I want to quiz him a bit. He has the potential to be our villain."

"Do you think so?" Margaret was startled. She had never imagined that Susan, so partial to the officer, could be considering him as a suspect. But she was so encouraged by this view, she agreed. "But don't be long. I don't want you the object of gossip, and we have a duty to our guests."

"Of course." Susan saw the wisdom of this advice. "I won't be missed. And here comes the earl to keep you company." She slipped out of the room, accompanied by Denzil, much to Stephen's discomfort. But he was a polite man and settled down by Prudence to pay her some attention and talk about Susan.

Denzil led Susan quickly from the view of the drawing room, toward the far end of the garden that was perfumed with the scent of roses. Susan, a bit discomposed, insisted they sit on a bench.

"What did you want to see me about, Denzil?"

"You must have guessed, Susan, that I hold you in great admiration. I have hesitated to call and plead my case because your mother does not seem to approve of me, a view I hope you don't share." He was about to continue, but Susan interrupted him.

"My mother is naturally concerned about my well-being

and my future." Her voice held a reproof, but Denzil ignored it.

"And so am I, Susan. I hope it is a future we can share. I am asking you to be my wife."

Thinking that a bit of persuasion might help his cause, Denzil took Susan in his arms and pressed a hot kiss upon her lips. She did not respond and unhurriedly released herself.

"That was unwise, Denzil. I have given you no reason to believe I would be receptive to such advances."

Before Denzil could protest and demand an answer, Stephen appeared. If he had seen the caress, he showed no sign of it, only announcing mildly that her mother wished her to accompany Prudence on the piano as the vicar's daughter had been invited to sing.

Susan leaped up, eager to comply, and a bit flustered. She hoped Stephen had not drawn an unwelcome inference to her tête-à-tête with Denzil. She felt confused, and annoyed. She had not liked that young man's kiss or his assumption that she would welcome it. What would Stephen think, and why did she care?

"Of course. Prudence has a lovely voice. Let us go in. Coming, Denzil?" she asked, noticing the sulky expression on his face and not liking it. She supposed she should feel flattered by his proposal, but instead she felt irritated. This was not a time for dalliance or suggestions of marriage. Could he not see that? And she had not liked his criticism of her mother. She took Stephen's arm and allowed him to escort her back to the drawing room, leaving Denzil to trail behind, cursing the interruption. He believed she would have assented to his proposal given a bit more persuasion. His attentions had never been received in such a cavalier manner before, and Susan was as susceptible as any female, he wrongly decided. Damn that Venner trying to queer his pitch, he concluded coarsely.

The rest of the evening passed without incident, and the guests bid Mrs. Woodhall farewell before midnight, thanking her profusely for the dinner party. After they had all left, the earl, Margaret, Stephen and Susan held a council of war.

"If our suspicions are correct, your attacker must be some fellow who has an interest in Edgebury," the earl said after they had gathered in the morning room. Margaret thought the intimate setting might be helpful, although she herself was none the wiser after the party.

"I can't believe any of our guests could be the rogue who shot at you, Stephen," she objected, fanning herself, for the evening was close.

"No, it seems unlikely. Haven't most of them been living here for ages."

"Certainly, the doctor and Mr. Pecksmith have been here as long as I can recall. Sir Edmund took up residence when Lady French's father died, some ten years ago. The vicar came into the living about six years ago."

"That leaves the colonel and young Capehart," the earl suggested.

Stephen was relieved that Denzil's name had been mentioned by the earl. He had not wanted to bring up that young officer's obvious claim.

"Sir Edmund is much too pompous and unimaginative to have thought up such a plot, and the vicar too unworldly. About the colonel I have little opinion, but I had considered Denzil," Susan admitted. It was obvious that the thought of Denzil as the perpetrator disturbed her. She remembered his proposal and wondered if it was greed not love that had prompted it, but that was an idea she could only discuss in private with her mother.

"He is certainly possible. We know little of his background," Margaret offered a bit tentatively. She did not want to anger her daughter, who she thought would believe her eagerness to accuse Denzil might spring from her general disapproval of him.

"You seem to know him best, my dear. Where does he come from?" the earl asked. He had a suspicion as to why Stephen was reluctant to push Denzil as his attacker, but certainly the officer was a prime candidate.

"He told me his parents were dead and that he came from up north, but he was very vague and did not entertain questions about his early days with any pleasure." Susan was honest enough to admit Denzil seemed to have all the qualifications for the role the earl had assigned to him. Yet somehow she felt she had to defend him. "But you know, we are forgetting a man who was not here this evening, but has a great interest in the Edgebury estates."

"And who is that?" Margaret asked.

"The earl's agent, Nigel Thorndyke. I was hesitant to suggest him before because I know, sir, that you have great confidence in him."

"Yes, yes I do." The earl looked taken aback, perturbed at this introduction of yet another possible miscreat.

"He has been with you just a short time, since your father's death and your return from the army, I understand." Margaret looked worried. She had not especially warmed to Mr. Thorndyke, but she had been guided by the earl's evident faith in him. "Of course you took up his references?" She turned to the earl for confirmation.

"Yes, and they were impeccable. He left his last post with one of the Percys in Northumberland because the heir wanted to try his hand at estate management." The earl frowned. Could his trust in Nigel be misplaced?

"And what about the colonel?" Stephen intervened, seeing his cousin's unhappiness.

"He has had a long career in the army, but that does not mean much, I suppose. He could have been biding his time and on the lucky chance of being posted here decided to cement his claims by ridding the world of Stephen." Susan's imagination was fertile, and the idea of a rival to Denzil as the attacker appealed to her.

"So we are little better off than before the party. Could you discover from your chat with the colonel and young Capehart any reason to think they might have been behind the ambush of Stephen?" asked Margaret, eager to be fair and soothe the earl, who seemed upset at the thought of his agent as their villain.

"Not really," the earl replied. The colonel knew several chaps I know when he served abroad in the Peninsula and spent some time in Paris during the occupation. Capehart appears to have had only peacetime duties. But that proves little. Oh dear, we are not any further in our quest, I am afraid."

"Well, it is late, and we must retire," Margaret said, looking around with a puzzled air.

"Yes, indeed. Tomorrow we must make a plan for Stephen to accompany me home. He has trespassed on your kindness long enough, and I want him to see Edgebury. Much as I have enjoyed our time here, I have been away far too long."

"I am certainly recovered enough to travel. I fear I have taken advantage of your hospitality beyond decent bounds," Stephen agreed.

Margaret hastened to reassure him. She wondered if his departure would serve as an incentive for another attempt to waylay him, but she did not want to suggest such a possibility. She realized, too, that she would miss not only Stephen, but the earl's comforting company. Still, she could see the necessity of them both departing.

"We will meet tomorrow, and now I must be on my way back to Bath. I rode out, so if you will call for my horse, I will be on my way," the earl insisted a bit gruffly. He did not want to leave Combe Manor and had every intention of keeping in close touch with the Woodhalls. He thought Stephen shared his view.

The company departed, all of them to troubled rest, for Susan, in particular, felt they had not heard the last of Stephen's attacker, and they were all worried about what lay ahead.

# *Ten*

The next morning, after their late night, Stephen, Margaret and Susan met for breakfast and tried to put a cheerful face on affairs. But any attempt to do so became fruitless when Jennings delivered a note to Stephen before he had even begun his deviled kidneys.

"This came early, Mr. Venner. One of the maids found it on the doorstep when she came down this morning. It must have been delivered at dawn," Jennings informed them. He withdrew from the room reluctantly, obviously very curious as to the message.

Stephen slit open the missive and then gasped.

"What is it, Stephen?" Susan asked.

"The fellow has gone too far. He says if I want to see the earl alive, I must meet him this morning at eleven near the Red Pheasant. It is signed by Coats."

"I knew he was behind this business. He or his ally must have apprehended the earl last night as he rode away from here," Susan exclaimed.

"Where is the Red Pheasant?" Stephen asked.

"It's a disreputable pub about five miles from here off the post road to the south," Margaret informed him. "Not a respectable tavern and mostly frequented by farm laborers and dubious types. You cannot go, Stephen."

"I must. Surely you can see that."

"Yes, if you insist, but you must take precautions. I will have Andrew gather up some of the men, and they will accompany you," Margaret pleaded. She, too, was concerned for the earl. She only realized now how much she had come to look forward to his visits, how much she admired his unfailing courtesy, his good sense and his generous nature.

"The note says I must come alone." Stephen looked angry and confused but not afraid.

"Oh, Stephen, I really think you must take some precautions. This could be a trap." Susan was impressed with Stephen's courage, but thought he was behaving in a foolhardy fashion. Naturally he cared about the earl's safety, but he must take some heed for his own.

"It probably is a trap, but as long as I am prepared, no harm should come to me. My first concern is the earl. And I think this confirms our guess that the villain must be the lost descendant who believes by removing me, and then the earl, he might be able to claim the estate." He spoke with resolution; now that the mystery appeared solved, he believed he could handle any problem connected with the mystery man's plots.

Neither Susan nor Margaret was so certain.

"I insist you take Andrew with you, at least part of the way. He will show you the direction of the Red Pheasant. It is quite out of the way, known only to the local inhabitants, I suspect," Margaret urged.

"Yes, I must waste no time in meeting the man's deadline. Who knows what my cousin might be subjected to by the rogue."

"I will send for Andrew." Margaret rang for Jennings, who appeared promptly from the servants' quarters, aware that some skullduggery connected with the note he had delivered might threaten the Woodhalls' houseguest. He was dispatched to summon the agent.

"It is just half after nine. You have plenty of time, and you must finish your breakfast." Margaret's practical and maternal nature was aroused. She knew she could not dissuade Stephen from his dangerous task, and though she was worried about the earl, Stephen needed her support, not foolish moanings and dire warnings.

After his breakfast Stephen awaited Andrew Baird, determined to set off in good time for the rendezvous. As a precaution, he first went to his room and rummaged in his chest of drawers until he found his pistol. Only once before had he had any occasion to use it, when a crazed fakir had attacked him in India, but he was a good shot and quite prepared to use his weapon in defense of the earl. When Andrew Baird appeared, a bit flustered and surprised, Stephen said firmly he would see the agent alone. He had no intention of adding to Margaret's and Susan's fears by allowing them to listen to his plans. They were alarmed enough, he could see, and his instinct was to protect them from further worry. Also he did not want to mention his chief concern, that his former valet might be in the employ of Denzil Capehart. If Susan genuinely cared for that dubious fellow, why add to her unease? And Stephen had decided that Denzil must indeed be the culprit.

He had met Andrew several times about the estate and found him a competent, cheerful man who would probably be a dependable ally. He explained what was involved. Andrew appeared to grasp the situation quickly.

"The Red Pheasant is a low dive, isolated and squalid, patronized by ruffians. Several attempts have been made to close it down, but the landlord, an ugly brute named Joe Riggs, has so far held off the authorities. You will be well advised to take precautions."

"I am prepared, I think, but my first concern is the earl." Stephen spoke in a hard tone, one that the Woodhall ladies would not have recognized.

Andrew Baird realized he was not dealing with the amiable and pleasant young man he had previously thought of little account. His whole personality seemed to have altered into a character it would serve him well to treat warily.

The pair set off a little after ten o'clock, alone despite Margaret's advice to take some of the grooms or farm laborers with them.

"The fewer people that know about this danger, the better," Stephen informed her firmly. "The earl would not appreciate the news of his abduction becoming common knowledge in the Pump Room."

"Oh, who could care about that when his life is in danger," Margaret protested.

"His life is not in danger. I am the target of this villain's attention. He has shown his hand rather foolishly. He cannot afford to harm the earl and dispatch me and then make a claim for the estate. The magistrates would immediately suspect foul play. I imagine he has a different role for the earl to play." Stephen meant to be reassuring, although he secretly believed, now that the man had recklessly shown his true colors, he must be desperate and prepared to commit any crime to assure his ends.

"Perhaps, but we don't really know what he is capable of doing." Susan made her own views apparent.

"Remember, the man probably has knowledge of the broken entailment, and I think that is a card the earl will play with some skill. After all, my cousin is an experienced soldier, not some craven fool who will submit tamely to any demands."

"I hope you are right, Stephen, but do take care," Margaret said and then, to Stephen's surprise, reached up and gave him a kiss on his cheek. Before he could respond to her gesture or the tears in her eyes, she rustled from the room, leaving him alone with Susan.

"I am sorry to have upset your mother."

"She is fond of you, Stephen—and, I think, of the earl."

Stephen yearned to ask her if she shared her mother's

sentiments, but realized he would be taking advantage of her apprehension. He could not ask her how she felt about him when he might be going out to remove the man he considered his rival, not only for his inheritance, but for Susan's affections. Stephen was thoroughly convinced that when he reached the Red Pheasant he would meet the sly Coats and Denzil Capehart, the organizer of the attempt to kill him. He took Susan's hands in a warm clasp.

"Try not to worry, Susan. I will be back before you know it with the earl. Comfort your mother." And before she could make any objection, he took her gently in his arms and kissed her briefly, his lips barely grazing hers, and then he was gone to meet Andrew in the stables. She stood looking dazed, wondering what the kiss had meant. It had not been a passionate caress, just a tender reassurance, so different from the bruising attempt at dominance by Denzil last night. He had shown concern not for himself, but for her and her mother. What a rare and considerate man he was, and Susan realized that he had made an indelible impact upon her. How dreadful if harm should come to him before he could tell her of his real feelings. She hurried to the hall and opened the front door, arriving just in time to see Andrew and Stephen riding down the driveway. She hoped he would turn for a final look, but he rode on, Susan forgotten as he turned his whole attention to what awaited him at the Red Pheasant.

Susan, mindful of her mother's disquiet, as heavy as her own, turned away with a sigh to join her. Oh, why could she not do something to protect Stephen, to thwart the greedy and dangerous man who was his enemy? She found her mother in the morning room, sitting disconsolately behind her desk.

"I cannot settle to any chore, Susan, with this dreadful situation facing Stephen and the earl."

"I know. I wish I could ride out and confront the murderer myself." Susan looked so fierce, Margaret was startled. Did Susan not realize that Stephen might be about to face Denzil Capehart when he reached that tavern?

"Sometimes I hate being a female. All we do when men are in danger is wait and wail."

"You don't look very timid, only angry and distressed."

"I am more than distressed. I am furious. To think that some criminal would attack Stephen once, then try again, and then use the earl as a bargaining tool. It's disgusting and heinous."

"Yes, but we can do little but put our hope in Stephen. He is both sensible and courageous. I must pray that all will turn out well. Andrew will help him."

"I just have this feeling that there is some aspect to this affair that we have not fathomed. All is not as straightforward as it appears." Susan made no mention of Denzil, but he was on her mind. Somehow she could not see him as the ogre behind all this business. She doubted he would put himself in a position where he would be forced to reveal his true character. She realized with a flash of insight that Denzil might not be the charming young man who courted her, but a possible murderer. No, vain, shallow, ambitious and concerned only for himself, he was all of that, but she did not believe he had what her old groom Jem called "the bottom" to face any rival and coolly kill him. He cared too much for his personal safety to boldly face harm. He would always take the easiest way, rather than work to achieve his ambitions. Susan now could ignore his charm and see him for the meretricious opportunist that he was. Brooding over her misreading of his character, she stood silent. Finally her mother, unable to conceal her worry, spoke.

"Do you think the mysterious attacker might be Lieutenant Capehart?"

"No, and not because I am so bemused by his attractions. I don't think he is either clever or ruthless enough to plan such a scheme. Denzil has grave faults, but not the determination or courage to attempt such a crime."

Margaret hid her relief at Susan's altered opinion of Denzil. Susan would not thank her for saying, "I told you so." Only a comparison with Stephen could have persuaded her daughter to see the officer in his true light, but she would not mention that. The two women sat silently, each absorbed in her own thoughts. Time appeared to be passing much too slowly. Susan finally jumped up and walked to the window which overlooked the drive, staring with unseeing eyes at the long vista of the driveway lined with lush lime trees. Then she noticed a figure trotting in the distance. Who could be calling at this hour?

"Mother, someone is approaching." Not waiting for her mother to respond, she rushed from the room and ran to the entrance, tugging at the door before Jennings, who had appeared noiselessly from the servants' quarters, could open it for her.

Poised impatiently on the steps, watching as the rider drew near, she finally recognized the earl. She stood aghast. If he was safe, where was Stephen? Oh, God, could he have been injured, even killed? As the earl dismounted and handed his horse's reins to a groom who had come up hurriedly from the stables, Margaret Woodhall joined her daughter on the step.

"What are you doing here, Godfrey?" she asked, shocked by his unexpected appearance.

"I told you I would call today. What's wrong? You both look distraught." The earl was taken aback by his reception.

"Come in. We have disturbing news." Margaret did not want the curious groom, who kept looking over his shoulder as he slowly led the earl's horse to the stables, to hear their explanation.

The earl followed them into the house, greeting Jennings politely and giving the butler his crop, hat and gloves, before following Margaret and Susan into the morning room.

"Now, what's the trouble?" he asked the two obviously upset women.

In her agitation Margaret paced the room, then turned to the earl and explained before Susan could voice her own fears.

"Stephen received a note from that nasty Coats this morning saying that you had been abducted and if he wanted to see you alive, he must meet Coats at the Red Pheasant at eleven o'clock this morning. He set off at ten with our agent, Andrew Baird, to show him the way."

"I see, an obvious trap to apprehend him or worse," the earl said, now as concerned as Susan and Margaret. "Did you notify the authorities, the village constable?" he added.

"We never thought of it. And Stephen would never have consented for fear of endangering you."

"I must ride to this Red Pheasant and rescue Stephen, the foolish boy, worried for my safety. If he had not been so overset, he would have recognized it as a ploy to harm him. But we have no time to waste. Where is this Red Pheasant?"

Somewhat reassured by the earl's calm reception of her news, Margaret hastened to explain. "It's a low tavern about five miles to the south, difficult to find, I understand. I have never seen it, but Andrew said it was the haunt of bad types and even criminals."

"Well, I will find it, if you will lend me a guide to its direction. Doubtless one of the grooms or farm workers knows of the place." The earl spoke calmly as if this were no more than a tiresome errand, hoping to calm the Woodhalls' fears.

"I will take the earl, Mother. I know the place. Jem

pointed it out to me once and warned me about riding near it." Susan, eager to take some action and fearing for Stephen, was determined not to spend any more agonizing moments waiting for news.

"I don't think that's a good idea, my dear. Perhaps this Jem could lead me to it." The earl thought women had no business involving themselves in dangerous missions, but Susan was not to be denied.

"No, I insist. I cannot just sit here doing nothing."

"You could soothe your mother," the earl said, his every instinct to protect Margaret and help her, as her usual composure had collapsed under this threat to Stephen.

"If I were a decent rider, I would come with you," Margaret insisted, "and I wish Susan was less reckless, but you cannot stop her. She will just follow you if you refuse to take her. She is a very intrepid girl." Margaret smiled a bit, although the strain of events was evident on her face.

"Quite right, Mother. Call for the horses. I won't be a moment. Thank goodness I am dressed for riding and we need not delay long."

Before either of her elders could protest, she had whirled from the room, leaving the earl looking at Margaret in dismay.

"Surely you could forbid her, Margaret. She could be in considerable peril."

"I have every faith that you will protect her, Godfrey. I think she has come to care for Stephen, and she would never forgive me if harm came to him and she could have done her bit to prevent it."

"She needs a firm hand." The earl disapproved, but he could see his warnings were to no avail. The Woodhall women were accustomed to managing their own affairs, and no matter what prudence dictated, they would not be denied.

"Yes, she does. She needs a strong husband, and a loving one. Perhaps Stephen is the man."

"Then we must rescue him," the earl hesitantly conceded as Susan burst into the room again, a pistol in her hand, dressed for their ride. She reluctantly relinquished the pistol to the earl, who looked at it, cocked it once, and then pocketed it.

"We will be back in no time with Stephen. Try not to worry, Margaret."

If Susan had not been watching, he would have given her mother more than a reassuring clasp of his hand, but that would have to wait. Jennings appeared to announce the horses were at the door, and without any ceremony, the earl and Susan left, trailed by Margaret to the entrance, where she watched them gallop off without any more than a hasty farewell. Turning as she saw them vanish down the drive, she found Jennings at her side, waiting for some explanation, although he would not ask for one.

"Mr. Venner has gone to a rendezvous with some villain under the misapprehension that the earl was abducted, Jennings. I know you will understand that there must be no gossip in the servants' hall about this dreadful crisis. I suppose it's hopeless to keep the servants from talking, but I rely on you to calm them and not dramatize the situation."

"Of course, madam. I am sure the earl will solve matters. He seems a very capable and courageous gentleman," Jennings comforted his mistress while wondering what this imbroglio was all about. He knew that Stephen Venner had been shot by some unknown assailant, and he suspected the culprit had determined to try again after his first failure to kill Stephen. He was not unaware that both Susan and his mistress had become attached to the young man and only hoped that a tragedy could be averted. Like all long-time retainers, the fortunes of the family that he served were very close to his heart, and he shared Mrs. Woodhall's fears for the safety of Stephen.

"Let me bring you a nice cup of tea. I know waiting is difficult and you want to take some action, but you must not try to impede the earl's rescue. And his last words to me were to watch over you."

"Thank you, Jennings. You are such a comfort. I will try to compose myself, but I cannot deny I am worried." Margaret smiled at Jennings, grateful for his understanding and prepared for what she knew would be an agonizing several hours.

# *Eleven*

Stephen had left Andrew about five hundred yards from the Red Pheasant, which at first sight confirmed its reputation, a tumble-down, faded wooden building, its grounds overgrown and the once proud sign peeling and faded so that the lettering was barely legible. Andrew had wanted to accompany him, but Stephen had insisted that he could not endanger the earl by not obeying Coats' instructions to arrive alone. Andrew had finally agreed to stay with the horses, concealed by a convenient stand of beech trees.

Stephen approached the entrance warily, for the tavern had a forbiddingly silent air. Upon entering, he could barely see, for the few small, dirty windows allowed little light to penetrate. He stood for a moment just inside the door, which he had left ajar, looking for the man who had summoned him there, and feeling for his pistol tucked into his pocket. There seemed to be no customers, which did not surprise him, and in the dim recesses he could glimpse the outline of the bar; but no landlord stood behind it. Where could the earl be confined? Beyond the bar, as he moved closer, he could see some rickety steps leading to rooms above, he supposed. He must be there. Before he could mount the stairs, Coats suddenly materialized out of the gloom and faced him in a menacing manner. Stephen drew his pistol.

"You don't want to do that, governor," Coats growled.

"Where is the earl?" Stephen asked, not intimidated, but fearful for his cousin, although determined not to give ground to this rogue.

"I reckon he's still in Bath living off the fat of the land and tossing his coins around to some fawning idiots," Coats sneered. "But you are here, just where we want you."

"I thought so. It was a trap, that note of yours, to lure me to this low hole."

"Quite right. You will be killed in a drunken tavern brawl, and no more than you deserve." Coats' hatred was evident.

"Why do you hate me so?" Stephen was curious. He could not believe this brutal blackguard was the same quiet, polite man who had been his valet.

"You toffs are all the same, never thinking of your servants as human with needs and desires and far better than you for all your gold. I have no real quarrel with you, but I want my share of that high and mighty earl's estate, and I will have it."

Stephen cocked the pistol. "I think not, my man."

"But I think so," came a hard voice from behind him, and Stephen felt the end of a gun poked into his back. "Give me that gun," the voice menaced.

Stephen turned and grappled with the man, whom he could not recognize in the gloom, but Coats came up behind him and grasped his arms in a throttling grip. He wrested Stephen's gun from him as Stephen stood amazed rather than frightened. Facing him from the threshold was Andrew Baird.

"Baird, I told you not to interfere." He could not believe that Andrew had not come to rescue him.

"Ah, I fooled you all. You are a nuisance to me, Venner, and I intend to remove you."

"Why, what have I done to you?" Stephen, shocked, could barely take in Andrew's appearance and his threatening stance. He must keep him talking. There was much here he did not understand.

"I have waited far too long to come into my rights. Now you turn up, a claimant to the estate that is rightfully mine. My grandfather was the earl's great-uncle, and so I will inherit it all when the earl sticks his spoon in the wall."

"And Coats here has abetted you in this attempt to secure what you consider your due," Stephen said calmly. His lack of fear annoyed Andrew, but the agent had kept his secret too long. Now he had the chance to air his grievances, and since Stephen would not live to thwart his plans, he saw no danger in boasting of his cleverness.

"You're a credulous fool, Venner. Did you never connect that attack on you with Combe Manor? I took this job some years ago, biding my time. I heard of you from a disgruntled servant on the earl's estate and laid my plans. I had hoped you would die conveniently in India, but you confounded my hopes. When I heard of your arrival in England to visit the Earl, I decided I would have to take drastic action."

Stephen looked with pity on the man. All this plotting and chicanery and for what. He did not know the entailment had been broken. Whatever deviltry he committed, he had no chance of inheriting.

"It's all been for naught, you know. Even if you dispatch me and some mischief should cause the earl's death, you will not get the estate. The entailment was broken a generation ago. The earl's estate is his to bequeath as he wishes, and somehow I doubt he would willingly leave it to you. You seem to have inherited your grandfather's criminal instincts. At least he was not a murderer."

"You're lying, trying to save yourself. Well, I am not gulled by such a fanciful tale."

"Suit yourself. And what will you do about Coats, now

that he has joined you in this murderous attempt on me? He could blackmail you for the rest of your life."

"I wouldn't do that, governor," Coats whined, not liking the tenor of the conversation.

"If I were you, Coats, I would watch my back. If Baird here kills me and you are the only witness, he cannot allow you to live either. Think about it."

"Pay no attention, Coats. This fool is trying to save his own skin." Andrew Baird had lost any vestiges of his cheerful, obliging air, and an ugly look passed over his face. He ought to shoot the fellow without any more palaver, but he could not keep himself from justifying his evil deed. Though he recognized Stephen's attempt to plant suspicion of his motives in Coats' mind, a clever tactic, to try to divide conspirators and set them arguing, he was more than a match for Stephen's useless stalling. With misplaced arrogance at seeing his plans within an ace of success, Andrew had to boast.

"Do you think I would be content to play the ingratiating, grateful agent to the Woodhalls for the rest of my life, when I could be the next Earl of Edgebury? I want to enjoy the good life, which is my birthright, not be patronized by people who should be bowing and scraping to me. If the earl dies intestate with no legal heir, then it does not matter about the entailment, for as the closest relative I will inherit anyway. I have studied the law. I have left nothing to chance. Only you stand between me and a life of wealth and prestige," he crowed. In his exhilaration he had not heard what Stephen had, the stealthy approach of someone just outside the inn.

"And the earl, of course," Stephen reminded him, hoping that whoever was on the threshold would do nothing foolish.

"Oh, he's no problem. He can be dispatched easily once you are out of the picture."

"Get on with it, governor, all this talk is wasting time.

Unless you are too lily-livered to pull that trigger," Coats urged.

Baird raised his gun, hoping to hear Stephen plead for his life. That would have given him great satisfaction. But before be could fulfill his murderous intent, a shot rang out, and he dropped his gun with an oath. Blood was coming from his injured hand, and Stephen picked up the gun before either Andrew or Coats realized what had happened.

"I think, Baird, you have mistaken your man." The earl spoke as he entered the room. He looked both capable and resolute, quite prepared to take further action if necessary. If he was surprised at the identity of Stephen's attacker, he did not show it.

"Keep the gun trained on the rogue, Stephen. I will take a look about to make sure there are no other villains waiting to ambush us."

"Thank you, sir. There is Coats. He's in this with Baird." But the former valet, seeing the collapse of his coconspirator's plan, had melted away.

"Well, I suppose we had better take this fellow to the magistrate and lodge our complaint. Too bad to lose Coats, but we have the chief villain, at least."

Baird stood glowering, nursing his wounded hand, and looked with loathing at the earl and Stephen. At that moment Susan entered the inn, took in the scene before her and reported in a breathless voice.

"That man, Coats, was trying to escape. I hit him with a piece of wood, and he's lying unconscious beyond the back door. One of you had better apprehend him before he tries to escape again."

"Well done, Susan. You are a brave girl," the earl commended with a twinkle in his eye. He might have suspected she would play a part in this dramatic episode.

"Susan, you shouldn't be here." Stephen looked at her with admiration and much more.

"Nonsense, Stephen. The earl would not allow me to come into the inn with him. I had to do something. We were very worried about you." She blushed, trying to hide the revelation that she was afraid she had just made.

But Stephen, recovering from his near escape, would not allow her to retreat behind any mistaken maidenly reserve. He crossed to her side, ignoring both the earl and Baird, took her in his arms and kissed her thoroughly.

"Thank you, Susan. And I have much more to say to you at the proper time," he said, as they both emerged from the embrace breathing hard and looking bemused.

The earl chuckled. "Enough of that. Your lovemaking must wait. We have a lot of clearing up to do here. I wonder where the landlord is; well-paid to absent himself, I suppose." Although he was pleased with the outcome of this affair, the earl had not forgotten Andrew Baird, who stood uncertainly, nursing his hand and wondering if he could manage to save himself from the inevitable charge of attempted murder.

"You shot me without cause. You will answer for that," he threatened the earl.

"I think not. I arrived in time to hear your plan to kill Stephen and your reasons. Do you think any magistrate would take your word against mine, especially when he heard the motive for your villainous plot. Come along. You will give no more trouble, I think."

The earl, paying no attention to Baird's pleas, secured his arms with a stout piece of rope, shepherded Susan and Stephen before him and left the tavern. On the way, he ordered Stephen to gather up the groggy Coats, who was just returning to his senses from the blow Susan had delivered so tellingly. It took some doing, forcing both the injured men onto horses and securing them to the saddles, the earl following closely behind Baird, Stephen behind Coats, and Susan trailing the quartet as they rode into the village. Stephen understood why his cousin had been such a successful officer. He met danger forcefully and with caution, but with no idea of defeat. The villagers were all agog to see the cavalcade ride up to the local hall with their prisoners.

In moments the earl had made the situation plain, and despite Andrew Baird's objections, both he and Coats were confined in a secure room while the earl made a formal complaint against the prisoners.

"They will have to be dispatched to Bath to await trial, my man," the earl informed the shocked constable, a sturdy, slow-witted man easily dominated by the earl, whose air of command as well as his title left no room for argument.

"Certainly, my lord. And you will be available to testify to the authorities," he added.

"Yes, indeed. I am staying at the Royal York, or you can reach me at Combe Manor."

Within half an hour Stephen, Susan and the earl had trotted out of the village on their way to Combe Manor and the waiting Margaret.

Margaret hailed them with tearful relief and a demand for explanations which were somewhat confusedly given.


Later, after a leisurely luncheon, Margaret heard more details. Amazed at Andrew Baird's duplicity and her false impression of a man she had always trusted, she shook her head in sorrow.

"How could I have been so deceived by him. He appeared so pleasant, so obliging, so good at his work."

"All a facade, Margaret, while behind it he schemed and planned his evil deed. A man, disgruntled and disappointed, believing life owed him a prize to which he was not entitled. Not content with his job here, he was greedy and nursing a grievance that he had inherited

from his father and grandfather. You cannot be blamed
for not seeing through his mask. He would have made a
fine actor." The earl comforted her. They were alone in
the morning room as Stephen and Susan, eager to be
alone, had departed to the garden.

Margaret frowned, still shocked by the turn of events.

"You need someone to look after you, my dear. You
have managed magnificently all these years, but you must
have been often troubled and lonely, bringing up two
fine children with courage and good sense. Susan is a
remarkable girl, as I am sure Stephen has discovered. If
I am not surprised, he is asking her this very moment to
be his wife, and she will agree. They will make a fine
couple. Now you must think of yourself. Is there any hope
you will reward my patience and deep regard for you by
doing likewise. In my clumsy way I am asking you to be
my wife." The earl's sincerity was obvious, but so was his
doubt.

Margaret hurried to reassure him. "Oh, Godfrey, I have
come to both admire and love you. Of course I will marry
you."


In the garden, Stephen, much less articulate but
equally determined, was persuading Susan of his love for
her. Taking her in his arms, he told her of his fears and
hesitation.

"I thought you cared for Capehart," he confided.

"Don't be silly, Stephen. Denzil has charm but little
else to recommend him. He would make an impossible
husband." She paused and then admitted. "At one time
I found his attentions flattering, I admit, but your arrival
changed all that. And then when I saw you riding off with
the odious Andrew into danger so bravely, I realized how
I really felt about you."

"I didn't acquit myself that well. If it were not for my

cousin, I would probably not be alive to ask you to be my wife."

"Nonsense. You would have contrived. I still can't believe that Andrew was such a knave, but you would have vanquished him." She smiled cheekily, all her fears and unhappiness melting in the knowledge that the cloud of danger that had hovered over him had at last disappeared.

"We will be married as soon as possible. There is no reason to wait, is there?" he pleaded, emphasizing his urgency with some passionate kisses.

Susan, reluctantly disengaging herself from his embrace, did not argue. But a sudden thought shadowed her face, and Stephen was quick to sense her withdrawal.

"Will your mother object, do you think?"

"She is very fond of you. But I hate deserting her. She has not had an easy life. My father was not an admirable or devoted husband."

"Well, don't worry. I suspect she will soon be planning her own trousseau. The earl admires her exceedingly, and I think he will ask her to become his wife. We might even have a double wedding."

Cocking her head and looking at him with a mischievous expression, she said, "You might be right. But I am not sure I want to share the biggest moment of my life, even with my mother. You are warned, I am a willful girl, who will lead you a dance."

"I will do the leading, my girl, never fear, but for now let us enjoy ourselves." And this they proceeded to do, only stopping their mutual congratulations on the outcome of their affairs when the earl and Margaret called them into the house to give them their own news.

# A GENTLE KIDNAPPING

Valerie King

# One

Evangeline Bradwell gave a strong tug on the reins and drew her plodding cart horse to a stop. Even though night had fallen heavily on the Gloucestershire countryside and the sliver of a moon cast only the barest shadows, she could not mistake the nature of the dark, lumpy figure sprawled on the grassy lane in front of her.

The inert form of a man barred her way of escape.

Her heart began beating strongly in her breast as a sudden fright came over her, not just for herself, but for the child next to her.

She felt a small hand touch her wrist above her leather gloves. She glanced down at the worried face beside her, just barely able to discern the wrinkled brow of young Lord Debriss.

"What is it, Evie?" he whispered. His fingers were cold against her skin. "Why did you stop the horse?"

"There is a man in the roadway," she said quietly. "I don't know if he's been taken ill, or what, precisely, but before we can proceed, I will have to find out what is wrong with him."

Lord Debriss rose to his feet, his carriage rug sliding off his lap as he peered over the sway-backed horse's head. The twitching ears of the old hack and the quick shiver along his back indicated his impatience to be going. "Oh, I see him," the young master cried.

"William," Evangeline whispered urgently. "Remember. Not a sound!"

"Oh, I say, I am sorry," he responded quickly, lowering his voice to a soft hush. "But who do you suppose it is? I'll bet it's some farm laborer in his cups returning from The Angel in Ozlebede." The Angel was located in the nearby village, where the fortnight fly to Bath was destined to arrive in just under an hour.

Evangeline should have reproached the lad for referring to the man possibly being inebriated, but since her object was to get him as quickly as possible away from his home, she handed him the reins instead. "See that old Jessup doesn't budge an inch, mind, or we shall all be in the basket—including the man in the road."

"I can manage Jessup," he said firmly, holding the leather straps laced masterfully through his small white fingers. For all the horrors of his upbringing, at least Lord Debriss had been permitted a thorough knowledge of horses and horsemanship. He was eight years old, lame, orphaned, and quite small for his age. He had been in the care of a ruthless, heartless guardian for the past year.

As housekeeper in his household, Evangeline had repeatedly sought redress with the younger of the lad's guardians—an indifferent, self-absorbed, Man About Town—who resided in London year-round, but to no avail. The good, the honorable, the beastly Mr. Fleming could not be bothered with the welfare of his nephew. Not once had he responded with even a single line of correspondence to her numerous letters.

Having witnessed the worst of barbarities a fortnight past, when a local physician placed a screw box on the foot of the young master—in a professed attempt to cure the child of his lameness—Evangeline Bradley had borne enough of Mr. Turley's guardianship. It was one thing for the old man to feather his nest by siphoning off the housekeeping funds and the young master's quarterly allotments, but it was quite another to inflict brutal punishments on his person for infractions as inoffensive as failing to recall his Latin lessons. When the curative of a screw box had been applied—and undoubtedly the physician's fees split between the pair of unconscionable men—Evangeline had done what any woman of fine sensibility and courage would have done—she had kidnapped her darling William, who had come to be like a son to her.

She carefully descended the cart, taking great care that her simple gown of gray stuff did not become caught on the splintery wheels or frame of the rickety vehicle. She peered through the dark shadows, the moon just barely visible above a thick line of tall, lofty beech trees. A cold, May breeze blew through the hilly countryside and ruffled her straw bonnet.

As she passed by Jessup, he shook in his harness and lifted his nose to her, indignant that he had been forced to stop in his journey. Leaving his warm stable in the middle of the night was bad enough, but being forced to draw an old cart along a darkened lane seemed offensive to him in the extreme. He stamped a hoof as though daring Evangeline to think otherwise.

The breeze freshened, and Evangeline held her black cloak together at the neck. The leaves overhead rustled, mocking her fright of the quiet spectre on the road. An owl hooted his warning in the distance.

Her heart was hammering against her ribs as she reached the man and stooped down to touch his shoulder. She gave him a gentle push, but her effort did not seem to awaken him. Taking a deep breath, she slipped her hand inside his coat in order to touch his chest. When she found his heartbeat and felt the steady rise and fall of his chest, she let out a sigh of relief so great that it resounded against the low, drystone wall which bordered the lane on the west.

He was alive.

Thank God for that!

She felt along his chest farther, hoping to discover if he was bleeding, or in what manner he had suffered injury; but she found nothing, nor did she smell the odors of whisky or rum on his person.

He moaned, a sound that startled her, but before she could withdraw her hand, a tight grip fastened about her wrist. The man rolled, pulling her over and beneath him in a quick, hard movement. She screamed, and at the same time she felt his fist glance off her straw bonnet as he struck at her.

"What the devil!" he cried, lifting himself away from her.

Evangeline scooted out from under him, hurrying backward like a spider on the grassy, dirt lane. He stared at her, grabbed his head as if he was in great pain, then toppled over in a faint on her legs.

"Oh, no," Evangeline murmured. The moonlight and dim starlight had been sufficient to reveal two things to her. First, the man had a terrible wound on his forehead, including a gash above his left eyebrow. And secondly, he was someone with whom she was well-acquainted.

She tried to slide backward, but his chest was pressing heavily on her legs, and his head had locked her knees in place. With all her might, she pulled backward and at last began to make slow progress.

"Evie, are you all right? Did he hurt you?"

"Don't speak!" Evangeline adjured her young charge, afraid that his voice would be caught up by the night breeze and carried to Mr. Turley's whiskered ears. Dropping her voice to a whisper, she continued, "I'm perfectly well. The gentleman swooned again. I'm 'fraid he's badly hurt."

At last she freed her legs and rose to her feet. She adjusted her bonnet which was askew from the gentleman's weak blow. She looked down at the hapless traveler, planted her hands on her hips and shook her head in disgust.

"Why did you have to come home now, Robert?" she queried softly. "And of what possible use can you be to me in this state?" She felt quick tears burn her eyes as her gaze drifted from his hatless head and black hair, to what she now believed were dark bloodstains on his neck-cloth, to his torn clothing and undoubtedly badly scuffed Hessian boots. She thought it likely he had been set upon by footpads and robbed; he appeared to have taken a bruising in an attempt to protect himself.

She didn't know what to do. She certainly couldn't leave him in the road. The night air would take its toll, and an inflammation of the lungs would undoubtedly follow so long an exposure to the unfriendly night elements. Yet, if she and Lord Debriss were to board the stagecoach on time, they couldn't delay much longer.

She walked quickly back to the cart and saw that the young master was holding his own with Jessup, sitting tall in the seat, his shoulders straight, his head erect. "You've done very well," she whispered.

He nodded, smiling. "Only what do we do about the man?" he asked, whispering in return.

"I'm not sure. I can't leave him, for I believe he would die since he is hurt. But the rest is a bit tricky, I'm 'fraid. He's well-known hereabouts." She didn't want to tell him the truth. "If I take him to the inn, even as far away as Croxton, he will surely be known to someone, and there will be such a kick up of dust as will bring unwanted attention to us. At the same time, I believe to take him home would mean disaster for our schemes."

"Does he live far from here? Will we then not make the fly at Ozlebede?"

Evangeline shook her head. "Whether we will reach the village in time is not certain. But as for this man, no, he does not live far, so to speak. The man in the road is Robert Fleming."

The boy blinked at her. "Uncle Robert?" he cried.

"Yes, but do hush," Evangeline again prompted him. She laid a hand on his arm and patted it. "He has suffered some sort of blow to the head. There is a gash above his eye."

Lord Debriss was silent apace. "We can't leave him here," he murmured, shaking his head. Evangeline had the sense that he was sorting it all out in his mind.

"No, we cannot."

"But if we go back, old Turley will likely discover us."

"Yes, he will."

"There is only one thing for it," William Debriss said, with a brisk nod of his head. "We must all go to Nanny's house. She will conceal us long enough to form a second scheme—and the village is not far from here, but farther yet from Ashland Park."

Evangeline stared at him and smiled. "You are quite a brilliant young man," she said at last.

"Of course I am," he responded. "I have had the best of tutors these many years and more."

"You are also an unconscionable flatterer."

The lad chuckled. Evangeline had taught him since he was breeched—at least up until a year ago when Mr. Turley took over his education. The affairs at Ashland Park had been in a sad state long before she had arrived to serve as housekeeper to the tenth viscount Lord Debriss, a year before William's birth. When his lordship, along with his wife—both indifferent parents—had perished in a coaching accident, what little order in the household had existed was soon cast to the winds with the arrival of Mr. Turley.

She had taken the man's measure at a glance, and he had formed a strong dislike of her from the first. How many times they had joined in battle were too numerous to count. She shuddered thinking of the pain she had endured knowing that her beloved William—a boy who was as much a son to her as any child could be to a woman who had cared for him since he was a babe—was being brutally punished by Mr. Turley in the name of discipline.

The household was in support of her, knowing that she alone stood between William and his guardian. Once, he had attempted to dismiss her, but the butler, the cook, the bailiff and the head groom had all threatened both resignation and Turley's exposure to William's uncle should she be dismissed. A cold, ongoing battle had ensued. The staff at Ashland Park had given her courage, and the majority of the beatings had stopped.

But he defied her to prevent his hiring of a physician to treat the boy's lame foot. One afternoon of William's screams when the screw box had been placed on his foot had convinced her that the only thing she could do to protect the young lord was to kidnap him. She had secured passage for herself and William to the Colonies, on a ship leaving Bristol in four days' time.

A ship they might yet make, even in the face of Robert's arrival, just as soon as they saw him tended to. Nanny's home would be as useful as any. Besides, the aged nurse had cared not only for William when he was younger, but Robert, now thirty-five, as well. There was no doubt in Evangeline's mind that Nanny would gladly take them all into her home for the night.

She turned her attention back to Robert, and after talking softly to him and ever-so-gently patting his face and rubbing his hands, she brought him round. He seemed to recognize her after a time and came to himself sufficiently to be led to the back of the cart. He crawled in and again fell into a swoon. Evangeline regained her seat and, with a slap of the reins, set the horse moving toward Nanny's house a meager five miles distant from Ashland Park and the odious Mr. Turley.

# Two

On the following morning, Evangeline stared down at the face she knew so well, taken aback for the hundredth time at the lines of strain fixed beside each closed eye. He was asleep on the sofa in the small parlor of Nanny's home in the village of Durspen. A thick quilt covered him in a warm embrace and was tucked about his legs and drawn up snugly beneath his chin.

His complexion was very pale, a strong contrast to his black hair. The gash over his eye had been cleansed and a sticking plaster placed on the raw wound. On his cheek was a hideous, swollen bruise varying in color from black to blue to purple to red. She would have accounted it a pretty sight had it not indicated a great deal of pain for her former love.

She could see by the circles beneath his eyes that Robert Fleming was no longer an innocent young man, full of youthful hopes and every security that the future would be as he wished it to be. Nine years had passed since she had first met and loved him. After which, they had parted, and later he had buried a lovely wife and baby daughter.

She sighed and drew forward a fine, old mahogany rocker. With a mug of tea cradled in her hands, she sat down to watch the man who had once held so much promise for her.

Her heart constricted in her chest as the memories began to flow through her mind, unbidden, unwelcome, unstoppable.

She had first met Robert at the assemblies in Bath nine years ago. The New Assembly Room had always drawn the flower of the aristocracy and the gentry into its many and august chambers. She had been visiting a cousin that vivacious summer and had been hopeful, as most young ladies of quality were, of making a match. Her tastes however were particular, her ideals encompassed nothing less than love and her dowry was nonexistent. Therefore, she had known from the first and had accepted with grace the possibility that she would quit her cousin's home at the end of August without love and marriage as part of her future.

But she did not repine her lot. Such was not her nature. In fact, if she did not contract a love-match with a gentleman of adequate substance, she fully intended, once the summer was concluded, to seek employment. She had always been quite good with numbers, exceedingly so. And she had a love of houses. Combining the two, she hoped to enter service as a housekeeper of some fine old mansion.

Her bedridden mother was unhappy with her scheme, but what loving parent would be content if it appeared her daughter was destined to become a spinster? No argument of her mother's in favor of a marriage outside of love had prevailed with her. She would love and be loved and marry within the gentry or she would earn her own keep as a housekeeper.

With her mind, her hopes and her heart fixed thusly, how shocked she was when Robert Fleming entered the ballroom of the Upper Rooms, promising by the beauty of his person, the intelligence of his speech, and the noble cast of his character to fulfill her every daydream. She could recall the moment exactly to mind.

She had dressed with great care that evening. She had

worn a summery, white silk gown embroidered with gold thread and bearing a ruff of tulle high at the back of the neck but descending to the décolleté of the bodice at a pretty, narrowed angle. The puffed sleeves of her gown were embroidered with seed pearls which matched her pearl eardrops and the necklet and cameo draped prettily about her throat. Her blond locks had been curled and gathered up into a delicate froth of a knot atop her head, and a single light pink ostrich feather was secured amidst the sweep of delicate curls.

Her cousin's maid had clapped her hands at the success of her toilette, and her cousin, Eugenia, had beamed with pride. She remembered having looked into the mirror that night, her heart beating with youthful enthusiasm as she scrutinized her reflection. She had large blue eyes, round and thickly fringed. Her brows were a pretty arch, her cheekbones were nicely formed, and her lips were bow-shaped, which made her the envy of her cousin and her friends. Her heart-shaped face completed what Eugenia termed fancifully as her *golden beauty,* high praise which helped her that night to feel that perhaps her schoolgirl's daydreams might just come true.

She could recall vividly the anticipation she had felt before she ever saw Robert that night, which made her memories seem even more sweetly romantic than usual. She sighed deeply at the form still sleeping quietly on the sofa. What an extraordinary moment it had been, when she had been giggling with Eugenia over some piece of nonsense, when her cousin had looked past her shoulder and gasped, and when Evangeline had turned around to catch her first glimpse of the dashing Robert Fleming.

Her whole world had turned upside down in that moment!

He had worn a coat of black superfine molded to broad shoulders, snug black pantaloons revealing athletic thighs, neatly starched shirtpoints which barely touched his cheeks and an elegantly tied neckcloth that was obviously the envy of several young gentlemen nearby who were heard to exclaim over the precision of the folds. His black hair was cut short and brushed nobly *a la Brutus*.

His features were refined rather than swarthy. His nose was straight, his gray eyes slanted attractively, his cheekbones high and cutting in a clean line to a firm jaw. He was handsome in the extreme, admired by every lady present. How the fans began to flutter, to attract his notice, to disguise the hurried whispers of excitement which flowed from lady to lady. Who was he? What were his prospects? Was he married, betrothed, in possession of a competence?

*Robert Fleming.*

*Five thousand a year.*

*Brother to Lord Debriss.*

*Handsome beyond speaking.*

Her cousin, dear Eugenia, was acquainted with his sister-in-law, the patrician Lady Debriss, one of Bath's leading hostesses during the summer months. An introduction could not be avoided. A quick blossoming of love had followed.

What a triumph it had been, a portionless female to have won the heart of such a man. Much she cared for that! Cupid had struck her, and struck hard. Love was the only order of the day to which she could devote herself.

What desolation when, after a betrothal of but a sennight and after having attended her mother for a fortnight following, to have returned to Bath and found that Mr. Fleming would have nothing more to do with Miss Bradwell.

How kind Lord and Lady Debriss had been. How utterly devastated they had appeared when they told her he had jilted her. He was gone to London. He would not return for some time.

Lady Debriss had shed many, many tears, weeping profusely into a delicate lace kerchief. Lord Debriss had worn a cold, pinched expression about his lips and would not meet her gaze, almost as though he was angry with her.

Six months later she had become the housekeeper at their home of Ashland Park north of Somerset in Gloucestershire. Over the years, Robert had visited there, of course; but whenever he saw her, he would incline his head coldly, and she would respond no less frigidly with a cool lift of her chin.

Another year and Robert married a London chit, a fine, well-dowered young lady from Kent. He was in love, he was content, and he could even greet her without ill humor. Within a year, however, his wife had died as well as a stillborn daughter.

That same year, Lady Debriss had given birth to William, her first and only child. What joy the birth of a son to Lord and Lady Debriss had brought to Ashland. He was doted on by one and all, and dear old Nanny was given charge of him.

But it was to Evangeline that the little, lame boy clung for nurture, for comfort, and for affection, especially in the long and frequent absences of his parents. Nanny slept more hours than she labored, and it was during her daytime naps that Evangeline and William would steal off into the countryside to explore and delight in the beauties of nature.

She taught William, she cuddled him during thunderstorms, she rejoiced in each lost tooth, and she read and read to him until he knew dozens of stories by heart. She drilled him in his sums, listened to his Latin verbs, and encouraged him to recite poetry in order to learn cadences, forms and rhymes. Evangeline was amazed at his progress and felt certain that what Nature had deprived him of in the stubby, twisted foot on his right leg, she had provided for amply elsewhere in the vivid imaginings and capabilities of his excellent mind.

She was as proud of him as if he had been her own.

If he stole off to the stables more than she would have liked, she didn't quibble. Once his formal education began at Eton, he would have need of at least this one physical accomplishment in order to keep the taunts and tormentings of the other boys at bay. And few things were more admired among young men than the ability to judge horseflesh or to ride neck or nothing at a fence.

Then Lord and Lady Debriss had perished in a coaching accident. The funeral had been a sore trial for everyone. Evangeline could still feel the grip of William's clutching hand as the good reverend sped the hapless pair onto their respective heavenly abodes.

But if the loss of his parents afflicted William, so much more the immediate arrival of Mr. Egbert Turley, his primary guardian, who moved his belongings into Lord Debriss's bedchamber almost before the tombs had been sealed in the family vault and the dust was seen skidding off the wheels of Robert's departing town chariot.

A rigorous form of discipline had been introduced from that very moment, of beatings for misspelled words and incorrect verb tenses, until every day saw a violent disagreement between Evangeline and Turley. A month more and he attempted to dismiss her, but the staff at Ashland Park had stood firmly behind her, threatening to travel together to London for the purpose of informing Mr. Fleming of his cruelties toward the boy.

Mr. Turley knew a little fear at that moment, and though his narrowed black eyes indicated he would do whatever he could while her skirts were turned away from him, the worst of his brutalities were now in check.

But the change in William over the course of that year nearly broke her heart. The brightness of his hazel eyes faded, the cherubic cast to his countenance paled and thinned to a mere shadow of unhappiness, and his shoulders grew stooped from a lack of exercise and an excess of study. The joy and love of learning and of acquiring knowledge had lost its savor, his limp became more pronounced, he never sang, and he forgot the stories of his childhood.

Evangeline encouraged him every night, and at least one evening out of every two she was able to make him smile and sometimes to laugh. She wrote Robert every day, begging and pleading for him to come to Gloucestershire and rescue his nephew from the barbarous hands of the tyrant.

In the sixth month she had learned of Turley's fleecing of the estate through padded merchant bills and through the seizing of William's allowance in order to dispose of it as he saw fit, an apportioning she was convinced meant that most of the largess saw its way into his pocket.

But at the end of a twelvemonth, when he had brought a physician to Ashland, a portly man of broad smiles, quick steps and soft handshakes, to examine William, only then did her concerns metamorphose into terror. She was not told of the doctor's intentions to apply a screw box to the boy's lame foot. Merely, she heard the screams—as did the entire staff—and her resolution to take him away from his monstrous guardian had formed then and there.

Needing time in order to make her escape with William effective, she had that night stolen the screw box and burned it in the large kitchen oven. Cook stood beside her, tears streaming down that good lady's face. Evangeline had no tears within her at that moment, only a blind rage that her beloved William had been tortured.

Turley had been furious that his supposedly well-intentioned device had been pilfered, but the physician assured him that he could have a new contraption constructed within a month.

One month.

One month to make William safe.

A sennight later she had taken a trip to the small village of Ozlebede, ten miles to the south of Ashland Park, and purchased two tickets for the stagecoach to Bath and at the same time passage for herself and William on a sailing ship, out of Bristol, to America. In addition, she had posted one final letter from Ozlebede to Robert Fleming informing him of precisely what she thought of his character for having refused to take even a particle of interest in his nephew's well-being and for ignoring the hundreds of letters she had previously sent him.

How odd, then, that on the very night of her departure from Ashland, with William in tow, she had stumbled upon Robert's inert form in the middle of an obscure country lane a mile south of Ashland.

She sipped her tea, rocked a little and again sighed deeply as she watched the steady rise and fall of Robert's chest. She had enjoyed her occupation as housekeeper at Ashland over the years, but she knew from the rumors that abounded that Mr. Robert Fleming was an unhappy man.

What would her life have been, she wondered, had Robert not jilted her? He owned a fine property in Berkshire, but of recent years he was rarely in residence, since his wife and daughter had perished there.

Evangeline set her mug on a polished table beside the sofa on which Robert rested. She slid off the seat of the rocker to drop on her knees beside him. She placed a hand on his forehead to see if a fever was upon him, but he was happily cool. Her throat began to ache with suppressed tears.

Too many memories, she thought, as a tear or two trickled down her cheeks. She swiped them away, then couldn't resist touching the backs of her fingers to the unbruised skin beside Robert's mouth.

He had kissed her several times when they had become engaged, kisses that had tasted of heaven and of springtime and of joy all at once. Her soul had touched his during their briefly shared betrothal; she was certain it had. She could not have been so utterly mistaken in that. Why then had he left her? Perhaps because she was a portionless lady with inferior connections and unworthy of the Fleming name.

Perhaps.

She didn't know.

He had explained nothing to her.

Yet, for the life of her she would never have believed Robert's character to have been so bad. How could he have jilted her, without so much as a single word of explanation, and left his sister-in-law to bear the ill tidings? The whole of it was still, even after nine years, incomprehensible to her.

He stirred slightly as she stroked his cheek and ran her fingers over his chin. These were the gestures she had once believed would have been hers to delight in, decade upon decade, as his wife. How much he stole from her, when he left Bath that wretched summer so many years ago.

She withdrew her hand, feeling desperately sad about the past, and sat back on her heels.

As she watched him, her thoughts took a new turn. She wondered just how he was going to explain to her why he had ignored her correspondence regarding the terrors of Mr. Turley's guardianship and whether or not he meant now to interest himself in the boy's hapless affairs.

As though somehow feeling the brunt of her thoughts, Robert opened his eyes and blinked, squinted, then turned to look at her.

"Evangeline," he murmured softly. "I had been dreaming of you. Or am I still dreaming?" He glanced at the plaster ceiling and all around the modest parlor. "Where the deuce am I? I take it this is not Ashland."

"You are at Nanny's home in Durspen."

"What? Old Nurse Nanny?"

Evangeline nodded. "I found you unconscious on a lane nearby."

"What?" he cried, clearly unable to recall the events of the night before or at least her involvement in them. He then winced. "The deuce take it, my head feels like the devil." He touched a finger gently to his eyebrow.

"You've a deep gash over your brow and a terrible bruise on your left cheek. A surgeon ought to tend to your cut. As for how you acquired your injuries, I can only suppose that you had been set upon by footpads, or do you have other recollections of your adventures last night?"

He fell silent, his brow furrowed in perplexity. After a moment, he said, "Yes, I believe it was footpads, three of them. I fought them off as long as I was able and then must have taken a blow to the head." He closed his eyes for a long moment, willing the memories away. When he opened them, he asked, "But how did I get here? I mean, why am I here?"

"I thought it best," she answered cryptically.

"But why did you not take me to Ashland? It couldn't have been very far, for as I recall, I was but a mile from the Park."

Evangeline heard steps on the stairs, and a moment later, William peeped around the corner of the stairwell wall. "Is he awake, Evie?"

Evangeline nodded and extended her hand toward him, still sitting on her heels with her knees resting on the floor. "Come. Say hello to your Uncle Robert."

William bounded into the room wearing a brown velvet coat and nankeens. His dark brown leather shoes were laced up tightly, and he had every appearance of a young man ready to travel. He moved swiftly toward the sofa

and slid directly onto Evangeline's lap, facing his uncle.
She placed gentle hands on his arms.

"How do you do, Uncle," he said shyly.

Evangeline wondered just how Robert would respond
to the changes in his nephew, or whether he would even
notice there was the smallest difference in the pallor of
his complexion or the hunch of his shoulders. She
watched a frown enter his eye, and he lifted a hand to
touch his temple. "I am very well," Robert returned politely, his gray eyes searching his nephew's features. "And
you? How do you fare?"

William turned back to glance up at Evangeline's face.
She saw that he was requesting a silent assurance of just
what he ought to say to his uncle. Evangeline nodded.
She felt William breathe deeply as he began, "Not well,
Uncle. Mr. Turley is a very mean man. I—I don't want
to stay with him anymore."

"So Miss Bradwell has informed me."

William was silent apace, then stated, "You don't believe her, do you, Uncle?"

Robert's gaze shifted from the boy and landed squarely
on Evangeline. "Sometimes it is most difficult to know
what to believe." So there it was. He did not trust her.
Perhaps he supposed that in her anger at having been
jilted she had purposely taken up the position at Ashland
Park in order to annoy him. If so, he would never believe
anything she might say.

"William," Evangeline said softly. "Cook has a little
breakfast waiting for you. You have only to show your
dear face in the kitchen and she will offer you something
to tempt your appetite."

"You are dismissing me," William said, scowling at her.

Evangeline lifted a brow. "I am," she returned firmly.

William smiled crookedly. "Oh, very well, but I take it
unkindly that you wish me to leave the parlor just when
you are to come the crab with poor Uncle Robert."

At that, Robert chuckled. "I can hold my own," he said, smiling and wincing at the same time. The bruise on his cheek would not suffer merriment lightly.

With that William rose from Evangeline's lap and headed toward the kitchen. Evangeline rose as well, her legs tingling from having sat on her heels—and that with William on her lap—for such a long time. She drew the rocker forward in order to better see Robert's face and his expression as she spoke with him.

She took a deep breath and would have begun remonstrating with the inattentive uncle, but he started before her, his eyes narrowed to slits. "What have you done to the boy!" he cried reproachfully.

# *Three*

"What have *I* done?" Evangeline cried, shocked. "What have I done? What manner of question is that? Have you no sense at all?"

"I can see that he is wretchedly dependent upon you, so much so that he has lost all physical bloom, or was that your intention, to keep him fixed by your side so that you would always have a place at Ashland Park?"

Evangeline was so thoroughly outraged that she could hardly speak. She opened her mouth to refute his reproaches, but she was too stunned to bring her thoughts properly to order. She was angry that he would accuse her of anything so absurd and at the same time furious that he had clearly disbelieved every one of her complaints against Mr. Turley.

"I have done nothing to William, except love him," she responded heatedly. "While you—oh, the very thought that you would render judgment when you have not been here in an entire twelvemonth so sickens me that I do not know where to begin in giving you answer!"

"Then stop speaking," he stated coldly.

She shook her head, her mouth agape, but continued to level her angry gaze directly at him.

"What?" he queried maliciously.

Suddenly, her anger faded, as quickly as it had blossomed. "You are so changed that I hardly know you anymore, Robert," she said quietly. "What happened to you?"

At that, his complexion altered completely, and his face became flooded with an angry flush. "How dare you," he murmured. "For above anyone else, you should know precisely what happened to me."

She was certain he was referring to his young wife and daughter and was mortified that she had not considered as much before leveling her own harsh accusation at him. She lowered her gaze to her ungloved fingers on her lap. Her knuckles were showing white, so tightly were her hands clasped together. "I have told you often that I was sorry for the loss of your family. But I would like to think that we could go beyond the sadness of your feelings in order to determine what might be best for William."

She heard him huff an impatient sigh. "So that is what you think I am referring to? How greatly mistaken you are, however. For I have grieved these losses. I have accepted that my dear wife and our child are in a better place, but there is one loss that will forever rankle, and you are the cause of it. You know you are."

Evangeline opened her mouth to speak, but couldn't fathom his meaning. A doubt began nagging at her, trailing her from the past. She knew he was referring to their betrothal of nine years ago, but why? Was it possible that he had jilted her for a purpose? Had she done something unwittingly to so wretchedly abuse him that he had felt he had had only one recourse, to desert her in Bath?

She skimmed quickly over every encounter they had enjoyed during their brief betrothal, but nothing came to mind that he could possibly construe as an offense against his character, mind, or sensibilities. What had she done, then? What could he be thinking?

Regardless, she was not sitting beside him wishful of tormenting either herself or him about matters that were best left buried in the past. "I'm not certain I know in what way I have offended you, but I beg you will set aside your wounded feelings and attend instead to a far more important matter."

"Very well," he murmured.

He withdrew his arms from beneath the thick quilt and rolled the top of the counterpane away from his neck. Part of his chest was visible from the center opening of his white shirt, and Evangeline bit her lip. She felt certain she shouldn't be alone with him given his state of undress, but there was nothing for it—she must speak with him about William; she must persuade him to remove Mr. Turley from Ashland. If this much could be accomplished, she would not need to take Lord Debriss to the Colonies. But so much distrust resided in her where Robert was concerned that she insisted on knowing his mind before she made her decision about the immediate future.

He folded his arms across his chest. "Your letter was quite offensive, Miss Bradwell," he said. "And now that I've seen how much the boy dotes on you, I begin to understand the whole of it. You spoke of Mr. Turley as a monster, but I tell you, miss, you are the one who has ruined his spirit. The meekness I have seen before me today is nothing more than the result of an overprotective female who has coddled a lame child from infancy. I wish to be very clear on that score. As for the hundreds of other letters you professed to have written to me, I can only suppose that you exaggerated—for I never received a one of these communications."

Evangeline had listened to his accusations with a rage that had, by the end of his speech, shrunk most happily to a cold indifference. He had reaffirmed his character to her. She understood him, and she had her answer. William must go to Bristol with her.

His comment about not having received her letters,

however, gave her pause. "Are you saying you have received only one letter from me over the past year?"

"Yes, dated a fortnight past."

Evangeline realized this letter had been posted from Ozlebede while the others had been ostensibly left from the closer village of Whitgreave, not a half mile from Ashland Park. She could only conclude that someone had tampered with her correspondence to Robert.

He continued, "I left my enjoyments of the London Season feeling that the excited speech you chose to employ in representing Mr. Turley's conduct warranted at least a mild investigation. But insisting you had sent hundreds of letters on William's behalf I find an absurdity beyond bearing."

She met his cold, gray gaze and responded, "Did it not occur to you, Mr. Fleming, that Mr. Turley might have been in some manner responsible for the fact that my letters did not reach you? He has been feathering his nest at William's expense and is a brutal taskmaster; but it is clear to me you are unwilling to put any faith in my word, so I suppose one might say this conversation is concluded."

"One might," he responded on a drawl. "I certainly have nothing more to say. Your word has been meaningless for these nine years and more. Therefore, surely you must admit that I can have no reason to believe anything you might say to me at this eleventh hour."

"*My word?*" she breathed, rising from the rocker, unwilling to continue arguing with him. "Well, if that isn't the pot calling the kettle black, I don't know what is!"

With that she turned on her heel and left the parlor.

An hour later, Evangeline bundled William up in his traveling coat of fine gray Merino wool, and having hired an old post chaise from a merchant at the top of the High Street, as well as one of his stableboys to act as postillion, they boarded the chariot. A few moments more and the wheels were making a fine, clackety progress up the High Street, in a southerly direction toward Bath and Bristol. She had told Robert she was taking William back to Ashland Park in the pony and cart and would send a proper conveyance to fetch him once she had arrived. She believed he wouldn't suspect treachery for several hours.

By dusk, Robert Fleming stood on the cobbles of the High Street staring east in the direction of Ashland Park. He was dizzy, very much so, from the wounds he had suffered upon leaving Ozlebede astride his fine black gelding. Though he was still unwell, his mind had cleared sufficiently to recall the attack. He had been assaulted not a mile from Ashland Park and had fought off the ruffians until a stunning blow to his forehead with the butt of a pistol had robbed him of his senses. He had also been robbed of a fine purse carrying fifty guineas. This, however, seemed of the present to be his least concern.

Ever since Evangeline had quit Nanny's house, ostensibly to take William swiftly back to his home and hearth, he had been reviewing his conversation with her. When she had first turned her heel upon him, he had been so angry with her that he had felt himself entirely justified in every harsh word he had said to her.

But now, the day having given him counsel, he began to wonder a little more. He had spoken rashly, and she had been so astonished at his reading of the situation that doubts now began succeeding his rage. Everything she had told him of Turley was, in a certain theoretical sense, possible, but so unlikely as to be ridiculous. Yet, her accusations were possible. Turley would not have been the first man in history to have abused a position as guardian.

But what nagged him most as he looked down the High

Street and wondered for the hundredth time where his traveling chariot might be was the odd circumstance of Evangeline having been driving a cart on an infrequently traveled lane, so very late at night—and that, with William in tow.

What had she been about? he wondered. Once or twice the thought had struck him that she might have been kidnapping the child, but this he dismissed as utterly absurd. Miss Bradwell was many things, she was faithless and unkind, but she was no kidnapper, nor was she so foolish as to risk her neck at the gallows for such a crime. He might believe she would go back on her word, but otherwise he had always thought her at least a reasonably sensible female.

So why was it, he wondered, as the gray clouds in the west grew pink with the descent of the sun, that a certain uneasy sensation began settling into the pit of his stomach?

When lights began to appear in the many windows about the lovely, golden stone village, he suddenly whirled on his heel and returned to Nanny's house.

He found the old woman sitting in the kitchen with her cook stirring a large pot over the fire. Both aged women had found a means of sharing a good retirement together, and the cook was just then ladling a fine trout stew into two bowls on the table.

"Little Bobby," Nanny called to him, with a toothless smile. "Have a little supper. I'm certain the coach will be along directly."

"You're telling whiskers again, aren't you, Nanny?" he asked kindly.

She hunched her shoulders and grinned. "I'll not open me budget to no man," she said, holding her crooked, white finger against her lips. "Miss Evie told me to hold mum, and so I will."

"Hold mum, eh?" he murmured. What the devil was Evangeline up to?

"Cook's stew is wery tasty," she said, nodding and grinning still, gesturing to the steaming pot over the hearth fire.

"I can't stay, Nanny. It's time I went home."

"Suit yourself, Master Bobby, but this time—do right by the lady. She always loved ye, ye know."

Robert was stunned by her words and wanted to ask what she meant by them. Somehow, however, he supposed that her mind had grown addled with age and that she was thinking of his pretty Olivia. Affection for his nurse from childhood washed through him in a sweet glow of fond remembrances. He crossed the room and, bending to place a kiss on her cheek, said, "I'll do right by her, never fear."

She patted his cheek. "You always was such a good lad. Now go away, afore m'stew takes a chill."

He chuckled and quit the house. The walk to Ashland Park would take an hour, perhaps a little more, but his mounting impatience with Evangeline Bradwell's antics was certain to sustain his stride the entire distance.

An hour and a half later, however, he sat on a tall stool near the fireplace in the kitchen, sipping a glass of Madeira, his spirits growing grimmer and more frightened by the second. Cook, who was as faithful a servant as any and who had been at Ashland Park for thirty years, spoke a tale that turned his blood to ice. Darnell, the butler, also an aged retainer who had served nearly as long as Cook, confirmed every word of Cook's speech, delivered between tears and sobs, a long recounting of such wickedness that caused his head to pound with the pain of guilt.

He began to regret and to regret again. He hadn't believed Evangeline. He had accused her of nothing less than hysterics and lies. But worse than anything was the fact that he had ignored his nephew entirely since his brother's death, and in doing so, he alone bore the responsibility of poor William's sufferings.

His eyes stinging with tears, his cheeks cramped with agony, he met Cook's red-rimmed gaze. "So you say she stole the screw box in the middle of the night and burnt it there?" He gestured to the wide-mouthed fireplace.

Cook nodded, sobbing a little more.

"But did you suspect she was kidnapping William?"

Cook shook her head. "Nay. But she were thinking only of saving him from suffering. Ye've got to believe as much."

He reviewed everything he knew about the events of last night, and he now understood that the reason a coach had not been sent back from Ashland Park to retrieve him from Nanny's house was because Evangeline had gone the opposite direction, probably heading toward Bath, where she could lose herself and the child in the densely populated city.

"And how long, do you say, has Turley been absent?"

Cook glanced at Darnell and gestured helplessly.

Mr. Darnell, whose mouth drooped and whose jaw worked strongly as he spoke, answered his question. "When it were discovered that t'young master, Lord Debriss, was to be found nowhere and that Miss Bradwell and her portmanteau were absent as well, he stormed through the house, kicking over chairs and sending two of the upper maids fleeing before his fury. That were about ten of the clock this mornin'. He took the best coach and Timothy coachman as well.

"Did he say where he was going?"

"Nay," was the quiet response.

He glanced at Cook. "Where would you go, with a child in tow, where you wouldn't be known, where you could hide?"

Cook shook her head and again wiped her cheeks. "I

dunno. A long ways away, I s'pose, especially since she's broken the King's Law."

"Yes," Robert murmured. "A long ways away." Bath enjoyed a fine road to Bristol and Bristol a fine sea path to the Colonies, where a wilderness could swallow up a woman and child more securely than even the limestone buildings of Bath.

He drained his glass of Madeira and bid Darnell have a bedchamber prepared for him. "But awaken me early and have the horses and Lord Debriss's curricle ready for departure by seven sharp."

"But ye're not well, Master Robert," Darnell returned, frowning, his gaze sliding over the sticking plaster on Robert's forehead and the bruise on his left cheek.

Robert shook his head and sighed deeply. "I've not made a push for a year," he murmured. "I'll not let a cut on my head stop what should have been my duty all along."

Once in his bedchamber, as he undressed slowly for bed, his mind returned to the sight of awakening to find Evangeline sitting beside Nanny's sofa and watching over him. His first thoughts had not been as hateful as his later words. When he had looked into her blue eyes, he had seen the young woman with whom he had tumbled in love so many years ago. A rush of fondness, of affection, of love had poured over him so feverishly that he was afraid if he did not immediately counter his vulnerability, she would again lay him waste with her indifference as she had that fateful summer in Bath.

He had understood himself in that moment, that ever since his brother had told him Miss Bradwell had broken off the betrothal, part of him had been dead to the world, to love, to affection. Only Olivia had succeeded for a brief time in awakening his heart. But her death had then driven the very light of his existence into the earth. Perhaps that was why, when his brother and sister-in-law had perished, he had refused to take on the mantle of William's care and had left the whole of it in Turley's hands. He had lost too much, and an attachment to William was a thing to be avoided—avoided, that was, until he had received Evangeline's wretched missive informing him of Turley's scurrilous conduct.

As he slid between the sheets, sleep heavily upon him, he knew he had only himself to blame. Tomorrow, however—God willing—he would rectify the whole of his cowardly conduct. That was unless Turley reached Evangeline and William before he could get to them. If that happened, given his current understanding of the vile nature of the man's character, he didn't know what might become of his nephew, or even of Evangeline.

# *Four*

"Mother," Lord Debriss said, slipping his hand into Evangeline's and giggling, "perhaps we could look about the Abbey before we leave Bath."

She glanced down at the boy beside her and met his twinkling gaze. Already he was much improved in both health and spirits. Despite the fact that he was certainly content to be away from Turley, Evangeline suspected much of the sparkle in his eye and the renewed quickness of his halting step was due to the fact that he was immersed in an adventure.

She understood him better because of it and squeezed his hand in response. "Well, *my son,*" she said, emphasizing the joke between them, "I should like very much to see the Abbey, but given the circumstances and the hour, don't you think we had best be on our way to Bristol?"

They had just visited the Pump Room because she wanted William to see the famous watering hole where so many of England's finest citizens enjoyed the bitter, vile mineral waters on what for many proved to be annual pilgrimages. More than this short excursion was proving impossible, however, given their time constraints. She would have liked to have shown him the Abbey and the Obelisk in the Orange Grove, as well as the Spring Gardens, but the stage for Bristol was due to arrive shortly.

The Pump Room had been an enjoyable experience. William had been suitably impressed with the fine statue of Beau Nash placed in a high alcove on the wall near the counter where the waters were dispensed. But he had seemed more delighted with the sweet smile and wink the serving girl gave him when he took his glass of water from her than with the elegance of the chamber.

With great boldness he had taken a hearty gulp, but unfortunately splayed the whole bitter mouthful onto the floor near the glossy boots of a fine Dandy who cried out in a high-pitched wheedle, "Here, I say! Good God! What have you done to me? Have a care, young pup!"

Leaving the Pump Room swiftly behind, they began a quiet march back to the White Hart, where they had spent the night. When they entered the foyer of the hotel, she was stopped suddenly by a tall, dark man with a patch over his left eyebrow, who caught her arm and whispered, "I shall come with you to your rooms, miss. No fuss now, mind, or I'll have you taken to prison on the instant for kidnapping my nephew."

Evangeline gasped, then scowled at Robert Fleming, who none too decorously drew her toward the staircase.

"Uncle Robert!" William cried, his hazel eyes wide with shock and concern, his complexion paling. "But how did you know? How did you find us?"

"Enough of your tricks, my little scamp," he said, smiling. He gave William a playful shove toward the stairs. "I am all agog to see your chambers. Will you show them to me?"

William stared at Robert as though trying to determine the precise state of his mind. His conclusions shone in the sudden twinkling of his eyes as he responded, "We have a pretty room with a view of the street below and a building across the way," he said excitedly. "I've never seen so many carts and carriages. I saw a gig which Mother—I mean Miss Bradwell—said was a light racing whisky. It had two wheels and hardly any padding along the back of the seat."

"That sounds like a whisky," Robert responded. "Now up the stairs, if you please. I'm anxious to hear about your journey."

William began a quick, though halting, ascent and soon left Evangeline and Robert behind.

Robert held Evangeline's arm in a firm squeeze. She met his gaze squarely. *"Mother?"* he murmured, his gaze and expression accusing.

"A ruse, only," she said, picking up her skirts of blue silk lightly in one hand in order to more easily mount the steps. "We agreed that he should address me thusly in order that we might travel together relatively unnoticed."

"And your travels have included kidnapping?"

"Yes, Robert, they most certainly have. Given the circumstances, I felt I had no choice. I know you don't believe me—"

"There you are out," he whispered urgently and sincerely. "I have a lot to say to you, including several apologies, but not here."

When he fell silent, she glanced at him, frowning. Several apologies? She felt her heart leap in her breast. Was it possible he had altered his opinions about her and about what he believed had happened at Ashland Park over the past year?

He did not speak again until they entered the small, tidy bedchamber and the door was shut with a firm snap against eavesdroppers.

William was ready to begin a recounting of their journey from Durspen, but Robert kindly explained that though he was wishful of knowing every detail, right now he had an urgent need to speak with Miss Bradwell. When William's face fell, Robert chuckled, caught up his chin in his hand and said, "You will have all my attention once I have finished conversing with *your mother,* I promise you."

At that William smiled broadly, then glanced at Evangeline. "You've already told him of our schemes, then?"

Evangeline nodded. "A little, but he and I do have a great deal to discuss. Why don't you settle yourself by the window as you did earlier this morning and watch the traffic below."

Since this notion appealed strongly to him, he limped to the window and planted himself on a chair arranged earlier for just that purpose.

Robert drew her as far from the lad as was possible, then launched into his speech in a quiet voice. "When I realized you weren't returning to Ashland Park, I immediately set out to walk the distance—"

Evangeline cut him off. "Oh, dear!" she began, properly stunned. "I never meant for you to be inconvenienced or forced to an exertion that would harm your already weakened state. I am sorry for that. But really, you ought to have hired at least a cart, or something."

"I don't give a fig for that!" he cried, lifting an impatient hand. "I was not so ill as you thought." His gaze drifted from her face to the boy by the window, whose nose was already pressed to the glass as he peered down into the street. Quite intently, he watched the passing carriages and for the present had his eye fixed on some object or other as though his life depended on it.

Robert returned his gaze to her. "Let me finish," he said softly. "When I arrived at Ashland, I found nearly everyone in a deeply sobered state. Cook and Darnell," here he paused as though nearly overcome, but continued after a deep sigh, "Cook and our good Darnell confirmed your history." He took a step toward her which brought him much too close to keep Evangeline in any degree of comfort. She understood completely how thorough his shift in attitude toward her was, and that knowledge was softening her heart in quick stages. He lowered his voice further, "I could not believe all that they told me. I am sorry, Evie, truly. I don't know why I said all the cruel things to you I did at Nanny's house. I was wrong, on every score—except perhaps one, but that is completely beside the point. I just want you to know—"

"Mother—I mean, Miss Bradwell," William called, interrupting Robert. "Would you object if I went down to the foyer to watch the horses and coaches from there? There's a high perch phaeton, driven by a very fat man, I wish to see."

Evangeline looked back at William, noting absently that his cheeks seemed a little flushed. "I have no objection, but you ought to ask your uncle. He is, after all, your guardian."

William turned an inquiring face to Robert, who nodded his acquiescence. Lord Debriss ran from the room, closing the door with a hard tug behind him.

"He is full of pluck, isn't he?" he said, a half smile on his lips.

"Like his father and uncle, I think," Evangeline said quietly in response, her smile equaling his own.

He returned his gaze to her face. Evangeline caught her breath, feeling just as she had the night she had met Robert Fleming for the first time, as though all the air had been squeezed from her chest. Much of his color had returned since the night of his scuffle with footpads, and in the warm, midday light, he was handsome in the extreme.

He wore a black, woollen, three-caped greatcoat slung casually over his shoulders, beneath which a coat of blue superfine, a white silk waistcoat, and fine buckskin breeches were partially visible. His top boots gleamed from a stiff brushing and polishing, his shirtpoints were properly starched and his neckcloth was arranged in the fashionable Mathematical. He was very much a fine gentleman and the very best of whom she knew him to be.

In that moment, as he gazed into her eyes, time seemed

to draw to a firm halt. She had a strong sensatIon that were he to take her in his arms, she would not only permit it, but would revel in his embrace.

Much to her shock, he seemed to read her mind. He gave a quick shove of his greatcoat which fell behind him to the floor, took a step equally as quick, and before she knew what was happening he held her in a fast embrace, his lips slanted hard across her own.

She struggled at first, overwhelmed by his actions, then in quick stages relinquished her soul to the sublimity of being held and kissed by the man she loved, by the man she had always loved. Her fists fell open, her arms began a slow sliding about his strong back, and her fingers slipped into the sleek strands of his black hair. The noise from the street below disappeared as the sunlight dimmed to a rosy haze all about her. The past suddenly merged with the future, and all of life stopped to wonder, to gaze, to exult.

She had forgotten how sweet the communion between them could be, as his kisses played a soft, gentle melody on her lips. How much she loved him! How much she had always loved him, even when he had treated her with such mocking, cruel indifference.

After a time, he drew back from her slightly, though still cradling her in his arms. "I have crushed your bonnet a little," he whispered.

She chuckled softly and caught her breath on a sob. "Why did you leave me, Robert?" she asked, posing the question she had feared to pose for so long a time. "What did I do that so grievously offended you nine years ago that sent you flying away from me as though coals burned your feet?" Tears trickled down her cheeks.

She was a little startled that a deep frown now creased his brow. "What do you mean?" he whispered. "I should be posing the very same question to you, not otherwise."

Evangeline felt dizzy suddenly. A certain horrible suspicion shot through her brain.

"What is it?" he cried, releasing her. "You are angry with me—I can see as much by the expression on your face."

"No, not angry," Evangeline tried to assure him.

"I knew this was hopeless; I shouldn't have kissed you. I can see that I have overset you." When she didn't respond, he stepped away from her. "I promise you, I won't trouble you again." He bent to retrieve his greatcoat.

"Robert, you are misunderstanding me," she said softly.

He smiled and waved a hand negligently. "You needn't explain. Right now, I only want to gather up William and to take him back to Ashland. But you may trust me when I say that I will not permit Turley to continue his torments. I shall prosecute him if I must."

Evangeline breathed a deep sigh of relief. "Then we are of one mind in that, at least."

He nodded. "Yes. Come. Let's take his lordship home."

Evangeline smiled and allowed Robert to guide her back down the stairs. Time enough in the long journey back to Ashland to settle the questions of the past, to speak about all that had happened nine years ago, and to discover in what way their betrothal had truly been disrupted.

Perhaps their hearts could be healed after all, especially if her suspicions proved correct and he had not jilted her after all.

But when they arrived in the foyer, William was not to be found. Instead, a large crowd was gathering outside.

Evangeline sensed that somehow William might be in the midst of the turmoil. She picked up her step, Robert walking briskly beside her, and hurried toward the crowd.

Even from the distance of the doorway to the Hart Inn she could hear William's voice. "Don't think you shan't suffer now, Mr. Turley. For my uncle is with me."

Robert quickly pushed a path through the crowd, and Evangeline followed swiftly in his wake. When they arrived at the center of the group, Egbert Turley was sprawled on the cobbled stones of the street, his legs, clothed in white stockings and sturdy brown breeches, sunk into a steaming dopple of fresh horse manure. His left eye was squinted shut and already turning a deep burgundy that promised to blacken shortly.

"Evie!" he called to her. "Look! It's old Turley!"

The murmuring, exclaiming crowd was gathered tightly about Turley, the child and a stalwart man of broad shoulders and intense bearing, all situated next to a high perch phaeton in a pretty shade of robin's egg blue.

Evangeline could only assume that the man had been the cause of Turley's black eye, having at some point stepped forward to aid William against his enemy. Robert surprised her by elucidating his identity, "So what happened, Mr. Jones? I take it he tried to kidnap the child."

The stalwart man nodded. "I was watching fer the man you described. When the lad come out of the inn and called out his name"—here he gestured with his thumb toward Turley—"I suspected what might follow, especially since the lad taunted 'im a bit."

"You taunted him?" Evangeline queried, opening her eyes wide as she turned her gaze upon William. "Well, that was quite bold of you, my dear, but not especially wise, eh?"

"I know," he murmured, shifting on his feet and lowering his head. "I shouldn't have done it. But when I saw him—and in such a rig—" He lifted his gaze and appealed strongly to her sense of justice.

Evangeline pinched her lips together and glanced at Turley. Oh, how she longed to plant a kick in his thick, soft belly—the monster! "How *did* you pay for your new phaeton, Mr. Turley?" she queried hotly of the old man.

He merely glared at her and came to a sitting position.

When he saw that his right leg was nearly buried in the vile manure, he started cursing, an activity that caused Mr. Jones to haul him up with a hamlike hand slid under the older man's arm and to bid him stubble it or feel the home-brewed again.

Mr. Turley wisely fell silent.

Returning to the White Hart, Robert explained to Evangeline that before he left London he had hired Mr. Jones from the Bow Street Magistrates Court to do a little investigative work where Mr. Turley and his affairs were concerned. His findings, which he had reviewed with Mr. Jones at the village of Ozlebede, two nights' past, had confirmed Evangeline's accusations that he had been robbing young Lord Debriss and his home of considerable largess over the whole of the last twelvemonth.

"What do you mean to do with him?" Evangeline asked on a whisper as they entered the foyer of the inn.

"I don't know," he murmured, glancing back at Turley, who was trying to brush the filth from his stockings with a glove he had pulled off his hand. "But I shall think of something suitable." When he returned his gaze to Evangeline, he smiled softly and added, "But as for the pair of you, if you would please return to Ashland, I would like to try to make amends. Would that be agreeable to you?"

Evangeline felt her throat constrict as she drew in a deep breath. "Yes," she breathed, her heart warming to the loving light in his gray eyes. "Very much so."

# *Five*

The return trip to Ashland Park was a jubilant one for Evangeline. William's spirits were so far restored as to give cause to wonder if he had ever suffered under Turley's tyranny. Knowing that Robert was seeing the old man safely stowed aboard a ship bound for the Americas solidified a general sense of well-being that pervaded their town chariot.

Three days later, Evangeline was playing a lively game of piquet with William in the blue drawing room on the first floor of the sprawling, golden stone Tudor mansion. The Aubusson carpet below their feet was in patterned swirls of predominantly blue and gold. The tall ceiling was stuccoed in acanthus leaves with the unrelieved portions painted a dramatic blue. Elegant paintings of landscapes and family groupings enhanced each of three walls which in turn were covered in a pretty dark blue silk damask. The remaining fourth wall was broken up by two long windows, each flanked in royal blue velvet draperies and trimmed with gold fringe. Scattered throughout the formal receiving room were elegant gilt tables of bygone years when brocades were the style. Two spindly settees, covered in a gold-and-white striped silk, were set at opposite ends of the chamber. But in the center was a large, overstuffed sofa of blue velvet that matched the draperies. The effect was slightly discordant, but comfortable. Near the empty hearth, while the last rays of a cloudy May day drew the chamber darker and darker toward nightfall, Evangeline sat opposite Lord Debriss at a small game table enjoying his squeals of victory as he threw his ace over her queen.

Their return had been celebrated by the staff with joy and laughter, and William's adventures had been recounted enthusiastically time and again. Now they had but to await Robert's return to feel entirely secure that the monster had been vanquished forever.

Just when Evangeline was about to claim a victory over her clever opponent, a carriage was heard in the drive. William nearly toppled over his chair as he pushed away from the table and scrambled to the window.

"It's Uncle Robert!" he cried victoriously, "driving the curricle at a spanking pace."

Evangeline felt her stomach fill suddenly with butterflies as she rose to her feet.

Why was she so nervous at the mere thought of seeing Robert again?

Because he had kissed her, of course.

Because he had spoken of making amends.

She pressed a hand to her breast and took a deep breath.

"Whatever is the matter, Evie?" William said as he glanced back at her.

"Nothing, dearest," she assured him, smiling and letting her hand fall to her side.

"What gammon!" he cried, "for I can see that you are overset. You are not still angry with Uncle Robert, not after all he did to get rid of Turley forever?"

She gestured for him to return to her with a wave of her hand. When he did, she took hold of his hand and pressed it. "Not by half," she said, smiling fondly down at him. He seemed taller somehow, after their adventures, and she realized he was no longer stooping as he had been just a few days earlier.

"Well, come, then," he said, drawing her toward the door. "Let's meet him in the entrance hall. I know he will want to see us, to tell us all that happened once we left him alone with Turley."

Evangeline followed him, feeling unsteady.

After a few steps, he turned to scan her from head to foot, then scowled. "You ought to have worn a different sort of gown, the kind mama was used to wear. Gray doesn't suit you."

"But gray suits a housekeeper very well," she reminded him.

He shook his head. "I don't want you to be a house-keeper anymore," he said.

"William," she admonished him with a half smile. "If you turn me off, even with a reference, how will I survive not seeing your sweet face every day?"

He seemed startled by her question at first, then smiled brightly. "Oh, you are just funning!" He laughed, but afterward his expression grew very serious. "Do you know, I think you should marry Uncle Robert, and then both of you could live here and you wouldn't have to be a housekeeper anymore." Seemingly having settled the future to his satisfaction, William led her once more toward the doors and the stairway.

"I've always enjoyed being a housekeeper," she returned, allowing him to hold the door for her, then passing through first. Turning back to him, she continued, "Especially here at Ashland Park."

"You know, Evie, if Uncle Robert won't marry you, I think I shall. Not for years, of course, but we could have a long betrothal."

They had reached the top of the staircase, and Evangeline looked down at him. "William, by the time you are of an age to be married, I shall be in my dotage with gray hair and a myriad of wrinkles."

When his eyes widened, she knew he was thinking of

dear old Nanny, and he voiced his fears, "But will your eyes wander as Nanny's do?"

Evangeline bit her lip. "Undoubtedly."

"I suppose that won't fadge, then," he murmured. "Well, I shall have to have a long talk with Uncle Robert." With that he gave a brisk nod of his head, again took up her hand and proceeded down the stairs.

Just as they had reached the first landing of the tall staircase, the front door opened, and Robert stepped inside tugging off his gloves. He looked up, smiled and waved, and William began a quick, halting run down the stairs.

Evangeline felt her heart pick up its cadence as she watched the man she loved. His cheeks were pink from riding in the cool May air, a contrast to the sticking plaster still fixed over his eye. He whisked off his hat, settled it on the table by the door, and tossed his gloves inside, all just in time to catch William up into his arms.

"We came down to greet you!" he announced, "Evie and I."

William looked back over his shoulder at Evangeline, then hugged his uncle hard about the neck, whispering something into his ear.

Robert smiled and responded, "That is an excellent plan, but you and I must discuss it later."

"Yes, of course," he said, as Robert set him gently down.

"Hallo," Evangeline said, stepping off the bottom step and moving toward him.

He took several steps in her direction as well. "You are in good health?" he asked, then glanced quickly at William. "The boy, too?"

"Yes. Perfect health. But how do you fare? I see that your bruise is nearly gone."

He nodded. "And I had a surgeon tend to the cut."

"Did he sew it up?" William asked, peering up at his uncle.

"Yes."

"May I see it?" he asked, his hazel eyes bright with curiosity.

Robert chuckled. "I'll show it to you later, if you truly wish for it, but not now."

"Evie won't mind," he assured his uncle, "if that is what you fear. She is full of pluck."

Robert returned his gaze to Evangeline. "You are right on that score, but I still refuse to remove the sticking plaster."

Evangeline felt the butterflies suddenly return in full flight to her stomach, diving, swooping, wheeling about until she felt dizzy. There was a warm light in Robert's eye, a light reminiscent of how he had looked just before he kissed her at the White Hart a few days past.

Robert turned quickly toward William and said, "There are several packages in the curricle, all for you, if you are of a mind to open a present or two!"

"Indeed?" he exclaimed.

"Yes. You may get them now if you wish for it."

William needed no further encouragement, but rounded his uncle in his familiar, brisk, halting manner, opened the door and swiftly disappeared outside.

Evangeline couldn't speak as Robert turned to settle his gray eyes on her. Every greeting, formal or otherwise, refused to move past her lips. For a long time she simply looked at him and he at her. Finally, he glanced about him and, seeing that the door to the library was open, took up her hand and quickly drew her inside. A shiver of gooseflesh tickled her neck and side at the thought that perhaps he meant to again take her in his arms.

Instead, however, he remained standing in front of her, as before, only this time pressing her hand affectionately and warmly over and over. She was overcome. She knew in her heart the thoughts running quickly through his mind. Was it possible that after nine long years, all would be settled in the manner it should have been from the first?

She felt as though she was dreaming. The library in which they stood was a small, cozy chamber, lined with books smelling of leather. The sun suddenly broke through in a final farewell to the day, sending sunny, golden beams through the front multipaned window of the chamber. He took a step toward her, entwining his fingers through hers.

"I have forgiven you," he said simply.

She frowned, feeling that his words were quickly dispelling the magical warmth of the moment. "What do you mean?" she asked.

He chuckled softly, then frowned. "What do you mean, what do you mean?" he returned awkwardly. "I forgive you for having broken off our betrothal."

Evangeline blinked, then blinked again. "You forgive me for having broken off our betrothal?" she reiterated, feeling that they were conversing as idiots might. "But Robert—" she began, then stopped. Her suspicions of two days ago flooded her in a sudden wave of understanding. If Robert truly believed what he had just said, that she was to blame for the ending of their betrothal and not he, as Lady Debriss had insisted. . . .

Lady Debriss.

She recalled to mind the very day she had returned to call upon Lady Debriss in Bath, after having tended her consumptive mother for a fortnight.

She drew back from Robert and placed a hand against her chest. She was seeing Lady Debriss's conduct in an entirely new light.

"What is it?" he asked, touching her shoulder with a gentle hand. "Why do you seem so distressed? Is this your way of saying that even though you might hold me in some affection, you are still disinclined toward marrying me?"

She turned her head to look at him and felt the blood rush from her cheeks and tears smart her eyes. "I believe there has been some grave error in all of this that so afflicts me now—to the very center of my heart—that I can hardly speak. For if what I suspect is true, then both you and I have been the objects of a terrible misdeed."

"What are you talking about?" he asked in a hoarse whisper, as though he, too, was beginning to comprehend what had happened.

She turned more fully toward him and faced him squarely. She placed a gentle hand on his chest. "I hope I won't give you pain by bringing this subject forward when your dear sister-in-law has been in her grave but a year. Only I should like to know that in your opinion did she seem in any manner opposed to our match—nine years ago? Or your brother?" She noted a certain quick tightening about his eyes.

"No, not really," he murmured slowly.

"What do you mean, *not really?* Your brother was a Peer of the Realm, and though you were fixed with an easy competence of your own, is it possible he disliked your having tumbled in love with an insignificant creature of few exalted connections and no dowry? You cannot hurt me by admitting as much, only I begin to wonder if some horrid mischance occurred so many years ago that had more to do with the will of others than with either your will or mine."

"You cannot mean what I think you mean," he said, his own complexion paling a trifle as well.

She drew in a deep breath, more tears biting her eyes. "When I returned to Bath from having tended Mama, after you and I had been betrothed for scarcely three weeks, I arrived at your brother's town house in Queen Square to pay my compliments to his wife. What I found there stunned me, for Lady Debriss met me with a tearful embrace and explained that you had decided against wedding me. Your brother could not look me in the eye."

"What?" he cried, shaking his head in disbelief. "But it was no such thing. Are you saying—then you did not—"

"Of course I did not abandon you. I loved you. But I couldn't have told you as much because you had already gone to London and—and I believed what your sister-in-law told me. Her explanations that you had thought better of the match given our disparity in station did not fail to make sense to me. I had always felt a nagging sense of agitation on that score."

"What a fool I was to have believed my brother," he whispered, gathering her up in his arms. "Your love for me was so pure. I had never known such bliss as when delighting in your company, my darling Evie. But I never suspected complicity, even for a moment, on their part. Otherwise—"

Tears now slipped down her cheeks. "And I was so cold to you after accepting the position as your brother's housekeeper."

He drew back from her slightly in order to look into her eyes and to wipe away the tears now trickling down her cheeks. "To think they lied to both of us, then hired you to serve them. I don't know whether to be enraged or disgusted."

Evangeline had long since known Lady Debriss to have been an indifferent mother to William and a quarrelsome wife with her husband. "Your brother was always kindness itself to me," she said, considering his treatment of her with new perceptions. She chuckled softly. "Now I realize how guilt-ridden he must have been. He always gave me a Christmas present of twice my wages at the end of the year, he forced me to take long holidays when the rest of the servants were denied as much, and he encouraged me time and again to make use of the entire house as my own. But most especially, when his wife would argue that I lavished an inordinate amount of affection upon William, he would tell her to stubble it. I begin to believe, even remembering the day that they told me of your disinclination to wed me, that he could not look me in the eye because he knew what he was doing was terribly wrong."

"Then he was a coward," Robert began harshly, "to have let his wife dictate the course of our lives."

"Perhaps, but he was also a good man."

"Evangeline Bradwell, will you marry me?" he asked suddenly. "And turn this terrible wrong into a right?"

"Yes, my darling," she whispered. "Yes."

He smiled, his own gray eyes misted with tears as he leaned forward and placed a kiss on her lips. She sighed, letting the soft, gentle touch of his lips become a balm to her wounded soul. Healing began to flow between them, sealing her heart to his once again. This time nothing would bar the path to their happiness.

"Is it settled, then?" William asked.

Evangeline drew back from Robert and would have slipped from his arms, but he would not permit her to do so. She glanced at him, surprised.

"I've waited too long to hold you in my arms again only to be separated from you just yet—even if it is most improper." She smiled, more tears brimming in her eyes as she laid her head on his shoulder.

"Why is Evie crying?" William asked, confused. "Or did you not beg for her hand in marriage as I told you to?"

Robert chuckled. "She's crying," he whispered, "because she's something of a watering pot and dissolves into tears at the slightest provocation.

"She does not!" William cried, deeply offended. "Do you, Evie?"

Evangeline withdrew from the comfort of Robert's

shoulder and sniffed. "Your uncle is being a wretched tease of the moment. Don't pay the least heed to him." When Robert took his kerchief from the pocket of his coat and handed it to her, she took it with a playful jerk of her hand and began dabbing at her eyes and her cheeks.

William screwed up his mouth, grimacing. "I think you are both being silly. Only tell me if you are to be married so I can tell Cook the good news."

"Yes," Robert returned firmly. "Now, did you find all the things I brought you?"

"Yes. I had Darnell take the packages to the drawing room."

"Darnell?" Robert queried, eyeing him askance.

"When I came into the entrance hall, he was standing near the doorway—just there." He pointed to a place beyond the open doors of the library. "Oh, I say! He must have been eavesdropping!" An excited glint entered his hazel eyes, followed by an expression of profound disappointment. "He will have told Cook by now, but not if I can help it!" With that, the child quickly left the library, his intentions clear. If at all possible, he meant to be first in communicating the happy tidings.

Evangeline chuckled, and Robert turned to look at her wonderingly. "This is all your doing, isn't it?" he queried. "You have been the boy's mother all these years. I find myself in awe. William is precocious, happy and bears a kind of deep contentment rarely seen in either children or adults. And he is amazingly energetic despite his lameness."

"And all this because he has had to endure the—how did you put it?—*an overprotective female who has coddled a lame child from infancy?*"

"Don't remind me of my earlier stupidities. In fact, if we are to be married, your first duty must be to make

**Say Yes to 4 Free Books!**

## COMPLETE AND RETURN THE ORDER CARD TO RECEIVE THIS $18.49 VALUE, ABSOLUTELY FREE!

(If the certificate is missing below, write to:
Zebra Home Subscription Service, Inc.,
120 Brighton Road, P.O. Box 5214, Clifton, New Jersey 07015-5214)

## FREE BOOK CERTIFICATE

**YES!** Please rush me 4 Zebra Regency Romances without cost or obligation. I understand that each month thereafter I will be able to preview 4 brand-new Regency Romances FREE for 10 days. Then, if I should decide to keep them, I will pay the money-saving preferred subscriber's price of just $14.60 for all 4...that's a savings of almost $4 off the publisher's price with no additional charge for shipping and handling. I may return any shipment within 10 days and owe nothing, and I may cancel this subscription at any time. My 4 FREE books will be mine to keep in any case.

Name _____

Address _____ Apt. _____

City _____ State _____ Zip _____

Telephone ( ) _____

Signature _____
(If under 18, parent or guardian must sign.)

RF1096

Terms and prices subject to change. Orders subject to acceptance by Zebra Home Subscription Service, Inc.

**ZEBRA HOME SUBSCRIPTION SERVICE, INC.**

120 BRIGHTON ROAD

P.O. BOX 5214

CLIFTON, NEW JERSEY 07015-5214

AFFIX
STAMP
HERE

the very most of every virtue you can find in me and to ignore my several idiocies."

Evangeline feigned having suffered a shock as she placed a hand to her cheek. "But what you ask is impossible! You are too laden with deficiencies. I would get nothing accomplished in the course of any given day. My hours would be full of striving to find anything good at all about you, all the while having to depress your faults, day by day, month by month, year by year. Oh, the labor of it! I can scarcely bear the thought—"

He did the only sensible thing and silenced her facetious exclamations with a strong kiss.

# SWEET COMPANION

### Nancy Lawrence

Antony Aylesworth St. John, Fifth Earl of Granfell, drove his very elegant curricle at a rapid pace up to Number Nine Grosvenor Place. He waited just long enough to bring his famous matched bays to a mincing and prancing halt before he tossed the reins to his tiger and leapt gracefully down to the flagway.

"Walk 'em, John," he said over his shoulder. "I won't be long. And mind you keep a bit of the edge on them!"

The front door to his mother's house opened magically at his approach, and he entered to find Mawson waiting in the hall, ready to divest his lordship of his hat, gloves, and fashionable many-caped driving coat.

"How is she this morning, Mawson?" asked his lordship out of habit. As was also his habit, he did not wait for an answer, but headed straight for the stairs.

Mawson did his best to warn him, saying in his most efficient butler's voice, "Beg pardon, your lordship, but I believe you'll find her ladyship—"

"In her room? Yes, I know, Mawson," said Lord Granfell, taking the stairs two at a time.

Mawson tried again. "Your lordship, I am rather afraid—" He stopped short as Lord Granfell disappeared from sight around the stair landing.

The earl gained the second floor and gave a peremptory tap at the door of his mother's bedroom. Again, he did not wait for an answer, but immediately swung the door open with all the usual blustery, good-natured style he employed whenever he visited her. He was halfway across to the bed before he realized it was empty and that the room had undergone a transformation. No longer did it look the least like a sickroom.

The draperies had been tied back to allow in the morning sun, and a very soft, refreshing breeze came through the open window to erase all the old familiar odors of invalidism. The bed was very neatly made up, and the table beside the bed was cleared of all the vials, tinctures, and treatments that had littered the table tops of his mother's bedroom for as long as he could remember.

His tall, muscular body drew up into a rigid line, and the color drained from his handsome face. He stood stock-still in the middle of the room as an unspeakable thought, long dreaded, came to him in a rush.

An almost overwhelming sense of regret enveloped him—regret that he had not planned his visit earlier; regret that he had not appreciated how seriously her health had declined; regret that she might have been alone at the end.

"Oh, Mother!" he uttered, hardly aware that he was speaking aloud.

"Antony? Antony, is that you? I'm in here, my dear!" came his mother's voice from the next room, so unexpectedly sweet and strong that he was half afraid he had imagined it.

He followed the sound of her voice to the sitting room, where he found her alone and quite comfortably established on a small settee drawn near the fireplace. Her legs were encased in their usual cocoon of blankets to keep them warm, and in her hands she held a book that bore all the appearance of a romantic novel from the lending library.

He fixed her with a penetrating stare of anger born of worry and demanded, "Have you any idea of the fright you just gave me?"

She smiled up at him and set her book aside. "Oh, don't look so astonished and come and kiss me!"

His frown cleared slightly, but his emotions were still in too much of an uproar for him to refrain from scolding her just a little. "I shall do so willingly—if I can be sure you are indeed my mother. But, you see, the mother I know has not in recent memory been outside the confines of her bedroom before—barring one very disastrous trip to Bath a few months back. You are not supposed to be without the presence of either your maid or your physician, both of whom—I might be forgiven to remind you—I pay a most handsome sum to ensure one of them remains with you at all times!" He bent over to tenderly kiss her proffered cheek, and his angry expression softened to one of concern. "What the devil gave you the notion you were well enough to get out of bed?"

"Now you are being unkind!" she said in the teasing voice she so often employed with him. "Here you find me in my very own sitting room for the first time since either of us can remember, and all you can do is read me a curtain lecture. I'm disappointed in you, Antony. I had been so sure you would see my improvement for yourself."

He drew up a chair close beside her, and his dusky eyes dutifully searched every detail of her appearance. "One cannot improve upon perfection," he said gently.

"Flatterer! You make love so readily and so sweetly, I cannot help but wonder why I still find myself without a daughter-in-law or grandchildren."

"A daughter-in-law I may not be able to present to you," he said with a quizzing look that never failed to charm her, "but grandchildren . . ." He allowed his voice to trail off meaningfully.

"Horrid tease! I refuse to be shocked by your nonsense! But tell me—when *will* I have a daughter-in-law?"

"As soon as I am able to find a young lady who is

enchanting and lovely and—well, a lady exactly like you," he said, and he was pleased to see her smile. And when she smiled, he saw it.

There was, indeed, a change in her. There was a sparkle in her eye he had not seen in years, and now, with the full light of day upon her face, he realized, too, that her color had improved. The faint, bluish tinge that had always lurked so insidiously just beneath the surface of her skin, signaling her condition, had lessened. In its place there was a rosiness, however subtle, to her complexion.

In that moment, with the remnants of a smile touching the corners of her lips, he recalled what a beauty his mother had been before a weak heart, made still weaker by the passing years, had changed her life and her appearance forever.

Even as a lad in leading strings he had thought her lovelier than any fairy-tale princess his imagination might conjure. But that was before he had seen her health decline at a sure and steady pace and had been powerless, despite his wealth and position, to do anything to stop it. Now, as she regarded him with bright anticipation, he saw a glimpse of her old self and he was warmed by it.

"I'll have you know I walked into this room of my own volition," she said saucily, daring him to scold her yet again.

"Remind me to sack your maid," he said darkly, but since there was no hint of malice in his tone or purpose to his expression, Lady Granfell laughed and promised him she would do no such thing.

"You wouldn't be so unkind!" she said with assurance. "Lighthill has been with me for years."

"But she's not with you *now*," he said pointedly, "and I've given strict orders you are not to be left alone."

"You worry too much about me," said the countess. "Besides, Lighthill was very much against my desire to walk even this short distance, and she refused to help me."

"So, with your usual stubbornness, you did it alone. What if you had fallen or injured yourself?"

"But I wasn't alone at all, for I have a new companion, you see, and *she* helped me."

His dark brows rose. "A new companion? One you hired on your own and without my assistance? Why, Mother? And what do you know about this woman?"

"Only that I owe my improved health and, yes, my very life to her!" said Lady Granfell. "And I'm convinced you shall like her excessively, Antony, for I very much want you to meet her."

Her son did not share her enthusiasm. He had always taken great pains to shield his mother from those who might take advantage of her because of her condition. Apparently his efforts had not been diligent enough. He regarded her with a look of frowning fixity and asked, "Who is this woman, Mother? And how is it you owe her your life?"

"Haven't you been listening, dearest? It is because of her efforts that I have been able to make such progress as you see. She has the most wonderful potions she concocts for me and—"

"Do you mean to tell me you have allowed some charlatan to quack you?" demanded Lord Granfell with awful calm.

"Oh, no, dear! She's not a charlatan, truly!"

"Nor, I'll wager, is she a physician."

"Well, of course she cannot be a physician, dear. She is a woman, after all."

For his mother's sake, Lord Granfell made a considerable effort to keep his patience under control. "Mother, I wish you would have consulted me before you brought this woman into your home. Much as you do not care to believe it, there are people in this world who would think nothing of trying to humbug you."

She laughed. "You are much too protective of me, Antony. And I think you are a bit too distrustful of others."

"I wish I had inherited that trait from you," he said, gravely, "for I think you trust others too well. You insist upon looking for the good in everyone—whether they are deserving of such consideration or not."

"You are very harsh, Antony."

"Merely practical. And it is the practical side of me that objects to your inviting some imposter into your home. I fear you've been taken in by this new companion of yours, Mother. Believe me, she has no power to cure you—just a bottle of some foul-smelling concoction and a few mystic chants that are nothing more than mumble-jumble in disguise. She's a charlatan, out to trade her witchcraft for your silver, jewels, and ready funds."

"Why, Antony! What a cynic you've become!" said the countess in a tone of wonder. "I shall have you know, I have not fallen victim to a fraud, and I have not been caused to drink foul-smelling concoctions."

He relaxed slightly. "Thank God for that!"

"I have been drinking very pleasant potions made of secret ingredients that I sometimes mix with my tea."

"I have heard enough, I thank you!" said her son grimly. "I hate to think how much money this woman has had from you, Mother, but I assure you, she shall have no more! I won't sanction a mountebank in this house, and I mean to have her put out this very minute!" He was on his feet in an instant, and made his way toward the bellpull. "I shall send a footman for Dr. Birtwhistle to come and examine you immediately. I can only pray he shall be able to somehow undo whatever damage that snake charmer has inflicted upon you!"

"But Dr. Birtwhistle *has* seen me, dearest," said Lady Granfell, effectively halting her son's hand before he gave the bell a tug. "In fact, he has seen me every day, just as he has for the past two years."

It was a rare event for Lady Granfell to see her son at a loss for words. In his usual mien he was a decisive, assured man of action, who could be relied upon to take charge of any situation. That came, she believed, from inheriting at such a young age his title and the responsibilities of a grand estate, two London town homes, and a sizeable payroll of servants. By the time he had reached the age of three and thirty, making decisions for others came to him as little more than second-nature.

In most matters, Lady Granfell let him have his way, for although she had been sometimes given cause to disagree with his decisions, she had never once been given cause to doubt the goodness of his intentions, especially where she was concerned.

He looked at her doubtfully. "Are you telling me that Dr. Birtwhistle approves of this woman's charms, chants, and nonsense?"

"He approves of her methods as much as he approves of her," said the countess emphatically. "They deal extremely well. Even Lighthill has warmed to her a little, I think."

Lord Granfell cocked one dark, sardonic brow. "Now I *know* this woman can raise ghosts! What magic spell has she cast over Lighthill?"

"You're talking nonsense, Antony, dear. She happens to be a very charming young lady. Why shouldn't Lighthill like her?"

"Because I happen to be in possession of a considerable amount of charm myself," he retorted, "which I have dispensed many times in Lighthill's direction. And never once have any of my efforts made the slightest chink in the armor of Miss Lighthill's grim, formidable expression."

Lady Granfell did her best to smother a smile. "Well,

perhaps Lighthill found it difficult to warm to you, dearest."

Perhaps. But as Miss Lighthill chose that moment to enter the room, Antony thought to seize the opportunity to hear for himself her opinion of his mother's new employee.

Miss Lighthill started slightly at the sight of him, and made a vain attempt to hide between the folds of her black bombazine skirts two slim books she was carrying. Her efforts produced the opposite effect, for Lord Granfell eyed her suspiciously.

An expression resembling guilt crossed Miss Lighthill's lined and stoic face. "Oh, beg pardon! I had no notion you were here, my lord. Shall I come back?" she asked.

"No, but you shall oblige me by telling me what you're hiding there," he said, advancing upon her.

"Antony, stop!" begged his mother, in a voice that was at once laughing and scolding. "You shall have Lighthill quaking in her boots under such interrogation! How suspicious you are! Lighthill has merely brought me two new books to read." She took them from Miss Lighthill and held them up for her son's inspection.

He scanned their titles and frowned. "Isn't that the romantic novel that set half of London on its ear a few months back? You never used to read such books."

"I know, and I am most distressed when I think of all the scandalous stories I've missed! Olivia set me in the way of them, bless her. They're quite diverting—especially when she reads them aloud to me, for she does all the voices so well."

His frown deepened. "Who the devil is Olivia?"

"You know very well Olivia is my new companion," said Lady Granfell in a chiding tone, "and very glad, indeed, I am to have her. She has a way of looking at everything through fresh and curious eyes. I daresay I have much to learn from her."

"Such as how to read romantic novels?" he asked, one dark brow sailing to a challenging angle.

She smiled rather ruefully. "I admit I am growing rather addicted to these little books now. Olivia reads them to me with such sincerity—such authority!—that she quite makes the stories and characters come to life. I'll admit they do have quite preposterous plots. But Olivia says we must rather concentrate on the beauty of the emotion the hero and heroine share for each other."

For a moment Antony could hardly credit he had heard her right, and peered at her as if she had just sprouted a second head. "I think you must be quizzing me!"

"Not at all! Love is a very powerful emotion that can strike one quickly and unexpectedly."

"I suppose you had that from Olivia, too."

"I did, indeed! Olivia is possessed of a rather romantic turn, I believe, and she is sometimes carried away by it."

"It sounds as if she has taken you with her!" he said, with a hint of a smile.

The countess cocked a quizzing brow. "Are you very much shocked to learn your mother harbors a romantic streak? You shouldn't be, you know. I have mentioned too often to you that I wish to see you married and presenting me with grandchildren."

"And what has that to do with romance?"

For a moment she was stunned. "Do you not wish to be in love with the woman you take as your wife?"

"I daresay I shall grow to feel some degree of affection for her after a suitable period of time—"

"That is not what I mean!" said Lady Granfell in an emphatic tone. "I am speaking of true romantic love that can strike suddenly and unexpectedly in the space of—of a single afternoon, for instance!"

"Fall in love in a single afternoon? What utter nonsense!" he said dismissively.

"Perhaps. Still, I should like to think such a lovely thing may happen."

He had never heard his mother speak so, and he didn't think he had far to look to find the cause behind her unusual words. He said, in a voice tinged with sarcasm, "Well, well, well! I see I have much to thank your new companion for! First she inveigles a place in your home; then she drives out the physician I personally selected for your care. And now I find she has undertaken to expand your mind with the sort of poisonous drivel you were never wont to think before."

"She has certainly brought a difference in this house, I'll grant you," said Lady Granfell, as if realizing the truth of her own words for the first time. "In almost three weeks since she's been here, I do believe she has even made Lighthill laugh one or two times."

Antony directed a look of patent disbelief toward his mother's staid and loyal employee, who had retreated with her needlework to her usual unobtrusive place in the far corner of the room.

Under his unwavering gaze, Miss Lighthill averted her eyes and pursed her thin lips together; then she said, "Couldn't say for sure. But the girl does have a way with her."

Antony felt his temper rise. He had always taken such care in managing his mother's affairs. Yet somehow, an avaricious charlatan had managed, through charm or chicanery, to secure a position in his mother's home. He could scarcely bring himself to think how much plate, cash, and treasure his mother's new companion might have pilfered in the short time since her arrival. And when he chanced to think how innocent his mother was of such treachery, he became quite furious indeed.

A mounting sense of outrage caused his voice to sound harsh as he said, "I've heard enough! Unless, of course, you'd like to explain to me, Mother, why you contrived to keep this girl hidden from me for the three weeks since she arrived in your home?"

"But Olivia hasn't been hidden, my dear," said Lady Granfell in a softly reasonable voice. "She spends days with me next to my bed or in this very room. Or she takes a turn about the gardens on her own, if the weather is fine. And in the evenings she is never from my side."

"Then how is it I have never seen her before?"

Lady Granfell held out her hand to him. He came forward and took it and felt her slim, delicate fingers tighten affectionately around his.

"My darling," she said in a gentle voice, "it has been at least three weeks since last you visited me."

It wasn't true. Antony Aylesworth St. John was a good son who loved his mother and visited her often. What in blue blazes did she mean by such moonshine?

He searched his memory and recalled that he hadn't visited her yet that week because he had been preparing to speak on an issue in the House. A further search of his recollection reminded him that the week prior to that had seen him at Ayleswood Park, his county seat, closeted away with his man of business in pursuit of a solution to an irrigation problem on the estate. And the week before that. . . .

Lady Granfell watched her son's expression of angry disbelief fade into one of dawning chagrin. She gave his large, strong hand another small squeeze of reassurance just as the door to her sitting room opened slightly and a young lady began to slowly back her way into the room.

She was very slim figured and dressed in a gown that appeared from the back to be nicely made, but plain indeed. Her chestnut hair was caught up on top of her head in a profusion of negligent curls. As she continued her rather extraordinary entrance, the sunlight through the windows caught the gold and red lights of her hair and lent them a healthy brilliance.

Once she was clear of the threshold and the open door, she began to slowly turn about and revealed that she was carrying a small tray laden with a slim medicine bottle, a glass of water, and three delicate little teacups, out of which most of the tea had been sloshed onto their saucers.

"Oh, dear! I've done it again!" she said, carefully advancing into the room with her brown eyes firmly fixed upon the offending teacups. "I shall never learn to carry without spilling!"

Lady Granfell said kindly, "I wish you would allow Mawson to carry that for you, my dear."

"Oh, it's no trouble, ma'am. I was in the kitchens preparing the foxglove, and I thought it would be quite simple to bring everything with me," she said, carefully setting the tray down on a table. Only then did she look up and notice Lord Granfell was in the room.

A not unattractive look of confusion swept over her face, accompanied by a very fetching tinge of color to her cheeks. Her large brown eyes, framed by dark lashes, grew larger still for the barest of moments, and she briefly caught her full lower lip between her even white teeth.

"Don't be alarmed, my dear," said Lady Granfell, "and come along and meet my son." She gave Antony's hand one more meaningful squeeze before she released it, and said, "Dearest, you will be pleased to meet Miss Olivia Charteris."

The lack of grace with which she carried a tea tray was more than compensated for by the curtsy Olivia sketched before Lord Granfell. She straightened and looked up at him in a rather appraising manner.

"How do you do?" she said in a very polite voice. "Am I intruding? Shall I leave you alone?"

Antony's gaze swept over her not once, but twice. This girl was nothing like he expected. He had thought his mother's new companion would be more in the gypsy mold, rather cronish, and chanting spells and hawking snake oils in a way that would easily explain why his mother was so bewitched by her.

But this girl was lovely, and he was a little disappointed that such a charming young woman should be so intent upon tricking his mother out of her wealth and jewels.

He saw that she was surveying him in as frank a manner as he was regarding her. In fact, after her first start of surprise at seeing him, she didn't appear to be at all shy—or impressed by him. Curious behavior for a girl he judged to be less than twenty summers.

Any other young lady of her age would have met his glance with a bit more deference. But then, any other young lady would not have been quite so well versed in the art of extorting money from his mother or wheedling a place into his mother's household.

Unlike the countess, Lord Granfell had no intention of being beguiled by Miss Olivia Charteris. To prove it, he moved forward a step and bowed slightly, offering her a look of cool civility.

But the countess smiled warmly upon her and said, "Nonsense! I have been wanting the two of you to meet. Leave the tray, my dear, and come and sit with us."

Olivia obeyed and claimed the chair Antony had vacated moments before. Her gaze rested affectionately upon Lady Granfell's face, and her fingers very gently touched Lady Granfell's hand in one soft, flowing movement. She seemed satisfied by Lady Granfell's appearance and turned her attention upon Antony.

"I'm very glad to make your acquaintance, my lord," she said in her low, rich voice, "for had it not been for you, I should never have had the pleasure of knowing your mother."

His brows went up. He didn't think he wanted to sit and exchange pleasantries with a rapacious woman intent on fleecing his mother. "Is that so? And how do you suppose that is?"

He had spoken with perfect civility; but the look he cast her was far from civil, and he saw her flush again slightly under the weight of his stare.

A person of lesser courage might have been flustered into silence. But Olivia met his gaze evenly with an expression of abject innocence and said, "You were the one who sent her on a trip to Bath a few months ago, were you not? I met the countess on her return journey to London, when she was too unwell to travel farther and took refuge in my father's house. So you see, if you had never sent her to Bath, I should never have met her and nursed her back to health. And she would never have invited me here to London to stay with her as her companion."

He flushed with sudden anger. So! The abominable bit of baggage intended to throw into his face his greatest folly! For folly indeed it had been to have sent his mother, under doctor's orders, to Bath. The journey should have brought a measure of relief to her suffering; instead, the trip had nearly killed her.

A vision of his mother, weak and drawn and failing from the rigors of the journey, haunted him still, and a familiar sense of guilt swept over him. Never again, he had vowed, would he allow his mother to leave her London home without him by her side.

He had a sudden notion that the girl, for all her appearance of wide-eyed innocence, was a master manipulator. Merely by the way in which she had put her words together, she had made him out to be somehow reckless with his mother's health—and had cast herself in the light of a healer.

Very well, Miss Charteris! The glove had been tossed! And he considered that he would take great pleasure in teaching her that she very much mistook the matter if she thought to ingratiate herself into his mother's household and purse.

But he could hardly do so at that moment, with his mother looking upon them both with the light of true affection in her eyes.

He said coldly, "I need no reminder of my mother's condition after that calamitous trip to Bath, I thank you!"

"In that case, I shall not raise the matter again," said Olivia, cocking her head to one side and observing him with interest. "May I tell you instead how much I am enjoying my visit with the countess?"

He shot her a penetrating glance. "Your visit? Are you a guest? I understood you were hired as an employee to serve as my mother's companion."

"Well," she said, rolling a look of fondness toward his mother, "that is not exactly right. You see, the countess very kindly invited me to stay with her here in London as a sort of payment for all I had done for her when—oh! But I promised not to speak of that again!—well, *you* know! But the thing of it is, my papa and I decided her offer was too good, too generous for me to accept. So I agreed to come to her only if I could be of help to her as—well, as a companion of sorts."

"Do you mean to tell me you have not accepted any wages? That you draw no salary in exchange for remaining by my mother's side day and night, and at her beck and call?"

"No, indeed! How could I, when it is my pleasure to be with her?"

"Admirable!" he said, with an expression of patent disbelief. This girl was much more shrewd than he originally gave her credit for. After all, what better way to thrust herself amid his mother's heart and purse strings than by convincing them all that she acted out of true affection? He said acidly, "I suppose next you shall tell me it is due to your ministrations that I find my mother's health so much improved."

"I think you already know that," she said, with perfect

calm, in the face of his anger. "I am very happy to see the countess faring so much better. I cannot think she was receiving the best of care before my arrival."

For a moment he was too stunned to reply. He said, "I suppose I know how I may take that! Tell me, have you any other criticisms you'd care to make?"

She blushed slightly. "I—I beg your pardon. I didn't mean that the way it sounded."

The look she cast him certainly appeared contrite, but he had no intention of allowing a pair of limpid brown eyes to disarm him into agreeing with anything she might put forward. He said, "Dr. Birtwhistle has been charged with my mother's care for years. He has no need of assistance, I assure you!"

Olivia held her tongue, as if divining most correctly that there was no use in arguing with him.

But Lady Granfell suffered under no such notion. "Antony, you cannot be so unkind!" she said. "You may not wish to recall that disastrous trip to Bath and how much I suffered because of it, but I think of it often. And when I think of it, I am well aware how indebted I am to Olivia. Had it not been for her, I shudder to think what might have happened!"

Lord Granfell controlled his anger with an effort at the same instant he realized that Olivia had again contrived to somehow appear favorably in his mother's eyes while he had been made to appear somehow lacking. "I collect I am in your debt, Miss Charteris," he said, rather coldly.

"Oh, pray, do not consider the matter," said Olivia, with an appearance of unconcern. She stood and sketched a small curtsy toward the countess and said, "Perhaps I should leave you now, ma'am. I believe I should like to take a turn in the garden while you visit with your son."

"Of course, my dear," said Lady Granfell kindly. "It is much too fine a day to remain indoors. Lighthill shall give me my drops, just as you showed her, so you must not think to hurry back on my account. Now, do go and enjoy yourself."

No sooner did the door shut upon Olivia than the countess directed a cheery look toward Antony and asked, "Isn't she lovely?"

He reined in his considerable temper, but could not refrain from cocking one dark, cynical brow. "*Is* she?"

"I'm quite taken with her, as are my friends when they come to visit me. Which puts me in mind of something I've been meaning to speak to you about, Antony. I shall need some funds against next quarter day."

"Of course, Mother," he said, "although I am a bit astonished. You've never outrun the carpenter before."

"Oh, the money isn't for me. It's for Olivia."

Antony stiffened slightly as he realized that all his suspicions surrounding his mother's new companion were about to be given credence. He asked darkly, "And how much money did you promise her?"

"Not a pence, for I doubt very much that she'd take it. But I do think if she is to stay on with me, she should be properly attired. You saw for yourself how she was dressed this morning. Admit it! The girl could do with some decent clothes!"

The girl could do with being tossed out on her ear, he thought grimly, and he would take the greatest pleasure in performing that task himself. If Miss Olivia Charteris thought she could squeeze one groat out of the Earl of Granfell, she very much mistook the matter!

And so Antony considered telling his mother. But one look into her face, so filled with affection for the girl, and he knew it would prove a mistake to try to convince her that Olivia's character was not of her imagining.

He resolved to take another tack: If he could not convince his mother to give up Olivia, he didn't think it would take too much effort—or ready blunt—to convince

Olivia, a young lady he considered of questionable honor and obvious avarice, to give up his mother. He would do it quietly, and with the best of taste. No shouts, no accusations; just a simple payment to the greedy little hoyden, and she would be gone, and his mother would be free of her influence.

He bent over to kiss Lady Granfell's cheek, telling himself that when the whole ugly affair was over and done, and he had rid them all of Olivia's presence, his mother would realize that he had once again acted in her best interest. For now, though, he said gently, "Of course. Rig her out in the best styles, if you like, and send the reckoning to me."

"Thank you, dearest," said the countess happily. "I shall have my dear friend, Lady Coniston, squire her to the shops. She will know just what to buy and won't be too extravagant with your purse!" Her expression changed as she looked up into his dusky eyes. She said earnestly, "I wish you could like Olivia a little, my dear."

"I was never one for first impressions," he said gently, not wishing to distress her. "Perhaps your Olivia and I shall come to an understanding in time. As a matter of fact, I was thinking of joining her in the garden for a few moments."

His mother's face lit. "Oh, I wish you would. And do take all the time you need. Lighthill will stay with me, so you need have no worry. Yes, an excellent suggestion, Antony. Olivia will be quite pleased!"

Olivia was not. Instead, her reaction, when she spied Lord Granfell walking with a powerful, lissome grace along the garden path in her direction, was rather more wary than pleased.

She had hoped he might conclude his visit with the countess and quit the house without her ever having to meet him again. From the little she had seen of him so far, he was just as callous and unfeeling as she had imagined he would be. And she had imagined him to be quite beastly indeed.

She had been in residence with Lady Granfell for well-nigh three weeks, and in that time Lord Granfell had not visited his mother once, despite her obviously frail health. Only a perfect beast of a son would have behaved so, and Olivia could not help but think the earl the most unfeeling man she had ever met. When the thought occurred to her that such a naturally cold-hearted monster might at times be cruel to the countess, he made her very angry, indeed.

He also made her nervous. She had never before met a Peer of the Realm, and she thought if only half of them measured up to the remarkable specimen now striding elegantly toward her along the garden walk, she would be most surprised indeed.

Cold and hard-hearted he may be, but he was, quite simply, the handsomest and most fashionable man Olivia had ever seen. As she watched him close the last distance between them, her knees were seized by a sudden and inexplicable weakness.

"May I accompany you on a turn about the garden, Miss Charteris?" he asked in a very charming tone, as he reached her side.

"Turn about the garden?" she repeated with surprise. She looked up into his face and saw that his expression no longer held any hint of the rigid disapproval she had seen while in his mother's sitting room but moments before.

But it did hold a wealth of purpose. He was fairly convinced he could buy the wretched young woman off and get her out of his mother's house in little more than ten minutes' time. At his most charming, he could probably have the whole nasty business over and done in only five minutes. He decided to use the charm.

"It is a fine day and a lovely garden," he said, meeting her gaze with an attractive smile. "A brief walk together will give me an opportunity to speak to you privately as I could not earlier in my mother's apartments."

Her brown eyes widened, and she could not mask the note of suspicion in her voice. "You wish to speak to me *privately?*"

His answer was a seductive smile that caught the corners of his remarkably chiseled lips. He gestured slightly with one well-manicured hand and said, "Shall we, Miss Charteris?"

Olivia moved quite mechanically down the garden walk, keenly aware of Lord Granfell's rather overwhelming presence at her side. She couldn't resist the impulse to cast him a sidelong glance and regretted doing so immediately, for she found his dusky eyes upon her.

Antony examined her critically and was forced to admit she was, indeed, a lovely young woman. He could well imagine that she would turn out to be quite a stunning beauty if only she were rigged in the latest fashions, as his mother planned. But he had no intention of allowing that plan to bear fruit.

He said, in his most appealing manner, "I notice my mother calls you Olivia. May I?"

She could hardly refuse; indeed, the thought barely crossed her mind, for she didn't think she had ever heard anyone pronounce her name so enchantingly before. "Of course."

"I notice, too, that my mother believes it is due to your efforts she is so much improved. I believe she considers you something of a miracle worker."

She looked up at him with a slight frown, for she thought she detected a hint of sarcasm in his voice. A search of his handsome face, however, revealed no malice in his expression, and she relaxed a bit. "I'm certain you know I am no such thing! But I am glad to be of help to the countess and equally glad to see her faring so much better."

"How do you do it? What potions do you give her?"

She smiled slightly. "You make me sound like a witch doctor!"

"Aren't you one?"

"Not at all, I assure you," she said, more amused than vexed by his opinion of her. "Would you be better satisfied if I chanted something nonsensical over the countess, danced like a savage about her bed, and hung a talisman from her neck?"

"Frankly, that is more along the lines of what I expected."

"You're speaking of quacksalvers," she said, frowning. "They rely upon spectacle and showy methods to convince their patients that their condition has improved or been cured."

There was a sudden, accusatory light in his eyes. "I believe the mind—especially the mind of an invalid—can easily be tricked into believing such tittle. And, if I'm not mistaken, the patient is usually so grateful, so enamored of the miracle worker who wrought such a change in their condition, that they are very willing to pay them handsomely for their trouble."

Olivia looked up at him sharply. That was the second time he had used the term *miracle worker.* This time he said the words disparagingly. The first time he had said them of her.

"I assure you, my lord, I am nothing of the sort," she said emphatically.

"What, exactly, are you denying? That you employ the arts of a shaman? Or that you have had some form of payment from my mother?"

"Both!" said Olivia, a good deal shocked.

"Are you telling me my mother has not pledged to somehow show her gratitude for all you have done to improve her condition?" he asked, and he was given the satisfaction of seeing a telltale flush cover her cheeks.

It was true, Olivia thought. Lady Granfell *had* promised to show her how grateful she was, and in the most extravagant manner possible. She had begun by buying Olivia trinkets and baubles—small gestures, really, that Olivia had blushingly accepted. But in the last few days Lady Granfell had spoken of shopping for Olivia and sending her out, under the aegis of her friend, Lady Coniston, to *tonnish* parties, drums, and routs. She had even spoken of presenting Olivia at court and holding a ball in her honor—a gift Olivia would never dream of accepting.

"Oh, but she didn't mean it!" said Olivia earnestly. "And I have begged her not to trouble herself! I assure you, I never would accept such an extravagant gift from the countess!"

Antony's steps drew to a halt, and as Olivia came to a stop beside him, he eyed her shrewdly. He considered her a remarkably good actress to protest her innocence so effectively. But it was a talent he found more irritating than admirable.

He said, "Let me be blunt with you, madam. I am prepared to double whatever sum you hoped to gain from my mother. In exchange, you will leave her house this day, and you'll have no further contact of any sort with her in future."

For a moment Olivia thought she could not have heard right. But in the ensuing silence that stretched between them, she realized that since the moment of their acquaintance, Lord Granfell had been less than civil. Now it was quickly borne upon her that he held a low opinion of her.

The realization that he considered her some sort of charlatan, intent on bleeding his mother out of her pin money, was a stunning one, and she was quite unable to speak for several moments.

Fleetingly, she considered assuring him, with mounting fury, that no power on earth would induce her to take a pence from him or his mother, and her fingers itched to slap his cold, emotionless face. But then she chanced to hit upon the happy notion that she might gain more satisfaction from making him regret having held such a horrid opinion of her.

She was a vicar's daughter, and she knew that revenge was a paltry and dangerous emotion; but at that moment she was far more interested in seeing if she couldn't make that hard, self-confident gleam in his eye disappear than she was of putting one of her father's sermons to practice. If Lord Granfell thought her a bad person when she had been at such pains to be on her best behavior with him, she didn't think it would take too much effort to show him just how bad she could really be when she put her mind to it.

"I am afraid, my lord," she said, with a controlled voice and the light of battle in her eye, "you cannot hope to match the offer the countess has made me."

He frowned. "What, exactly, did my mother promise you?"

She took a deep breath and looked him full in the eye. "A title!" she said and was pleased to see that he was looking back at her with an appalled expression.

"A title? Do not tell me she has pledged to make you her ward, or some such nonsense! I swear to you now, I shall never allow you to become a member of this family!" he said unpleasantly.

Olivia fought back an impulse to assure him she would rather die penniless in a gutter than ever be a part of his family. Instead, she said in a gently chiding tone, "You have a very poor opinion of me, indeed, if you think I would be satisfied to remain your mother's ward for the rest of my life!" She cast him a flippant look, then resumed strolling along the garden path at a leisurely pace that Antony was forced to match.

"Then how do you intend to use my mother to gain a title?"

"The countess has promised to present me at court. This very morning she began making plans and drafting guest lists for the ball she intends to hold in my honor. I believe she is so engaged, even as we speak," said Olivia, secure in the knowledge that since she was not really lying but merely stretching the truth only a little, God should not strike her dead.

"I don't believe it!" he said savagely. "My mother will never be well enough to escort you to the queen's drawing room!"

"Perhaps not. But Lady Coniston is in perfect health, I assure you, and she is quite willing to squire me about."

A muscle pulsed in Antony's jaw as he recalled, with stunning effect, that his mother had already mentioned that Lady Coniston had been tapped to take Olivia shopping. But his mother had only mentioned buying the girl a few dresses and furbelows—a prospect of a much lower order than rigging her out for a season of presentations, balls, and assemblies.

"I won't stand the blunt!" he promised.

"But your mother shall," said Olivia, noting with satisfaction the rush of angry color in his face. "The countess has promised me a most dazzling season in which I shall attract only the most eligible of suitors. I mean to marry a title out of it all and remain most comfortably established for the rest of my life. Frankly, my lord, I do not see how any sum you may propose could possibly tempt me to abandon my plans to be presented from your mother's house."

A look of disgust crossed Antony's handsome face.

"Very fine talk, indeed! You have proven yourself to be much more mercenary than I gave you credit for!"

Once again, her fingers itched to slap him, but she forced herself to think instead of the immense satisfaction she would gain from making him squirm just a bit longer.

She said, in a voice of reckless bravado, "Only be reasonable. You must see I cannot whistle past your mother's generous offer if there is any chance I may gain a rich and titled husband out of it. I am, after all, almost twenty years, and I have a keen desire to be established respectably."

"A wife from a snake-oil wagon! No man of society would bear it!"

"Oh, but I am not out of a snake-oil wagon," she assured him. "My father is not a gypsy, but a vicar."

"I don't believe it!" he said grimly. "You behave nothing like a vicar's daughter!"

Mulishly, she shrugged her slim shoulders and let out a long, theatrical sigh. "I suppose there must be at least one bad seed in every garden."

Antony's strong fingers gripped her elbow, and he drew her to a stop, forcing her to face him. He looked down into her eyes and saw a brightness there that he had not seen before, and he took it as a signal of her coldness and calculation.

"You would do well to reconsider my offer, Miss Charteris," he said, in a low, measured voice. "I hold a considerable influence over my mother and her friends. You shall find no husband among them."

"If your influence over the countess were as you claim, you would not be trying to bargain with me now," said Olivia, doing her best to ignore the manner in which her heart had begun to flutter the moment he touched her.

He stared down at her for a good while before he released her, but there was no masking that telltale muscle that still pulsed in his jaw, signaling his anger. "Bargain? With an empiric who never should have gained an entree into my mother's house in the first place? The only reason you are here is because you had the good fortune to be born beautiful! Were your face and figure otherwise, your wiles and arts would not be so well received, I assure you!"

It was rather curious circumstance to discover that the Earl of Granfell could think her beautiful while at the very same moment his expression was filled with enough anger to throttle her on the spot. She was woman enough to be pleased when a man thought her attractive, even though *this* man made it quite clear he did not admire her for it.

"Oh, I know you cannot be so cruel as you would have me believe," she said in a cajoling voice. She had a sudden and keen desire to see how far she could push him. "Come now! Say you won't begrudge me one or two ball gowns! Did I tell you? I've already chosen the material for the gown I shall wear to the ball your mother is giving in my honor! I mean to make the gown up in red-shot silk. Lady Coniston drove me out to the Pantheon Bazaar where I found the most cunning yellow plumes that I mean to dress in my hair. Oh they were so tall!" She made a sweeping gesture, stretching her slim fingers up over her head as far as she could, and she looked up into his face. His horrified expression almost caused her to laugh aloud. "I daresay I shall attract quite a bit of attention!"

For the first time since he could remember, Antony found himself shocked beyond words. But a sudden and appalling vision of Olivia dressed in the outrageous manner she had just described, and greeting his mother's guests at the top of the grand staircase, temporarily robbed him of his powers of speech. "You—you cannot be serious!" he managed to say at last.

Then he saw it; a spark of amusement glimmered

within the depths of her brown eyes, and he knew she wasn't serious.

But she *was* toying with him, and he wasn't sure that he cared for it. Since his earliest memory he had been treated with deference and respect by everyone within his orbit. Miss Olivia Charteris, however, stood looking up at him with the light of laughter in her eyes and a pointedly provoking expression. He didn't know whether to be diverted or vexed. He was certainly confounded and, somehow, oddly charmed.

"What an abominable young woman you are!" he said at last.

She did laugh then, and there was no mistaking the fact that she was enjoying his confusion.

"You deserved it!" she said.

He ran his hand through his hair in a distracted fashion. "Let me understand you. Was none of what you just told me true?"

She shook her head and cast him an impish look. "Sadly, no. There is no red dress. And there are no yellow plumes. Disappointed?"

"I should say not!" he said. He tried to sound gruff, but only succeeded in making her laugh again. "I fail to see what you find so devilishly amusing!"

"I beg your pardon," she said, though he didn't think she looked the least bit sorry, "and I am willing to cry truce, if you are. May we not start our acquaintance over again, without all the misunderstandings? I think we have been less than reasonable in our dealings so far."

"I am *always* reasonable," he said rigidly.

"No," she said with a small shake of her head. "A reasonable person would not have jumped to false judgment so quickly. A reasonable person would have noticed that since my arrival three weeks ago, there has been a marked improvement in your mother's appearance."

He had noticed. Her improved color, the light of life

in her eyes, her ability to walk from room to room—his mother's *appearance* had improved; but he knew that charlatans had the ability to trick their patients into thinking themselves cured, often with disastrous results.

"My mother's heart has always been weak. If she were to think herself well, she might tax what little remaining strength she has left and then—" He broke off, unable to complete that most dreaded of thoughts. He said harshly, "I won't allow you, with your charms and chants, and deviltry, to bewitch her into thinking herself well."

"Deviltry?" she repeated, in a tone that was at once shocked and amused.

He looked a bit triumphant. "My mother told me you concoct magic potions for her made of secret ingredients. I've no doubt you utter a few chants over her and cast the odd magic spell to convince her your healing powers are genuine. I, however, am not so easily persuaded."

His tone had been ruthless, his expression, severe; and he fully expected that by the end of his speech, Olivia would be reduced to a compliant, very repentant young lady. But he was fast learning that Miss Olivia Charteris was anything but compliant.

She laughed again, a rich, throaty confection of a laugh that left him with little doubt that she was greatly entertained and not the least intimidated.

"Oh, I beg your pardon," she said at last, "but you must admit it is rather wondrous that such an intelligent man as you could come by such idiotic notions! Magic spells, indeed! I believe you have read many more gothic novels than even I have! Next you shall accuse me of dancing like a heathen about her bed!"

Antony Aylesworth St. John, Fifth Earl of Granfell, had never before experienced the feeling of having someone laugh at him, and he resolved that it better not happen again. It was all he could do to keep his temper under control. Or to keep from grabbing her by the shoulders and giving her a richly deserved shake.

"You may laugh at me and flatter my mother as much as you like, but you will not alter the fact that nothing will come of your schemes!" he said furiously. "If you think to tease me into offering you a larger sum to leave my mother's house, you have not succeeded, Olivia. I shall not pay you a penny! I am not a pigeon for plucking."

She looked him straight in the eye and said, in a voice of quiet strength, "And I am not a scheming charlatan."

Something in her tone arrested him for a moment. Still, he couldn't bring himself to believe her. "Do you honestly expect me to believe you are living with my mother—caring for her—and you expect no compensation? No payment of any kind in return?"

"Of course I expect no payment," she said. "How could you think such a thing of me?"

"Very easily!" he retorted. "You must admit it is rather incredible that a young, attractive woman would closet herself away to care for my mother and expect nothing in return."

She frowned and regarded him with a searching look. "Have you never known anyone to act merely out of kindness or affection?"

"No!" he said baldly.

Her eyes never wavered from his face. "Then I feel sorry for you."

He was a little stunned; then his gaze raked over the cheap, unfashionable gown she wore. *"You* feel sorry? For *me?"*

She ignored his insolent look. "Yes, I do. And I wonder how many opportunities for friendship and affection you have missed merely because you are so mistrustful of others."

"Very few, I thank you!" he said, suddenly angry. "Missed opportunities, indeed! It might interest you to know, Miss Olivia Charteris, that I am possessed of a goodly number of friends who——" He stopped short, suddenly aware that this abominable young woman had somehow managed to set him on the defensive. He took a deep breath and made a vain attempt to count to ten before he said, "Do not try to change the subject. It so happens, madam, that I alone am responsible for my mother's care, and I don't recall figuring you and your magic potions into her plan of treatment. You will oblige me by packing your things and leaving this house today."

Olivia's brown eyes widened with astonishment. "Leave? Today? Oh, no!"

"I shall arrange your passage back to wherever you came from," he said ruthlessly.

"But the countess—I cannot leave her now!"

"You can, and you will!"

"But my papa sent me to care for her. If I go home now, I shall be quite disgraced, and the countess won't have her medicine and—oh, please don't send me away!"

He looked down at her face, so filled with concern, and he hardened himself against it. "You needn't worry that your time here will have been for naught. I shall see that you are paid something before you leave," he said firmly, and with an eye toward her reaction to the promise of a little silver.

But her brown eyes didn't glint at the mere prospect of money, as he had been half afraid they would. Instead, her eyes gained a measure of softness, then blurred slightly; and he realized, with a good deal of alarm, that she was very close to tears.

It was a turn he had not expected. Even less expected was his reaction to it. In an instant his amazement gave way to an overwhelming sense that she was very young, rather vulnerable, and quite attractive.

"Olivia," he said, shaken by the knowledge he was the cause of the wounded look in her eye. He took a step toward her and stopped, then said in a rather disjointed voice, "Pray, do not—! Perhaps I spoke hastily—! For God's sake, I didn't mean it!"

Those words, once uttered, were as confusing to him as they were unwelcome, for he suddenly doubted his opinion of her. Could he have been so wrong about her methods and motives? Or were her tears yet another ploy of hers to get money out of him? He struggled with that notion, assuring himself that he still had good reason to mistrust her.

Yet a large measure of that resolve fled when he saw her raise her hand to her cheek, and realized she did so to dash away a tear.

For the first time in a great many years, Antony had no idea what to do next. His impulse was to touch her, to comfort her somehow, and that notion warred directly with his more realistic nature that told him that no logical good could come from allowing this impertinent young woman to remain in his mother's home.

He said in a grave, but gentle voice, "Olivia, it was never my intention to hurt you so. But I am a practical and reasonable man. With a bit of effort, I think you can well understand how I might be suspicious of your presence in my mother's home."

She sniffed and wished she had for once followed her mother's advice to always carry a handkerchief. "No, I cannot understand."

"Be reasonable," he said coaxingly, and he drew his own kerchief from his pocket and pressed it into her hand. "Don't you find it rather odd that a mere slip of a country girl could succeed in improving my mother's condition, where England's best physicians have failed?"

"I don't find it odd at all," she said stubbornly, "and I think you are very harsh."

He recognized those words as an echo of a similar sentiment his mother had voiced earlier that day.

"Only when I am given cause to be. You laughed at me and behaved as if you believed my concern for my mother was somehow amusing. You were very willing to let me think the worst of you!"

"*You* would not believe me when I tried to tell you the truth!" she accused, fighting back another tide of angry tears.

He had no excuse to offer in the face of this argument, and an unwelcome sense of guilt caused his next words to sound harsh.

"I am responsible for my mother's care and well-being. I have worked very hard to establish an order and peace about her. And when I come to visit, what do I find? A young woman—a stranger—established in my mother's home, spilling tea, talking of come-out balls and prescribing medicines and potions!"

"I am not a stranger!" said Olivia, with mounting anger. "Your mother's household and her friends have known me very well these three weeks. And I assure you they all would be very much shocked to hear such accusations as you have made today."

Antony felt his face color slightly. "Do not try to make me feel guilty for protecting my mother! You know very well your appearance in her home might be considered highly suspicious, not to mention all this talk of potions and medicines mixed in her tea!"

"Then you have no need to suspect me. Herbal cures and medicines have been with us for ages, and are not new merely because *you* have never heard of them before."

"Perhaps, but my mother's physician *has* heard of every available cure—legitimate or otherwise—and would have employed them if he thought it best."

A telltale spark of anger lit her brown eyes. "So you still think me a charlatan!—a faker!—who would dally with your mother's health!" she said roundly. "I suppose

I could assure you, once and for all, that I am nothing of the sort and have no designs on your mother or her purse. But I think I shall save my breath to cool my porridge, for you, my lord, seem quite determined to think the worst of me no matter *what* I say!"

He was a little stunned by her outburst. No one, to the best of his knowledge, had ever addressed him in such a tone. Little spitfire! What the devil did she mean by speaking to him so?

She wasn't about to let him find out. Olivia turned on her heel and walked away, leaving him standing alone on the path.

"Wait!" he exclaimed.

She stopped and turned to face him with a burning look. "Why should I?"

He couldn't think of a reason. He knew only that he didn't want her to leave. It went against his better judgment, but he didn't want her to leave.

He said, "Tell me what you give my mother. What is the potion you make for her and mix into her tea?"

"It is *not* a potion!" she retorted. "It is a medicine drawn from the leaves of the foxglove."

"And how do you know of this medicine? And why does Dr. Birtwhistle—a trained physician—*not* know of it?"

She gave a sigh of exaggerated patience. "Dr. Birtwhistle is very familiar with foxglove, but he has never used it before. It can be very dangerous, even deadly, if not properly prepared and administered."

"You, I suppose, know how to prepare it properly?"

Olivia ignored the faintly acid tone in his voice. "I do," she said with an unwavering look.

"And how is it that you possess this knowledge, and one of the most learned physicians in the land does not?"

She eyed him measuringly. "Do you *really* want to know?"

He frowned, for he was suddenly not at all sure that he did. But he said, "Yes, I really want to know."

"Very well. I was taught herbal cures by a mystic who lived in our village."

His lip curled slightly. "A *mystic?*"

She laced her arms together beneath her bosom and fixed him with an icy look. "Do you want to hear this story, or don't you?"

The last time anyone had used that tone of voice with him, he had been a mere lad caught running truant from his Latin lessons, and he was caught a little off guard. "I apologize," he said just as he had years before to his Latin tutor. "Tell me how you came by this knowledge."

"Only if you promise you shall not interrupt again."

Outrageous girl! Who in blazes did she think she was talking to? A feeling of resentment flared within him, then quickly died as he saw she was looking up at him with a rather engaging expression of exaggerated patience. He didn't know whether to be infuriated or charmed. He was certainly intrigued, and said evenly, "Very well. I promise I shall not interrupt you again."

She looked as if she didn't believe him, but she began her story anyway. "When I was growing up, there was a woman who lived just outside our village. We called her Dark Mary, for her skin was quite brown from the sun and her eyes were black as night. She spoke with a very pronounced accent, and she was very old when I first saw her; so I really don't know her age when at last she died. But her face was very wrinkled, and her back was very stooped."

"Do you mean to tell me this woman was a gypsy?" demanded Lord Granfell, quickly forgetting his promise.

"I cannot say, for certain. But the thing I remember most about her when I was a child was that she had a very mysterious presence. All the children in the village were quite terribly afraid of her, and the adults, too, avoided any contact with her. Until, of course, one of the villagers fell ill. We had no physician in the village, you see, and as many of our neighbors believed Dark Mary was something of a sorceress, they would call upon her to mix up medicines and cures for ailing villagers."

"And did her medicines cure them?" asked Antony.

"Yes, they did, and Dark Mary's reputation as a healer grew. Whenever a villager fell ill, some terribly brave soul would apply to Dark Mary for a healing medicine. And Dark Mary never failed. Even though she was quite shunned by everyone in the county, whenever they needed her or her cures, she always obliged. Then one day, Dark Mary fell ill herself. Since my father was the vicar and went to visit her regularly, he sent me as his eldest daughter to nurse her."

Antony frowned. "Weren't you afraid of her, like the other children?"

"I was terrified! But my father insisted, and—believe it or not—I am a very dutiful daughter!" She saw a slight smile lift the corners of his lips, and she felt herself utterly disarmed by it. She had to force herself to concentrate on her story. "So off I went to Dark Mary's cottage all alone. Dark Mary was confined to her bed for the first days I was there. But she told me everything I must do to make her well. She gave me a leaf and sent me out to her garden behind her tiny little house, telling me I was to find the plant with matching leaves. When I had done so, she instructed me in cooking the leaves of the plant to make a medicine she could take."

"So you saved her!"

Olivia nodded. "I stayed with Dark Mary for a little more than a week. I learned about making medicines, and I learned that I and all the villagers were wrong about Dark Mary. She was not a sorceress, nor even very mysterious. She was simply a very old lady with a very special knowledge. When she was well, I returned home, but I went back to her cottage every day to visit her. We became friends. And she taught me all she knew about the plants in her garden and making different medicines and cures."

Antony looked down upon her animated face with a grave expression. "That is how you came by your knowledge of medicines, and that is how you know what to mix in my mother's tea. It was a very important lesson to learn."

Olivia shook her head slightly. "No, the important lesson was that I learned not to judge others by their appearance or even by the first impression they might make."

He glanced at her sharply. "I suppose that was meant for me."

She cast him an impertinent look. "I suppose it was," she said saucily, and she resumed her slow perambulation down the path.

He stood for a moment, wondering if the atrocious little bagpipe intended to make a habit of speaking to him so. Then his attention was captured by the sight of her gown swaying easily over her slim hips as she moved slowly away from him.

He was mesmerized by it. All his much-vaunted practicality could not drag his gaze away from the faint outline of her figure beneath her gracefully swinging skirts. The plain blue dress, which he had looked upon so scornfully earlier, quite captured and held his attention. He couldn't have felt a greater desire for her if she had been gowned from head to toe in the finest silks from London's grandest couturier.

He was strangely and utterly attracted to Olivia. She was beautiful, but not in the same way as the women with whom he usually surrounded himself. Those women were idle and self-absorbed, concerned with gowns and jewels and learning the most fashionable dance steps. Olivia

Charteris was none of those things. Yet she moved just as gracefully and held her lovely head at just as regal an angle as the most highly born female of his acquaintance.

Shamelessly, he watched her until he realized she had moved quite a distance away. Then he caught up to her with a few long-legged strides.

"I shouldn't have to ask your forgiveness for having my mother's best interest at heart," he said. "I know I can be rather too protective of her, but my intentions are well-founded."

"I'm sure they are," she replied, ignoring the rather defensive tone to his voice. "But by being overprotective, I think you chase away those who might be able to help her."

"I didn't chase *you* away."

"No, but I am much more stubborn than most people," she said, casting him a very charming smile.

"That I can well believe!"

She glanced up at him, and detected the intriguing hint of a smile at the corners of his mouth. "Even if I were not so stubborn," she said, "I could not leave your mother now. She needs me and she relies on me."

"To give her the foxglove in her tea?"

"And to be her friend. I think she is lonely sometimes, with only Miss Lighthill for company. Sometimes her friends do visit. Lady Coniston is especially loyal and tells the countess some very entertaining stories about some very fashionable people. Still, I think she gets lonely. I know she would like to see you more often."

As soon as the words left her lips, Olivia knew she had said the wrong thing. Lord Granfell stiffened visibly and looked down upon her with a cold gleam to his eye.

"You may be interested to know that I *do* visit my mother—and frequently!"

"I'm sure you do," she replied with unimpaired calm,

"but I am equally sure I have never seen you visit her, and I have been in the house for these three weeks."

"I do have responsibilities in other areas," he said, striving to maintain an even tone.

"Are those responsibilities more important than visiting your mother?"

"My dear young woman! You have no notion what you are asking!"

"And you have no notion what it is like to watch your mother sit beside her window all day, hoping to hear the sound of your carriage pulling up before the house! Or the sound of your footstep on her stair!"

He felt an odd pang of conscience, but he wasn't about to let her know it. "Footstep on the stair," he repeated scornfully. "You may be interested to know that my mother is very aware that my duties take me from town for days at a time. Besides, if my mother wanted me to visit, she would have said so!"

Olivia raised one finely arched brow. *"Would* she?"

He flushed, and stared at her with hard, grim eyes. She was right. His mother would never dream of summoning him to visit, any more than she would consider complaining of her condition or moaning over her fate as an invalid.

Good God, was he really as callous a son as Olivia made him out to be? "I visit my mother frequently, and I'll thank you to remember that!" he said stiffly.

"But you haven't visited in the last three weeks. And when you sent the countess to Bath and she came to our vicarage because she was too ill to travel, you never visited her once!"

"Good God, must you throw that in my face, too? I was traveling to my hunting lodge and was halfway to Scotland by the time I received word of her condition!" he retorted furiously. "Don't you think I would have been with her if only I had known?"

Olivia cast him a skeptical look. "Perhaps."

His teeth ground together almost audibly. "I may not have seen my mother as often as I should during the last few weeks," he admitted coldly, "but I am here now, and I have every intention of making this visit of prolonged duration!"

He had the satisfaction of finally having the last word over Miss Olivia Charteris, but that satisfaction was fleeting.

No sooner had he finished speaking than he looked up and caught sight of Mawson coming toward them down the path with a slow butler's step and a look of apology on his face.

"I beg your pardon, your lordship," said Mawson, from a stately distance away, "but your groom was growing concerned and asked if I wouldn't speak to you on his behalf."

Antony frowned. "My groom? John? What the devil has he to be concerned about?"

"Your horses, sir. The bays. John Groom has been walking them up and down in front of the house as your lordship instructed, in anticipation of a rather short visit. You've been here some time, however, and John Groom is having difficulty holding them. He would like your permission to drive them back to your stables."

A dull color swept over his cheeks as Antony recollected that he had indeed arrived at his mother's house with the intention of staying only a few moments.

But Miss Olivia Charteris, with her wide brown eyes and mocking ways, had changed all that—and he wasn't sure whether he should bless her or curse her for it.

He did his best to erase all trace of emotion from his expression, but he was feeling very angry indeed. Angry with himself for having thought he could treat his mother in such a cavalier style; angry with Olivia for having divined that his devotion to his mother was less than he had claimed; and angry with himself for thinking, for one brief, appalling moment, that he wanted very much to show to advantage in front of Olivia—and had failed to do so.

It was almost a full minute before he could trust himself to speak. "Tell John to drive the bays home, Mawson, and send the barouche back for me in an hour."

Once Mawson had retreated, Antony braced himself to turn and face Olivia, convinced that he would find her looking up at him with a mocking smile of satisfaction. Instead, he found that she had very discreetly moved along the garden walk and was making a great show of examining the blooms on a rose hedge.

He knew full well she had overheard everything Mawson had said and he chose to mask his mortification with anger. "If you think I shall apologize or explain to you my actions, you much mistake the matter," he said ruthlessly.

She cast him a curious, unreadable look and moved a bit farther down the walk.

He thought her silence more condemning than any words she might have uttered, and he was unsure whether or not to follow her. His hesitation lasted only a moment.

He caught up to her with a few quick strides. His hand on her arm forced her to stop and face him. "Go ahead and say it!" he demanded. "You might as well, for I know you think I'm a great, unfeeling beast!"

He looked down upon her, bracing himself against the criticisms he knew she had every right to make.

But they didn't come. Instead, he saw that her face had flushed a very vivid color and she could not bring herself to meet his eye. He frowned. "What is it? What's wrong?"

For a moment he didn't think she would answer; then at last she said in a tight, little voice, "I'm sorry."

Those two simple words threw him quite off his stride. *"You're* sorry?" he repeated, his voice full of deep confusion. "What the devil are you talking about now?"

"I had no right to criticize your conduct," she said in a rather stricken voice, "and it was wrong of me to accuse you of neglecting the countess."

By now he should have been well enough acquainted with Olivia to know that she never spoke or behaved in the logical, sensible manner he anticipated. He should have known by now that the girl was nothing if not surprising.

He should have recalled such things—but he hadn't. So he had no one but himself to blame when he found himself wholly bewildered by her words.

"Don't you see what we are doing?" she asked, looking up into his dusky eyes with unmistakable sincerity. "We're fighting over the countess, you and I. It's really very senseless of us to be in competition with each other, for I think we each love the countess so very much."

Antony ran one distracted hand through his hair and muttered, not quite to himself, "You're the most unpredictable young woman!"

"Does that mean you agree with me?" she asked, brightening.

She received no answer to her question, and to gain his attention, she slipped her small hand confidingly in his.

The responding pressure of his long fingers tightening about hers made her hopeful. "You *do* agree with me!" she said.

He gave a short laugh that held little humor. "Yes, you atrocious young woman! I agree with you!"

"And you do see that I'm not trying to take your place in your mother's affections?" she persisted.

"But you did intrude upon the care her doctor prescribed," he said. "That I cannot allow, Olivia. You must not ever give her any medicines or draughts of any kind without my knowledge!"

"But the foxglove has improved her condition—"

"I know that."

"—and Dr. Birtwhistle quite approves of it!"

"And you may continue to give it to her, but nothing else. Don't mistake me, Olivia for I shall not be crossed on this. My mother's health is of paramount importance, and I have vowed that I shall never again see her in the condition she was in when she returned from that near-fatal trip to Bath."

Olivia watched the shadow of worry cross his face, and her fingers instinctively tightened about his. "You feel guilty for having sent her on that trip, don't you?"

He didn't think he wanted to drag up that all-too-painful memory. "Wouldn't you?" he said in a harsh, strangled voice.

She looked up at his handsome face, at his expression so consumed with guilt, and her heart went out to him. His was not the face of a callous, unfeeling son, as she had once supposed. In his eyes she saw gentleness and affection and devotion—and she was filled with a sudden and keen desire to see his face reflect those same emotions whenever he looked upon her.

She said in a tender, probing voice, "I think you have been trying to make it up to her ever since. I think you feel her health and well-being are wholly up to you, that it's your responsibility to care for her."

"No," he responded quietly. "It is my privilege to care for her."

Olivia looked up into his dusky eyes, and she felt again that sudden swell of emotion. She could hardly drag her gaze away from his handsome face as a light fluttering began to dance within her breast. At that moment, she wanted nothing more than to stay with him forever, and she thought of the words he had flung at her in anger.

"You—you won't send me away, will you?" she asked in an uncommonly tentative voice.

He had forgotten about that petty resolve and knew a

sudden feeling of alarm that she might have taken him
at his word. "No, I won't. In fact, I hope you will stay,"
he said and realized immediately that his voice had be-
trayed how much he wanted her to stay.

She smiled brilliantly in return. "I promise not to be
a charge on you! I—I shall tell the countess I cannot
agree to her scheme to present me. And I shall tell her
firmly that she is not to send me off to parties with Lady
Coniston."

He shook his head slightly. "Let her have her enjoyment of it."

"Do you mean you will allow her to present me at the
queen's drawing room?" asked Olivia, afraid to trust that
she had heard right.

"Yes, I'll stand the blunt for it. And tell Lady Coniston
there is to be nothing nip-cheese about your presentation.
I confess, I should like to see you properly gowned."

Olivia's heart quickened, and she couldn't prevent herself from taking a small step toward him. "Would you?"
she asked in a slight, breathless voice.

He looked at her with a sudden light glimmering within
the depths of his dusky eyes. With an effort he forced
himself to ignore her tantalizing nearness and the feel of
her slim fingers, still twined with his. He said, rather
sternly, "We're straying from the point."

Her gaze never wavered from his. "What point is that?"

He was having the devil of a time concentrating on
anything except for the fact that she was standing so
close. "The point is that I am responsible for my mother's
care and well-being," he said, trying hard to sound gruff.
"And I did very well with that responsibility until you
came along and upset all the peace and tranquility I have
worked so hard to establish!"

She was far from cowed. Instead, her brown eyes widened with sudden amusement. "What new crimes are you
accusing me of now?"

He couldn't very well tell her that she left his emotions in a state of turmoil every time her eyes met his, or that the closeness of her slim body made his fingers burn to touch her. He said instead, with a notable lack of conviction, "You—you read my mother romantic novels!"

She laughed. "But the countess *likes* them! She is a true romantic, I assure you. She dearly loves to think all men are as dashing and all women as brave and lovely as those within the pages of a gothic adventure."

"They're not," he said reasonably.

"But they *could* be, with just a bit of effort. At least, that is what your mother and I believe. Haven't you ever supposed a man and a woman could fall instantly and hopelessly in love?"

He hadn't thought so earlier in the day, but after a mere matter of hours spent in the company of Olivia Charteris, everything about his well-ordered and logical life had been reduced to little more than rubble at his feet.

She was the most abominable young woman, but she was also intriguing and astonishingly lovely. And when she smiled and laughed at him, his body responded with a radiant warmth that seemed to touch his very soul.

"Never mind. You needn't answer," she said, saving him from the trouble of forming a sensible reply. "I think I have a very good idea what a practical and reasonable man as you will think of such emotion!"

She laughed again, and his attention focused on the delicate curve of her lips. In that moment he wanted nothing more than to kiss her, and he couldn't think of a single reason why he shouldn't. Slowly, alert to her reaction, he lowered his head toward hers.

Olivia had never been kissed before. Her father's profession had always provided an adequate armor against the advances of any of the neighborhood dandies who might have been attracted to her.

But she knew Antony was going to kiss her the moment she saw his dusky eyes looking down at her with an odd fire glittering within their depths. As his lips neared hers, she didn't resist, for she wanted to see what his kiss would be like.

It was not at all as she expected. His lips brushed hers lightly, tantalizingly—and then they were gone. Gone so quickly she could hardly be sure she had been kissed at all. But she must have been, for her lips were parted in wonder and she was filled with a keen desire to be kissed again.

Antony watched her reaction, and a rather triumphant smile touched the corners of his mouth before he dipped his head to touch his lips to hers once more. This time, his kiss was lingering and tender and stirred a response within her that seemed to feed his own ardor.

His kiss grew more insistent as he let go his hold of her hand to gently tangle his fingers in her chestnut curls. The feel of his touch at the back of her neck sent a wave of sensation through her. Instinctively, she raised her arm to encircle his neck, and she felt his other hand at her waist, gently pressing her up against the hard, muscled wall of his body.

How long he held her in his thrall with that touch at her waist and the caress of his lips on hers, she really had no idea. But when at last his mouth left hers, she felt suddenly bereft and a little bewildered by the overwhelming feelings surging within her.

Antony looked down at her and smiled slightly. "Well? Were those the actions of a practical and reasonable man?"

She looked up at him with a becoming flush to her cheeks. "No more than mine were the actions of a vicar's daughter!" she said, bemused. "Are you very much shocked that I let you kiss me?"

He shook his head slightly. "No. But I'm very much pleased."

Still blushing, she said in a rather dazed but happy voice, "I hope your kissing me means you are at last convinced I am not a gypsy. And that you don't think I'm a charlatan intent on stealing from your mother."

He frowned. "Forgive me. I don't think I ever really thought so of you."

She cast him one of her teasing looks. "Horrid man," she said but there was more affection than censure in her tone.

He didn't think such a loverlike tribute should go unrewarded, and he promptly pulled her into his arms and kissed her again. But this time, his kiss was more demanding, and his hold about her slim body was thrillingly possessive.

Moments later, Olivia struggled from an embrace that threatened certain suffocation. "Oh, dear! What if everyone is watching us from the house?" she asked.

"You've picked a deuce of a time to be the practical one," he said; but he released his hold of her a little, and she slipped rather reluctantly out of his arms.

"Your mother shall think I am lost to depravity!"

"My mother shall think only that I have come to love you just as she has."

Olivia regarded him with serious, searching eyes before her kiss-bruised lips parted into a dazzling smile. "And I—I think I love you, too," she said in a tone of happy wonder. "Even though you will insist upon being logical and practical!"

"We do have our differences, don't we? Who would have thought a few hours ago that we would come together like this?"

"Your mother, for one," said Olivia pointedly. "Frankly, I think she was very hopeful that we should make a match of it."

Antony thought back to earlier in the day when his mother had spoken of Olivia with such affection. "Good God, I think you're right! What a calculating woman she is, to be sure!"

"I would imagine," said Olivia, "that a loving and devoted son would not keep his mother in suspense, but would tell her she was right to think all along that we should suit."

"I have a rather dreaded notion that I shall spend the rest of my days being manipulated by the two of you," he said grimly.

But Olivia found a way in which to soften the prospect of such a horrid fate by once again stepping within the circle of his strong arms and raising her lips toward his in a most inviting manner.

Antony spent several very pleasant minutes kissing Olivia before he left her in the garden with the promise of his speedy return.

He entered his mother's apartments to find her in her bed and Lighthill arranging her pillows and blankets comfortably about her.

Lady Granfell dismissed her maid and said, "Lighthill has given me my sleeping draught, so you shall have to speak quickly, my dear. I fear I shall soon be fast asleep!"

"Shall I stay with you until you drift off?" he asked gently as he drew a chair up to the side of the bed.

"I should like that. Tell me, did you enjoy your walk with Olivia, dearest?"

He gave a short laugh. "It was more revealing than enjoyable, I think. What an extraordinary young woman she is, to be sure!"

The countess smiled, sleepily. "I *knew* you should like her. Did I not tell you so?" She cast him a defiant look and said, "I mean to present her at court, Antony."

"I know. She told me."

"And you don't object?"

"Being well-acquainted with that stubborn streak of yours, would it matter to you if I did?"

Her smile grew brighter. "Not at all!"

"Why do you want to present her, Mother?"

"Because only then will she be acceptable to all the very best families."

"So you mean to find her a husband?" he asked, and silently cursed himself for not having uttered that simple sentence in a more casual tone.

She gave him a meaningful look from beneath her sleepy eyelids. "I am hoping I won't have to look far."

He was a little startled for a moment; then he said, "I imagine I know how to take that!"

"I imagine you might."

"So you intend to play the matchmaker with us, do you?"

She ignored the question and said, "Olivia is a very attractive girl. Well, *isn't* she?"

There was no use denying it. "Yes, she is attractive."

"And you always told me you would gladly give up your bachelor state and marry if ever you made the acquaintance of an attractive young lady who was just like me."

"And so I shall," he said with a soft smile of affection.

"Then I intend to hold you to your promise, you horrid flatterer! Olivia *is* just like me."

His smile disappeared slowly. So she had divined what was in his heart, had she? Well, he wasn't yet ready to admit that her matchmaking scheme had been successful. With an eye to her reaction, he said, "Olivia is abominably headstrong and stubborn!"

"As am I. You have reminded me so on many occasions."

"And she blurts out whatever nonsense comes into her

head—either that, or she's attempting to manipulate my mood by teasing and cajoling!"

"A complaint you have often voiced in my direction."

"No, I thank you! Olivia Charteris is much too impertinent and much too critical of me to ever form any regard for me."

"Critical of you?" repeated Lady Granfell, her attention arrested. "Why, dearest? What did she say?"

He recalled that his mother had always been a perceptive woman, and he tried to parry her probing question by responding with his most charming smile. "Oh, it's nothing. You know how Olivia is, I'm sure. She blurts out whatever nonsense has got into her head."

"I think you must be right," said the countess. "She has such a tender heart, I think she can be quite censorious of anyone she suspects of cruelty."

"Like me," he said quietly. The words Olivia had flung at him earlier had been lurking just beneath the surface of his consciousness. Now, her words came back to him in one rushing wave of guilt. He stood suddenly and took an agitated turn about the room. He felt unaccountably restless and tired of exchanging nonsensical banter with his mother when there was a more pressing matter on his mind. And Olivia, he realized, was the cause of it.

He went to the window, trying to summon the courage to ask the question he really wasn't sure he wanted to know the answer to.

Gazing out into the garden, he saw Olivia, still slowly strolling the pathway, awaiting his return. The light of day shone brightly on her chestnut curls, and the sun sketched a faintly provocative outline of her slim figure beneath the blue material of her dress.

Guilt and a burning recollection of everything Olivia had said to him at last drove him to ask the question he had been dreading. "Mother, have I been a neglectful son? Have you been very much disappointed in me? Be honest with me now!"

She was startled into opening her eyes very wide. "Neglectful? My dear, whatever put such a nonsensical notion into your head?"

He hesitated, his gaze still directed upon the garden and its lone occupant. At last he looked up and said without any trace of his usual confidence, "Perhaps I have not visited as often—there might have been times—if you were ever lonely—"

She stretched out her hand to him, halting his rather disjointed speech, and he went to her immediately.

"What talk is this?" she asked briskly, drawing him down to sit beside her on the bed. "Lonely, indeed! With Lighthill and now Olivia circling about me day and night as if I were a maypole?"

"Lighthill is an employee!" he said rather scornfully. "She is paid to be with you!"

"When you put it that way, she sounds rather mercenary. Of course, Olivia is *not* paid to stay with me. Neither is Lady Coniston, and she remains quite constant in her affection for me."

"Lady Coniston is not a member of this family," he said pointedly.

"No, she is not, but I should shudder to think of any member of our family being forced to hang on my sleeve!"

"But—but are you never lonely?"

"Antony, I beg you will not tease yourself over such thoughts! If you are asking if I think you have provided well enough for me, the answer must certainly be, yes. I have this very lovely house, which, I daresay, you paid much more for than you will ever admit to me when you know very well I would have been quite content to have the dower house. And you provide me with a household

full of servants and a shocking allowance that is the envy
of all my acquaintance."

He looked doubtful. "But from the moment I established you here, I have visited you not above once a
week."

"And for that I am truly grateful!"

He was a little startled. "Do you mean you do not want
me to visit you?"

"Only if it pleases you, my dear, but never more often
than that. Don't you know I could have no more pleasure
than to see you happily settled in life and busy at your
own affairs? I would much rather you had many more
better ways to fill your days than keeping your mother
company."

"How would you rather I spent my time?"

"Filling your nurseries with my grandchildren!" she answered promptly.

That made him smile. "Do you never give up?"

"No! Not when I am so close to having my dearest wish
come true. And if each of those dear little grandchildren
should have dusky eyes like yours and chestnut hair the
very color of Olivia's, I shall be very well pleased."

He tried to frown discouragingly. "If you think for one
moment that you shall find a daughter-in-law in that
abominable bit of baggage walking the garden lane . . ."
He stopped when he saw the rather knowing gleam in
her eye.

"You may bluster all you like," she said, in a rather
faint voice that still managed to convey an air of authority,
"but don't think you shall dissuade me from hoping that
you and Olivia might make a match of it."

He was quiet for a moment, then said, "Do you know
that earlier today I accused Olivia of being something of
a scheming temptress?"

"Did you? How horrid of you!"

"Exactly!" he said in a gently amused voice. "Because

I see now that it is *you* I have to fear! Tell me, Mother, has that been your plan all along? That Olivia and I should make a match of it?"

She nodded slightly. "From the moment I first saw that dear girl at the vicarage, nursing me with such tender concern, I have thought of nothing else but that she should suit you very well indeed!"

Antony watched her close her eyes again and realized the medicine she had taken was having its effect and that she was having a difficult time staying awake.

He leaned over to bestow an affectionate kiss upon her forehead. "I can see it shall do me no good to resist you and your monstrous schemes. I suppose there is nothing for it but that I return to the garden and see if Olivia will have me."

She gave a sigh of great satisfaction. "Then leave me, for I am very close to sleep, my dear. And you, I believe, are very close to losing your heart."

"What makes you think I haven't done so already?" he asked gently.

She opened her eyes just long enough to cast him a teasing look. "In the space of a single afternoon? What utter nonsense!"

He smiled again and bestowed one last affectionate look upon her before he left the room.

The countess was feeling very well pleased with herself when at last she slipped off into a deep sleep, filled with quite the nicest dreams she had had in years. Vivid dreams, they centered around a nursery filled with grand-children, each with dusky eyes and chestnut curls.

# *DARLING DAUGHTERS*

## Jeanne Savery

# *LOVE*

Thinking he heard girlish laughter, Lance Atterley pulled his sorrel gelding to a stop well within the edge of the woods. Hidden there, he listened carefully. Was it possible? *Could he possibly be hearing what he thought he heard?* He heeled Thor, setting his mount to a walking pace, and peered between the trees until the happy scene in the meadow was revealed.

It *was* possible! Lance smiled to see his darling daughters so happy, laughing as they pranced around and around a woman he had not met. A closer look revealed her to be a young woman he had noticed whenever he had managed one of his erratic appearances at the village church.

Then, as his youngest, almost five, dropped to her fanny, his fist clenched around Thor's reins. But as he watched, his seven-year-old swung her arms out and stilled while the eldest, all of eight years now, dipped, spread her hands wide, and lifted one foot. All three froze, and Lance relaxed as he realized it was merely a game they played.

Elizabeth stared between the trees straight into her father's eyes. Her gaze widened as she realized who was watching, and she wobbled disastrously, her face turning bright red. "It's Father," he heard her hiss to the others.

The three girls, even little Mary, instantly turned into the prim and proper young ladies they had become since their mother died and his grief left him unwilling to be near them for any great period of time, beloved though they were. All three looked far too much like Beth and were painful reminders of his lost love.

But that alteration in his behavior had been temporary, and he knew, now, he should never have put such distance between himself and his unhappy children, all of whom were becoming strangers to him. He had said as much in his last letter to George. His elder brother had testily advised him, as he had done more than once in the past, to rewed.

Which was, thought Lance, rather insensitive of him—especially given George's own plans to remain *unwed*, once his much beloved wife succumbed to the dread disease that had hold of her!

Lance's thoughts reverted to his daughters' unhappiness, and he wondered if it had been an error to remove the girls from the home they had known as babes. But he himself had found it impossible to stay where Beth had been the bright and guiding light of their days. He had felt impelled to go somewhere he wasn't known, somewhere he could put his life back together.

The minor and previously unvisited family estate, Redding Manor, where he knew no one and no one knew him, had seemed the perfect solution. Sunk in a grinding grief Lance allowed no one to touch, he had ignored his new neighbors' early visits of ceremony, and now, though it seemed absurd, he found himself forced to continue living in the isolation he had once craved. An isolation that continued simply because he had not obeyed propriety's stringent rules and left cards on those same neighbors in return!

One flouted propriety at one's peril, however. By the rules, no future invitations could be tendered to him or by him. Which was too bad, since the need to be alone, something very real two years earlier, had waned. As he had been told at the time of his Beth's death, grief eased, became bearable, and then, although it never totally disappeared, became something one noticed only if it were called to mind.

At least it had for him. Sometimes he wondered if his daughters would ever recover, would flower and grow and be the happy children he vaguely remembered from before their mother died.

He looked again at the frozen scene in the spring-lovely meadow, and in some confusion, he realized they *had* recovered—*just not when they were near him*. He didn't understand that, but he would get to the bottom of it. And the first step, perhaps, was to discover the identity of the young woman who had achieved this miracle.

Lance decided he rather liked the way the stranger's little chin set at a determined angle at his approach, the way her eyes flashed a warning. Although he didn't quite know *what* warning. But he definitely approved of the protective way she held Ellie's hand, her other laid on Elizabeth's shoulder while little Mary backed up against her until he wondered the child didn't push her over. Their behavior told him his children liked and trusted the young woman. Which was good. They had not seemed to trust anyone much for a long time now.

"Good morning," he said politely, dismounting and leading Thor nearer. "You were playing at statues, were you not? I seem to recall that it's a very good game."

*Good heavens, why do they stare so?* he wondered.

"Good morning, Father," whispered Elizabeth. She seemed tense, holding herself stiffly erect, trembling, he would guess, under the stranger's hand. "Miss Christian taught us," she said and added, a trifle hesitantly, "We didn't mean to . . . to . . . be disrespectful."

Disrespectful? Lance frowned. "In what way do you fear you've been disrespectful?" he asked sternly.

*Oh, Lord, did she have to flinch? What did I say or do to make her so afraid of me?*

"Tell me, child," he said more gently.

"Because of Mama . . ." The words trailed off, and she bit her lip.

"It's been two years, Elizabeth, since your mama died," he said when it appeared she would say no more. Taking pains, he spoke gently, but didn't think to erase the frown. "No one expects you to grieve forever. Besides, playing and being happy *isn't* disrespectful to your mother's memory. She'd *want* you to be happy." He glanced from one obviously disbelieving child to another. "Who has told you otherwise?"

"Madame Beaumont, Papa," piped up Eleanor, stepping forward and putting her hands behind her back. "She is always telling us we must not be loud and boy-something . . ." She glanced at Elizabeth.

"Boisterous," whispered Elizabeth.

"That word," said Eleanor, nodding. "Besides, she says noise gives you the headache."

A muscle jumped in Lance's jaw. *"Did* she, then?" he asked when he had put reins on his temper. How dare the woman tell his beloved daughters such a bouncer? And in what other ways might she have lied in his name! He glanced at the young lady hovering over his children. "I don't believe we've met," he said a trifle shortly, still angry.

Her chin rose a half inch farther. "I am Miss Christian Pelling, sir. I do not hold with young children being forced to sit still and mind their needle all day every day or that they be allowed nothing in the way of exercise or some part of each day in the fresh air. It is not healthy."

"I don't hold with it myself," said Lance, drawing surprised looks from his offspring. "Is this something else your Madame Beaumont has laid at my door?" he asked politely, thinking this young woman had a delightfully forward spirit that she would chide him in such a way. Why he found it both amusing and proper instead of pert and unpleasing, he hadn't a notion. Perhaps it was that she defended his young from a woman he had quite suddenly taken in strong dislike!

Eleanor, who appeared to be the leader of the nursery party, looked from her older sister to her younger and back at her father. "You don't get headaches when we're noisy and boy—that word?" she asked with only a trifling hesitation.

"I wouldn't know, since I've never been tested," he responded, trying for a touch of humor. "You girls have never behaved so loudly I might hear you! In fact, my darling daughters, once or twice I've been strongly tempted to come up to the nursery to see if you still live there!"

He noticed Miss Pelling relax at his wry words. What, he wondered, had the girls said to her that she had looked at him so? It had been rather unpleasant to have such a very attractive young lady watch him with such fierceness and what he was forced to interpret as disapproval; he felt a warming pleasure now that the censure had disappeared.

Still, not one of them relaxed their guard to the point they would continue their play. Lance felt it unfair to interfere in a treat much enjoyed by his daughters, and failing to come up with a notion that allowed him to enjoy it with them, he decided he must be satisfied he had accomplished more here than he had managed during weeks of mulling over the problem of the girls' unhappiness. While blaming his loss of their company, the loss of their affection, on his own behavior, he had not had an inkling how to change the situation.

But now, with new information to think about, he would leave them to their joy. Besides, it was imperative he have a chat with the dragon he had hired to see to his daughters' welfare. Although he knew he had faults, putting off a distasteful duty was never one of them, and now, while his daughters played, would be just the time to interview the woman.

Lance gathered his reins into his left hand. Still overly quiet and far too wary, the three girls and Miss Pelling watched him mount Thor. He tipped his hat, and all four curtsied, the young lady with grace and his daughters with a deal more awkwardness than he thought necessary!

Frowning once again about that last tidbit of information—what was the Beaumont woman about not to have taught them a proper curtsy?—he rode off, pretending to care nothing about what they did. He didn't look back until he was well into the woods. There, where he could still see but not be noticed himself, he pulled Thor up and twisted around.

The four had their heads together, talking. He wished very much he could hear what was said. . . .

"But you see he is *not* so very disapproving," Christian was insisting. "You are wrong about that."

"But Madame says . . ."

"I've a notion about *that,* too," said Christian, interrupting. She went on more slowly, asking, "Do you suppose it isn't your father who gets the headache, but your governess herself? Is it possible she blames *her* disapproval of noise on *him,* because you will not like to upset your father, but you *might* he willing to disobey a governess?"

The girls thought about that, Mary with a finger in her mouth looking from one older sister to the other, the latter staring into each other's eyes in silent communication. Again it was Eleanor who spoke first. "But if that is so . . ." She trailed off and looked at Elizabeth.

Elizabeth, her brows slightly twisted, asked, "Miss Christian, what do you think we might do about it? I mean, if Father does *not* wish us to . . . to . . ."

"To behave like sticks because he, too, thinks that shows respect for your mother as your Madame Beaumont has taught you?" The two older girls giggled, Elizabeth covering her mouth with her hands. "You know, girls, there for a moment I thought your father was wishful of joining us in our play," said Christian whimsically, and then she sobered, looking from one girl to the next. "But we weren't very welcoming, were we?"

"Papa? Play a game?"

Eleanor looked doubtful, but Elizabeth, old enough to *almost* remember how it was before their mother died, swallowed. Hard. Her eyes glistened. "He used to do so! *Then*. I remember once he put me up on his shoulders and . . ."

The tears overflowed. Christian pulled the child into her arms, rocking her back and forth.

When Elizabeth's cheeks had been wiped and little Mary's sympathetic tears scrubbed off as well, Christian asked what their mother had been like. "Did *she* play with you?"

"She read stories," said Eleanor, doubtfully. "Didn't she?"

"Yes," said Elizabeth. "And she'd sit and watch us, her sewing in her lap. And she'd laugh with us and she'd sing."

"Oh, yes. I remember her singing," said Eleanor, brightening. "I do remember that."

"And was Madame there?"

"Oh, no," said Eleanor firmly just as Elizabeth said, "We had Nurse then."

Again Elizabeth's easy tears spilled down her cheeks, Mary joining in for company, and again Christian wiped away the moisture, this time with a handkerchief that was a trifle damp.

"Do you know what I think?" asked Christian, sitting in the grass and pulling Mary onto her lap.

"Tell us," said Elizabeth.

"I think your father didn't know what to do when your mother died. I think he asked someone for advice and I think he was told to hire someone to take over the nursery and I think he advertised, and when Madame came he read the letters of recommendation she gave him and they were very likely unexceptional; so he hired her. And then"—Christian hugged little Mary—"he was so unhappy about your mother dying, he didn't think to see if Madame really was the sort of good woman he wished to have a care for you."

"So what do we *do?*" asked practical-minded Eleanor.

Christian swallowed. She suffered, herself, from such losses, first her mother and then, within months, her father. She could empathize not only with the girls, but with their bereaved father. Still, it was one thing to come up with *why* the overly stern and emotionally cold Madame Beaumont was given charge of the children, stifling normal childish behavior in every way possible. It was an entirely different thing to decide what one might do about it.

Did Mr. Atterley know how his nursery was run, what a tyrant had charge of it? Should he be told? Did she *dare?* Oh, dear. She was coming to love these children very much indeed. Too much, perhaps! In any case, she must do something.

"Miss Christian?"

"I'll think about it," said Christian brightly.

Did she have the nerve to march up to their father after church next Sunday, formally unintroduced, as they were, and speak with him? Explain to that stern man about his girls? Assuming, of course, that this was one of the rare Sabbaths he kept by coming to church! For that matter, would she have the opportunity if he did appear. Her aunt had no liking for the sun and was usually unwilling to stay in the churchyard, as many of her neighbors did, gossiping and then discussing the sermon with the vicar—and returning to their gossip the instant their rather scholarly vicar moved on to another group of parishioners.

"So tell us what you think we should do while you think about it, please," said the persistent Eleanor, tugging at her skirt. Eleanor was the sort who liked to be certain she understood things thoroughly.

"I think . . . maybe go on as you have? Things *are* better now, are they not? She lets you come out with me, so the tedium of your day is not so great. It was," she said brightly, "a very good thing, her bringing you to that children's party where we met, was it not?"

"Yes, a very good thing," said Elizabeth solemnly, nodding her head in a rather portentous manner for such a young child.

"She *wouldn't* have," added Eleanor severely, "except the invitation was addressed to our father instead of to the nursery party and *he* said she *must*, that it was time we made friends in the neighborhood."

"Right then you should have realized he isn't such an ogre as you've believed," exclaimed Christian, pleased to learn the man had expressed concern for his girls.

"Why, so we should," said Elizabeth, obviously surprised.

"Except," objected Eleanor, "Madame said we'd been too noisy so he wanted us out of the house for a while, and *that's* why we had to go, remember?"

"Yes. I remember now," agreed the too easily led Elizabeth.

"Ah!" Christian resisted laughing. Elizabeth could not yet laugh at her own foibles. "But now you *do* know better, do you not?"

The girls nodded, although they cast each other one of those questioning looks so common between them.

"And now you need not be afraid of him, do you?"

Elizabeth and Eleanor gave each other a longer look. They turned back to Christian. "It wasn't hard when *you* were here, like today," said Eleanor, "but he frowns so."

He had frowned. Quite fiercely, remembered Christian. "Do you think he was frowning at *you?*" she mused out loud.

Still again, the older girls consulted each other silently, their gazes locked. Eleanor turned back to Miss Pelling. Carefully, she asked, "What do *you* think?"

"I think, maybe, he frowned mostly because he didn't like what he heard about Madame Beaumont. Maybe he'll have a word or two with her and she won't be quite the dragon she's been."

*And,* added Christian silently, hopefully, *maybe I won't have to find an answer to what you can do to change things!*

Again Eleanor and Elizabeth exchanged that odd stare. "I don't know . . . ," said Eleanor after they had communed for a time. "Madame Beaumont . . . well . . ." The girls' eyes met again, and their thoughts set their mouths tightly shut. They looked at their feet. Eleanor took in a deep breath and looked back to Christian. "I just wish, maybe . . . you *might* decide what we can do? Just in case? Please?"

Christian wondered that children should be so cowed, but decided it wasn't a good idea to ask what they had *not* told her about their governess. Not when so much emotion had already flowed. Better if they were to get back to behaving like little girls! She set Mary on her feet.

"Well"—she got herself up from the ground—"what I've decided *right now this minute* is that we should have a race to see who can first reach the pond and our picnic basket!"

As usual Eleanor won the race, Christian, holding Mary's hand, coming in last. Mary plopped down on the rug Christian had spread when they had first come out to the meadow, and Christian took a moment to study the older girls.

Their complexions were rosy and their eyes bright, unlike when she had first met them. Thank goodness she had volunteered to help organize that neighbor's children's party. The Atterley offspring had arrived just a little late, and she had immediately tried to lead them into the noisy game of blindman's bluff which had been going on for some time, but they had hung back. They had continued to do so when asked if they preferred to play London bridge is falling down.

Christian had been deeply shocked to discover the Atterley girls didn't know the rules of the simplest games! When they had first met, the girls had been too pale, as quiet as little mice and just as shy, without the least notion of how to go on. Feeling compassion for the silent creatures, she had taken it on herself to help them in every way she could.

She had talked with their Madame Beaumont during the period when, for once as contented as all the rest, the girls ate the feast provided for the party goers. She pretended interest in the governess's problems, learned she was another who disliked the sun, and asked permission to take the children for walks. Madame Beaumont, pretending to hesitate, rapidly agreed when Christian pretended to take back the suggestion.

Thus the afternoons in the outdoors began. Although it had been nearly a month now, they still didn't know all Christian thought they should about play, but they were healthier-looking, their skin no longer pasty, and their hair had come alive, was more lustrous, better groomed. Christian thanked her aunt's cook for their health, her picnic baskets packed with the fruit and cheese and meat.

The better grooming was her doing: after the girls ate, she would brush first one child's hair and then another's as she told stories, making up tales about three little girls who liked to dance and sing and play and never never never had to think about being quiet!

Miss Christian's opportunity to speak to Lance Atterley came—and went—without her contriving anything at all. In fact, the situation so surprised her, she was unable to take advantage of the moment when, eschewing his usual practice of leaving the instant services were ended, Mr. Atterley walked up to her uncle, Lord Merkham, and brusquely asked if they might make an appointment so he could speak with his lordship.

Mr. Atterley didn't so much as look Christian's way until he had made the desired arrangements and then, a quick glance and sharp nod, and he had walked to where his daughters waited in the charge of a young maid.

"Well," said Lady Merkham, her eyes popping. "What do you think *that* is all about?"

Her mild-mannered, softly spoken husband, whose spine, however, was made of good cold iron, responded, "I've no notion in the world, my dear. I assume I'll discover his purpose when he comes by later this afternoon."

"Probably has to do with some boundary he's decided isn't right," suggested Lady Merkham with a sniff. "The man hasn't a notion how to go on in the county. Why, he's never said so much as a friendly hello to anyone that *I've* heard of. Not even on those rare occasions when he manages to drag himself to church!"

Lord Merkham smiled sardonically. "You hit the nail on the head, my dear. Even today he didn't say so much as a friendly hello. He straightaway asked when it would be convenient to see me, did he not? Obviously you are correct and he hasn't a notion how to go on."

"I believe I will *not* provide refreshment which was my first thought," mused her ladyship. "When you are finished, my lord, you may show him the door. I see no reason to trouble myself to do the polite when he can make not the least effort himself!"

"Very sensible, I'm sure," agreed Lord Merkham, guiding his lady toward their carriage. He glanced back to assure himself his niece followed.

She didn't.

"Christian, my dear, come along now," said Lord Merkham when he discovered she stood like a stork, staring after Mr. Atterley.

Christian was watching Mr. Atterley gather up his offspring, who awaited him in the charge of a plump little maid, and lead them toward their carriage, but her uncle's words startled her out of her circling thoughts.

"What? Oh, yes. Yes, of course, Uncle."

*Was Mr. Atterley going to complain about me?* Christian wondered. Was it her little scold that had him frowning that day they met and not what he had learned about Madame Beaumont? Had she irked him so much he meant to have words with her uncle? And come to that, where *was* Madame . . . ?

"And don't dawdle," ordered her aunt. "I cannot abide this sun. You, Christian, spend far too much time out of doors. It cannot be good for one, I am sure," she continued when everyone was seated in the carriage. "You *must* take better care not to become brown as a berry, which, if you do not remember your bonnet when you go out, you *will* be, and then what shall I do with you?"

"But," asked Christian, perplexed, "what has my complexion to do with anything?" She settled herself more comfortably on the forward seat and looked, inquiringly, across at Lady Merkham.

"Good heavens, Christian, are you all about in your head? You will be very nearly twenty when you come out of black gloves and one is finally allowed to present you. Not that we'll do anything fancy, of course," she warned, and added, "but then you can *expect* nothing very much, can you, the way you are situated? I expect we'll do quite well enough for you at the local assemblies. There are several widowers round and about who may think you capable of taking on the responsibilities of their nurseries for instance. Or a farmer who will think having you is a step up the social ladder. We'll see . . ."

"But why would I need to go to assemblies to find a position in a nursery?" asked Christian, bewildered.

Her aunt stared at her. "Do not be absurd."

"But I don't understand. I mean, even a governess doesn't, surely, go to assemblies?"

Lady Merkham stared. "I speak of *marriage*, of course. I wouldn't have such a close relative known to be a mere nursery maid or governess."

Christian felt a twinge of panic rise up in her breast, choking her. She fought it down. "You speak of . . . a marriage of convenience?" she asked diffidently.

"Something of the sort can be arranged, I'm sure," said her aunt complacently, but her expression then hardened as she went on, "*assuming* you do not ruin your complexion!" Waving her hand limply, Lady Merkham yawned widely. "I do not know how it is," she said crossly, "but I believe the vicar becomes more long-winded with each passing Sunday. I believe I'll go directly to my room as soon as we've eaten." She yawned again, patting her lips with her fan.

Christian judged there would be no more talk of her future, but wondered how she was to avoid the fate her aunt planned for her. Marriage without love, or at the very least without some caring, would be intolerable.

Surely, if she made herself useful, her aunt wouldn't thrust her into an unbearable situation merely to be rid of her. She had tried so hard to make a place for herself in her uncle's home, but it was difficult when her aunt so obviously resented her existence! Once or twice the notion that her aunt actually wished her ill had floated to the top of her mind, but, as she told herself, that must be an absurdity.

Christian recalled how despairing she had felt when her father died and how hopeful when her uncle had appeared at his funeral and whisked her off to his home, telling her he would take care of her from now on. He did, of course. He fed her and clothed her, and since even a marriage of convenience must require a dowry of some sort, then he would very likely dower her . . . but his wife made her feel as if each bite she ate was a bite stolen, and the woman appeared to grudge each ell of the black wools, and more lately, the gray and violet summer-weight cottons, that had been made up into proper mourning. So, if those reasonable and necessary expenses bothered her ladyship, what would she say to the outlay of a dowry which would be many pounds more than a simple wardrobe . . . ?

Christian's firm little chin set in the way it did as she put her mind to a problem. She would come up with a notion or two, she decided, and then find a moment when she could discuss her ideas with her uncle. Sometime when her aunt was not near! If nothing better occurred to her, perhaps her uncle would help find her a position with an elderly woman who required a companion. That would be far better than a marriage in which there was neither love nor respect, but only duty.

After all, if she must simply do her duty by someone,

then she would prefer to be paid for it, thank you just the same!

Later that afternoon Lancelot Atterley dismounted and glanced across the frontage of Lord Merkham's manor. A well-kept estate, he had decided months earlier when, absent-mindedly, he had allowed Thor to stray onto his neighbor's land. Now he saw that the house, although not huge, was just as well-kept, a plain man's neat country residence.

Atterley guessed he would probably like Lord Merkham. He hoped all went well today and that they could get to know each other and, perhaps, become friends?

He handed Thor's reins to a waiting groom and started up the shallow steps to the front door of the brick and stone house. There was a touch of the Netherlands in the architecture, common enough for the period in which it was constructed, but the casement windows were a newer development and had been installed sometime in the fairly recent past.

As Atterley studied the house, the front door opened, a footman bowing him in. "I believe I'm expected?" he asked, handing over gloves, crop and hat.

"Yes, sir. Right this way, sir."

Atterley followed, softly thanking the servant when the man opened the door to a long, narrow room, a combination library and study. Lord Merkham sat behind a wide desk dipping his pen into an ornate inkwell, but he looked up as the door opened and immediately wiped the nib on a pen wiper. Setting his writing instrument aside, he rose to his feet.

"Welcome to Merkham Manor," said his lordship.

"Thank you." Atterley reached the chair he was waved toward, and both men seated themselves. "It was good of you to see me so quickly."

"Think nothing of it." Merkham offered a variety of refreshments, all of which Atterley denied. A silence fell, and the men looked at each other, his lordship waiting for Atterley to open his budget.

But the silence became a trifle awkward, and Merkham cleared his throat. "What may I do for you, Mr. Atterley?" he asked, trying to decide whether he was amused or irritated by the man's inability to come to the point. He watched, with interest, as blood flooded his visitor's neck.

"I'm sorry," said Lance, startled. "I've fallen out of the way of behaving properly in company, and since I've the added difficulty of deciding how to introduce my topic when we are so completely unknown to each other, I, as is my habit, said nothing. The fact of the matter is, I have determined that . . . No . . ."

The guest broke off, biting the corner of his lip. He sighed.

"Well . . . ," he said, starting again, hesitantly, "I don't know if you are aware that your daughter has been kind enough to take a interest in my children? That she spends some of each pleasant day with my darling daughters?"

"I have no daughter," said Merkham calmly. Atterley made a movement as if to rise, but his lordship continued before his guest could complete the motion, "I've a *niece*, however. Christian Pelling, my brother's daughter. She was orphaned when her father died nearly a year ago."

Atterley relaxed. "I see."

After another moment's silence, Merkham decided he was going to have to help this awkward man along or they would never get to the core of this meeting. "Are you *unhappy*?" he asked, "that Christian takes an interest in your daughters?"

Again a startled look crossed Atterley's features. "Oh, no! To the contrary!" He looked down at his clenched fist, then back up. "This is so absurd! Why is it so difficult," he asked, smiling slightly, "to simply ask if you would be so very generous as to give me your dau . . . er, your niece?"

Merkham blinked and wondered if he had to do with a madman. "*Give* her to you, you say?"

The blood rose again in Atterley's neck, finding his ears this time. "In marriage, my lord. I would wed her."

"Wed her . . ." Merkham finally realized why his guest was behaving in such an odd fashion—after all, a man in love! But even so . . . his lordship eyed Atterley. "I wasn't aware you even knew her!" he said sternly.

"I know enough," said Atterley, remembering their meeting in the meadow—and the fact he had been unable to get the attractive young woman from his mind since that day. "I know she'd be very good for my daughters, and I know they need someone like her who will teach them, among other things, how to be happy again."

"Teach them?" Merkham pounced on the words as he eyed his guest. "It sounds as if you require a governess. Why, then, do you not simply hire her? My brother-in-law was something of a scholar, and to be perfectly frank, I rather fear he overeducated his only offspring. But, given that is true, I suppose it means she'd do very well as a teacher."

Startled, Atterley blinked, squeezed his eyes tightly shut and then blinked again. Finally he shook his head slightly, indicating indecision. "You would prefer that I *hire* her to *wedding* her?"

Merkham smiled as he realized his guest couldn't decide whether to feel insult, as indicated by a stiffening in his neck and shoulders, or to give in to laughter, which was revealed in his twinkling eyes. Laughter appeared to win over the first inclination, and Atterley grinned. Merkham liked that in the man, that he had a sense of humor. But it wasn't enough.

His lordship sobered. "It is a simple fact that I do not know you," said his lordship quietly. "So, in a word, yes, as things stand at this moment, I'd prefer you to hire her."

Atterley frowned.

"She could *leave* a position, you see," explained Merkham, "if things went wrong, but it is not possible to leave a marriage."

The frown faded, and the incipient smile returned. "I am pleased you have Miss Pelling's interests at heart, my lord. I assumed that as your daughter, marriage would be far more suitable than to offer a position . . ." A hint of the frown returned. "Surely the fact that she is your niece does not change that conclusion?"

"Perhaps I am odd in that I believe marriages should be made in heaven," said Merkham dryly, thinking of his own which was *not*. "The parties to a marriage need to know something of each other and to feel some affection for each other so that there is a chance of that. To know that their values are the same and their goals and their needs . . . ?"

Atterley nodded, drifting off into thought again and silent a trifle too long. He was brought back to attending his host when that gentleman cleared his throat, making of it a querying sound.

"Ah!" said Atterley, looking up and reading the questioning expression his host wore. "You wish to learn something of me and my background which is understandable. My lord," he continued abruptly, "will you think it very odd in me if I ask that you not pass on to your neighbors what I tell you?"

"Good heavens"—Merkham's brows climbed high up his forehead—"you alarm me, sir! Have we an escaped murderer among us? A bankrupt? Or, perhaps even worse in the minds of some"—Merkham thought of his wife!—"a well-heeled cit who would play off the airs of the gentleman he is not!"

"You mock me, my lord." Atterley relaxed at Merkham's quick shake of the head. "Or perhaps it is that you jest. Quite simply, I've no wish for the neighborhood to learn that I am heir presumptive to an earldom. George Atterley, the Earl of Morningside, is my much elder brother, you see. My courtesy title, which I don't use, is Lord Longtown."

Merkham frowned, trying to understand. "You do not believe you'll continue his heir and therefore wish that it not be puffed off?" he suggested.

"To the contrary. My brother married his childhood sweetheart, who is a poor thing and of a consumptive habit. He's cared for her for many years, but she's deteriorated badly recently and won't live much longer. George swears he'll not rewed, that it is my duty to provide an heir." A sad smile marred Atterley's expression. "You'll feel no surprise that George was not pleased when my wife died of a putrid sore throat before providing the necessary son!" He straightened, his face less revealing. "However that may be, I believe my antecedents are such they cannot offend, and my solicitor will convince you my income is more than adequate to keep a wife in the elegancies of life, all the pretty things a woman craves. I will, of course, make an adequate settlement so that if anything happened to me, Miss Pelling would not find herself in financial straits which, if I understood you, she does now?"

"I've set aside a dowry for her. It is not so large as a prospective earl might expect, but a decent sum, I believe."

"I suppose it is not in my interests to say so, but I'd require no dowry. What I *need* is the woman who, in a very brief time, turned my daughters back into the delightful children they'd nearly forgotten how to be!" Again that sad smile crossed Atterley's face. "I am deeply at fault. I believed I'd provided for my children and could indulge my grief for their mother, but all I actually did was give a sinecure to a beastly woman who should never have been allowed near anyone's children! I still don't see how she came to have such excellent testimonials," mused Atterley. "Ah, but you can have no interest in that except that I am much in need of your niece!"

Lord Merkham settled back in his chair, his lids slightly lowered over his eyes. Tenting his fingers, he tapped them together. "So," he said slowly, "you wish to marry again for the sake of your children."

Atterley nodded.

"At least in the first instance?"

Atterley felt his cheeks heat still again. "I do not understand you."

"Of course you do," retorted Merkham. "It could *not* be a marriage in name only. Not if you are still in need of an heir."

"That is correct."

"Hmm." Merkham tapped his fingers several more times. "I rather like my niece. She has often entertained me of an evening with a surprisingly good game of chess. She also has an excellent voice and even my wife deigns to listen when she reads aloud. I've had her by me less than a year and do not know that I'm quite ready to let her go. Besides, she is not yet out of black gloves. No, I do not think I can give you permission to wed my niece." He smiled at Atterley's obvious disappointment. "What I *will* do, is provide you the opportunity to court her."

Atterley perked up.

"I think we might begin this very afternoon when I'll suggest she show you my rose gardens." A duty his wife would avoid, given she hated sunshine. It would allow the young people time alone in unexceptional surroundings. "I am exceedingly proud of my roses, you see."

Atterley nodded. "You would give the girl the opportunity to know me before wedding me. That is reasonable. But"—he frowned—"how long?"

"Would a guess that you've given notice to your governess be amiss?" asked Merkham, smiling slightly.

"I doubt you need *two* guesses!" said Atterley, speaking with a certain dry humor. "She packed the day I spoke to her and was gone the next. Which leaves me in a dilemma. I lost my temper after a very short discussion with the woman. The situation was, of course, not *entirely* her fault. I should have discovered long ago what was happening and corrected the problem. But those references! Truly, I do not know how I *could* have known. What to do now, though . . ." Atterley shrugged.

"You'll discover I'm a bit of a busybody in our region, Mr. Atterley. So I've a suggestion for a temporary cure. Our neighbors to the east, the Tempests, have recently retired their nurse. The woman, a Mrs. Brown, has the use of a cottage in the village and a pension, but even so, my niece tells me she's unhappy. I suspect she's too young to have retired, but is, on the other hand, too old to find a new position easily. Your children are, you'll say, beyond the need of a nurse, but may I suggest you offer her a temporary appointment? I think you'd like her. She loves children and is very good with them."

"May I admit surprise that you know so much of the woman's situation?"

"I suppose," mused Merkham, "that it is more usually the province of the females of the house to know such things, is it not?" He sighed. "I'll confess to you, Mr. Atterley, that I deeply regret not having had a large brood of children of my own. I have, over the years, paid more attention than I otherwise might to my neighbors' nurseries. I'm known to many local children as an honorary uncle!"

"I see."

"If Christian weds you," said Merkham, "although in view of my niece's streak of independence"—he remembered the surprising interview he had had with her only an hour earlier in which she'd insisted she'd not accept a marriage purely of convenience—"it is not a foregone conclusion that she *will*, I'll be happy to add three more children to my long list of honorary nieces and nephews. Come to that," he mused, smiling, "I suppose I will even if she does not!"

As he spoke he rose to his feet, reaching for the bell-pull which hung by the fireplace behind him.

"I'll order refreshment in the back parlor which looks out over my roses. I enjoy looking at them, and it will give me a reason for suggesting you walk out with Christian." He turned and caught Atterley's eye, holding his gaze. "You will not," he said soberly, "take it wrongly if my wife is not so welcoming as you might like? She feels you have not made a proper effort to become part of the neighborhood, you see, and affects to feel insulted."

"I certainly meant no insult, but she is correct that I've been lacking in proper attentions to my neighbors. When I first arrived, my grief was still too new and I didn't care for company. I ignored those who left cards on me. Then, once I began to feel restless and perhaps ready to acquaint myself with those around me, I freely admit I hadn't a notion how to set about it."

Merkham chuckled. "I wondered if it might not be some such thing. I will undertake to introduce you around now I know you would not dislike it. There is, for instance, a sale in Burford next week. Most every man I know will be there. Perhaps you'll go with me . . . ?"

Merkham glanced at the door which opened after a light knock.

"Ah, John," he said, "please ask Cook to contrive something, a light refreshment suitable to the hour, and convey it to the garden room. Also, send up word to Lady Merkham and Miss Pelling that Mr. Atterley and I will join them there presently."

Merkham asked if Atterley were interested in horticulture, his own passion, and when he discovered the topic not unpleasing, he launched into a discussion of the problems of growing roses which lasted them until it was time to join the women. . . .

Lady Merkham was still grumbling when she and Christian reached the parlor. ". . . I do not understand it," she complained. "I am certain I informed his lordship I'd not offer that man so much as a glass of water! Why has he done this when he is aware I do not wish for the connection? Now it will be impossible to avoid it. It is too bad of him, but it is ever the way of the man. No consideration, Christian. Never a thought to my sensibilities. It is all him and his wishes which must be—"

She broke off as the door opened, but it was only the footman and two maids bringing in trays from which they arranged platters and bowls on a serving chest. The footman and one maid pulled the two halves of the table away from the wall, either side of the chest, and joined them together near the window, before laying the table for four.

All the time her servants worked, Lady Merkham fumed and fussed. The door finally shut behind them, the footman giving one last look to see that all was ready.

". . . and on top of that," continued her ladyship, raising her voice now the servants were gone, "he did not even ask if it were convenient. He might at the very least have sent a maid to see if I were resting before inviting a guest to stay. He knows it is my invariable occupation in the afternoon. But no. I'm certain it never crossed his mind. Instead he must—"

Once again the door opened, and Lady Merkham broke off in the midst of her tirade. She straightened, becoming quite stiff and adopting a disapproving look which did not soften by so much as an iota when introductions were made.

". . . and this is my niece, Miss Pelling. Christian, you have, I believe, made friends with Mr. Atterley's daughters?"

"They are very nice children," said Christian, not raising her eyes much above Lance's cravat. "I enjoy playing with them of an afternoon."

"So that is where you disappear to!" Lady Merkham's shrill voice grated on the ears. "It is too bad of you, Christian. You are never here when I need you."

Christian cast a startled glance at her aunt, looked quickly toward her uncle, and let her eyes drift toward Mr. Atterley. He smiled a commiserating smile, and she found she could not quite help smiling back. "I am sorry, Aunt, if you had need of me, but I thought it your unvarying custom to rest in the afternoon. You said, when I first came—"

"That is *not* relevant. You *should* be here in case I were to need you, but—" Lady Merkham seemed to realize her scold was not quite the thing with a stranger present. "I will not rebuke you. Instead, I believe this is a good occasion for you to practice pouring the tea. Do so now."

Once again startled, Christian stared at her aunt. She swallowed. "Are you certain?" Lady Merkham had made it *very* clear upon Christian's arrival that she was *never ever* to encroach on Lady Merkham's place at the tea table!

"Would I have said it otherwise?"

"Come child," said Lord Merkham soothingly, touching Christian's shoulder gently. "Do play mother for us. I will like to see your cheerful face above the teacups, my dear."

"Which is to say you are tired of my *sour* face there," said Lady Merkham coldly.

"You will have your little joke, my dear," said Lord Merkham, his hand a trifle hard around her arm as he drew her to the table. "My friend?" he said, looking at Atterley. "If you will take that place?" He indicated the chair to the right of Christian, seated his wife across from his niece and took the last chair. "How cozy. My dear, Mr. Atterley has expressed an interest in my roses. Christian," he added, turning from his wife, "you must take our guest around the beds after we've eaten."

"I expect Christian to read to me then," contradicted Lady Merkham, glaring at him.

"Christian will do as I've suggested and give Mr. Atterley a tour of my roses," repeated Merkham with a touch of the ice that meant his wife went too far. "I would go myself, but I've a letter which must be finished today as Mr. Atterley knows, since I was occupied with it when he arrived."

"You are imposs—" Lady Merkham gasped, shut her mouth tightly for a moment and then, sitting back, refused to eat or drink, holding to a disapproving silence, asking no questions, seeming not even to listen to the discussion of the region, all one could do and see around and about.

". . . the ruins at Minster Lovell where something of the church remains, and the old dovecotes are of interest," said Merkham. "Then, although His Grace is not in residence, his librarian is quite happy to take anyone interested in art or architecture around Blenheim. Too, there are assemblies in season in Oxford which we attend upon occasion. You will think them a trifle provincial perhaps, but we find them amusing enough, especially since we no longer go into London for the season."

"I returned to London for a few weeks last spring," offered Atterley, "and found it a dead bore. My brother asked me to visit, you see. But it is so full of toadies and climbers and not at all so comfortable as it once was. Or perhaps," he added with a quick, self-deriding smile, "it was merely that I'd no wish to be there and therefore refused to be pleased, seeing only the bad?"

"Surely you attended the opera? And you patronized the bookstores, did you not?" asked Christian, startled into speech.

"You would like to visit Hatchards, perhaps?" asked Atterley gently, remembering Merkham's comment about her education.

"My uncle is kind enough to take me into Oxford where there is an excellent bookstore, the scholars at the colleges requiring the very best, of course. I do not repine that I've never seen Hatchard's bow windows."

"Are you, perhaps, a scholar yourself?" asked Atterley, becoming curious about her interests.

"Oh, no. Not at all. I very much enjoy books written by those who have traveled in foreign climes. And I like biography and some history."

"Sermons?" questioned Atterley, assuming that would be of interest to a vicar's daughter.

Christian cast a shy glance at the handsome man speaking so kindly to her. If she didn't know how deeply he grieved for his much beloved wife, she feared she was likely to develop an infatuation for him . . . despite his children's opinion he was cold and withdrawn and not very loving. But, as to that, she had decided they were wrong, had she not?

"Do you like sermons?" he repeated.

"I fear I've not the proper sort of mind to enjoy sermons," admitted Christian primly, blushing slightly for the thoughts that had been running through her head which were far, indeed, from the topics covered in sermons.

Just then her aunt, proving she *was* listening, looked daggers at her, and Christian's blush turned into a painful flush. Perhaps she should not have admitted a dislike for reading sermons; but it was true, and surely one should not lie.

"Have we finished, my dear?" asked Lord Merkham, also noting his wife's sharp glance and wishing to prevent the sharper words that might follow. "Then, as that is so, you, Christian, should run up and find your bonnet and take Mr. Atterley out to view my roses. They are especially fine this year. You will remember which he likes best, Christian, so that I may have cuttings taken at the proper season and sent over. Or I will," added Merkham only half joking, "if you've a gardener who understands roses?"

Lord Merkham smiled broadly when Atterley assured him that if he did not, he would acquire one! His lordship watched Mr. Atterley hold the door for his niece. His company smile faded, although a hint of it remained in place as he laid plans for his niece's future. He wondered if she would have *several* sons—and if he might adopt a younger boy for his own heir. Not, of course, for the title, but his property was unentailed. Such an arrangement was common enough . . . although not perhaps at the level of society that Atterley occupied. Ah well, something to think about when the time came. If it ever did!

". . . you are not listening!" finished Lady Merkham, jerking on her husband's sleeve. "I am not pleased, sirrah! You *know* I had decided to have nothing to do with that man, and yet you force me to serve him at my table! It was not well done of you!"

"Have nothing to do with him? But my dear"—Merkham deliberately widened his eyes—"I do not see how you'll manage that. No, I do not see how that can be."

"I'll manage very easily," said Lady Merkham smugly. "I will ignore him."

"No, no, you do not understand. It is impossible. You cannot ignore my niece's husband!"

Lady Merkham's mouth dropped open. She closed it

with a snap. "Husband!" she repeated scornfully. "Surely you jest."

"I would never jest about such a thing," said Lord Merkham with a certain coldness. When assured his wife would not respond, he added, "You did not, you see, ask what he wished to discuss with me. That is it. A marriage."

"You've no notion who the man is! I'd not be at all surprised if he were a cit! You'll not wed your niece to a cit!"

"He has satisfied me as to his pedigree, my dear, and that is all you need know."

"You've agreed?" She didn't wait to see how he answered that. "You didn't think it proper to ask *me*?"

"Ask *you*? Ask *what*, pray?" Merkham's tone was touched with acid as he continued. "It is *my* business to see to my niece's future, is it not?"

Lady Merkham had first heard that slightly dangerous note in her lord's voice not long after their marriage, which, to the distress of both, had been forced by their families. She had quickly learned it meant she had reached ground over which he would allow her no trespass. As usual, her resentment at such treatment knew no bounds, and very nearly shedding tears of temper, she turned on her heel and left the room.

*Marry his nuisance of a niece to that handsome young man?* she thought. *Never.* By the time she was done, the chit would have nothing to do with the encroaching fellow. Whoever he was!

"I don't believe I've ever seen such lovely roses," said Lance, eyeing his guide's cheeks.

Christian, never slow, caught his compliment, and her sun-touched complexion turned a darker red.

"Such a lovely combination of colors, too," added Lance, teasing her.

"Uncle," she said primly, "has worked for many years to achieve the effect you see."

She waved toward the beds where one color faded into the next and that into another until one could barely understand how at one end of the long garden the roses had been yellow and at the other were bright red.

*So, the little Pelling is not a flirt,* thought Lance, and he wondered how one courted a woman who didn't flirt. "It is very impressive," he agreed, changing to a more normal conversational tone, and found himself pleased when Miss Pelling relaxed.

Christian concluded she had been wrong to think her uncle's guest flirted with her and wondered at herself for having suspected it for even a moment. She knew the neighborhood gossip about how deeply the man mourned his dead wife and sternly admonished herself that she was not, under any circumstances, to allow the growing admiration for him to become something deeper. But she must say something. It was impolite not to instigate conversation. But what and how? His children. . . .

"I hope you did not come to my uncle to complain about my playing with your daughters," she ventured when they had strolled a bit farther, stopping now again to admire a particularly lovely rose.

"Complain! Never. If anything I came to thank you for paying them much needed attention. I, to my great sorrow, somehow managed to lose touch with them and can't seem to get close to them again. I've been very worried about them, but hadn't a clue what to do about what I thought a very unnatural grief on their part. Some months ago I asked Madame Beaumont for advice, but she claimed it *was* natural and I was not to concern myself and"—his jaw clenched quickly once or twice, and his voice harshened—"fool that I was I believed her!"

"At first appearance, she has," said Christian slowly, "a natural authority which makes disbelieving her difficult.

She spun me a story when I asked permission to take the
girls out which—" Christian sent a quick sideways glance
toward Lance, noted his look of curiosity and, taking a
deep breath, finished, "which made me think you an
ogre! She insisted you wished your children trained to be
quiet as mice and, like mice, rarely seen. It was only when
I said I'd take the children to the far meadow that she
reluctantly, I felt, agreed to my doing so. Now I wonder
if she only pretended to be reluctant to be rid of them
for a while or, alternately, if she feared she'd lose control.
I cannot like the woman."

"Nor I now I've seen her for what she is. She's gone—"
His brows rose at her startled look. "You didn't know.
Your uncle kindly suggested a temporary replacement for
her, whom I must see when I leave here. Or—" He had
a sudden notion for prolonging their time together. "Perhaps you'd come to the village with me? I am to speak
to the Tempests' old nurse."

"Oh, yes. The very thing!" Christian turned a glowing
face his way. "Brownie will do very nicely! She loves children, so they cannot help but love her back; and where
there is love there is happiness, is there not?"

"It was certainly true for . . ." Lance looked away,
searching his mind for a way to finish which would not
refer to his dead wife.

". . . you and your wife," she said, sighing softly.

He sighed equally softly. "Yes."

Hands behind his back, Lance strolled on. Finally he
glanced her way and discovered her face set in slightly
sterner lines. He wondered at it, feared that reminding
her of his first wife had undone any closeness they might
have achieved that day and wondered how to regain lost
ground. Then, too, he wondered why it had become important that he reach his goal of wedding Miss Pelling.

It was, was it not, merely for the sake of his girls? The
fact she was an attractive young woman only a bonus?

"You did not answer me. I don't suppose," he said a bit tentatively, "that a walk to the village appeals to you so late in the day, but I would appreciate your assistance in explaining to the woman just what is needed and why I hope she'll come to us immediately . . ."

"I will be happy to do what I can," said Christian promptly. "If you can wait a moment, I'll tell my uncle where we go and collect my maid, who can accompany me home again when we've finished. Excuse me?"

"Oh, I will escort you home again, Miss Pelling. We walk to the village, and I must return for Thor, must I not?"

"Thor?"

"My horse."

"Oh. Well." She gave him a sideways glance. "Yes, but . . ."

"But, for propriety's sake," he finished for her when he noticed how flustered she was, "you must have your maid. I understand."


The next day Atterley joined Christian and the girls when they went out to play. And the next day. The following day it rained, and with no more notice than a note carried by a groom, Atterley and his daughters arrived at Merkham Manor to take up Christian and a maid and drive into Oxford, where she was to help choose material for new dresses for his daughters . . .

And so it went.

Lady Merkham continued set against the marriage and took every opportunity to stick a spoke in Atterley's wheel. "He only wishes a free governess for his brats," she said one day when certain her husband was truly gone beyond hearing.

Then: "He's still deeply in love with his dead wife and ever will be."

Another time she elaborated on the same theme: "You would go through life never knowing the meaning of love between a man and a woman," she said.

And on another occasion: "You've no knowledge of his family, Christian. Why, they might be the worst sort of manufacturers. Will you wish to spend the rest of your life in such society as that? Once wed to a cit, you'd no longer have entrée to polite society, you know."

And still again: "The man is a monster if he wishes to wed you, Christian, forcing you to become something far less than you are. He can have no respect for you, no affection, to draw you down into the mire he inhabits . . ." It had, by now, become a settled thing with Lady Merkham that Mr. Atterley was a jumped up cit!

Christian took in all her aunt's words, added a grain of salt to temper the spite, but even seasoning the bitter woman's advice with a dose of common sense, she knew Lance's proposal was for his daughters' sakes. He was pleasant to her. Occasionally he turned her a neat compliment in that teasing way he had. But he had attempted, in no way, to show her the least hint of affection, and she well knew she could never ever take the place of his beloved first wife.

The knowledge hurt. It hurt a great deal in fact, since she became more and more enamored of Atterley as she got to know the loving father, the honorable and intelligent man.

Unfortunately for her peace of mind, he was correct that his girls needed a woman's guiding, loving touch, so that although she felt she was foolish to put herself into the danger and pain of loving him when he couldn't love her back, she felt a need to help his girls. And then, late in the summer, the girls discovered their father meant to ask Christian to wed him.

". . . but you will, will you not, Miss Christian?" asked Eleanor, her great eyes shining with hope. "It is good that Madame has gone, but it would be ever so much better if you come live with us."

"Please?" asked Elizabeth softly.

Little Mary stuck her finger in her mouth, came closer, and leaned into Christian, looking up at her with those same huge eyes. Removing the finger, she said, "Pleath?" which was a great deal for a little girl who almost never said a word.

The girls needed her, yes, but, Christian wondered, *dare* she wed their father? Her emotions, whenever he came near, were almost more than she could manage. But perhaps, she thought, it was merely an *infatuation* and would go away when given no encouragement? How difficult it was to know since she had never before experienced the sort of feelings he roused in her.

However that might be, she *did* love his daughters, so when the time came and, among Merkham's roses, Lance made his formal proposal, she could not say *them* nay, even though, deep inside, she feared she would find nothing but pain by agreeing.

So, her eyes well open, Christian agreed to the marriage—or so she thought. She took to heart her aunt's lectures concerning Lance's deep grief for his lost wife and that it was nothing more than his love for his darling daughters that led him to take the drastic step of wedding again, and she warned herself sternly that she must never forget it.

Never forget, Christian reminded herself for the umpteenth time as she waited at the back of the church.

Her uncle, standing beside her to walk her down the aisle, watched her with slightly worried eyes.

Atterley's exceedingly excited girls, each holding a basket of rose petals to strew before the bride as she went down the aisle, waited as well, but they had no doubts of any sort,

His beloved daughters. Constant living reminders of his

first wife, Christian told herself. Studying them, she decided that it was their mutual love for the *children* that would be the glue holding their marriage together. If there could be no other relationship between herself and the man who awaited her at the altar, then there must be a good rapport based on their mutual affection for his girls.

## *MARRIAGE*

Lance watched his daughters romping in the long meadow grass as Christian laid out their picnic. "You know, my dear, you were quite correct to suggest we not take a wedding trip just now. My girls are adjusting much more quickly, I think, because we've remained here to reassure them they are important to us."

"Knowing they are part of a family is important to children," said Christian. She sat back on her heels and looked up at her husband of several days. Except, in one sense, he was *not* her husband. He wasn't looking at her, and given the opportunity, she stared for a moment, feeding those emotions she knew should be starved. Chiding herself, she returned to laying out the food.

The task finished, she called to the children and dished up everyone's luncheon. When they had eaten she told the girls their father meant to teach them to fish, and they all strolled toward the pond.

"You are frowning again," muttered Christian, just loudly enough for Lance to hear. He wiped the creases from his forehead and grinned at her before turning to his children, who watched warily. "Now, girls," she said, "your father will give you a lesson in fishing. Fishing is a delightful occupation one may continue all one's life, you see, and one which can be indulged almost anywhere one goes. Yes, Mary," she added, encouraging the overly

silent child's hesitant question, "it *is* true you must be
quiet or you will frighten the fish."

"But that is no problem for you girls, is it?" asked their
father, teasing them. "You have all learned so very thoroughly how to be quiet, have you not! You see? Not even
the awful Madame Beaumont's teaching is entirely to be
wasted!"

Eleanor giggled, but Elizabeth glanced at Christian before nodding. Mary actually stepped forward and grasped
her father's hand. "But we don't have to be quiet forever
and ever?" she asked softly.

"Only so long as we are fishing," he told her gently,
"and you need not fish for very long if you do not like
it."

Much to Christian's surprise, the girls did like it, but
she soon guessed why. They had been so suppressed, for
so long used to inactivity, that they had become accustomed to it. The fishing, therefore, was a novelty that did
not ask more of them than they knew how to give.

In fact, before very many days passed, Elizabeth and
her father would occasionally sneak away all by themselves
for an hour's fishing. Elizabeth began to blossom.

Mary, especially, looked forward to the late afternoons
in which, at Christian's suggestion, Lance joined the girls
in their nursery. He would ask to be informed when the
children's supper tray went up to them, and while the
girls ate their evening meal, he would read to them.

As soon as Mary finished eating and Nurse Brownie
wiped her hands and face, Mary would run to him and
ask to be taken up into his lap which, happily, he did. In
fact, the feel of the little girl snuggled against him, listening to his words, had love swelling in his heart until
he felt it might burst.

The only thing lacking from these occasions, from
Lance's point of view that is, was Christian. She told him
it was better if he had the time alone with his daughters,

that they would get to know him faster if she were not there.

"I mustn't complain, of course," Lance explained in a letter to his brother a few weeks into his marriage. "It was, in the first instance, for the sake of my daughters that I contemplated remarrying, and my relationship with them *is* changing, rapidly and for the better. So for the girls' sakes I must remember to take things slowly with my lovely but very young wife. Which means that under current circumstances, we remain at Redding Manor.

"Besides," he continued, his pen scraping across the paper, "if I understood your last letter, the situation at Morningside is deteriorating, and I will not put you to necessity of welcoming visitors. I was sorry to learn that my sister is so unwell, but, because of that, I'll not burden you with an introduction to my Christian. Eventually, when you feel able, you will come to us, of course."

Lance looked up from his letter at the sound of happy voices, glancing out his window when his attention was caught by movement. He thought back to when he had first seen Christian playing with his girls, much as she was right now. He had liked what he had seen then, but during the weeks courting her, he had grown exceedingly fond of her serious mind and the joyful and generous nature of his wife to be, to say nothing of more than a little attracted to her pert figure. Then, when she had diffidently suggested they not take a wedding trip, he had assumed she meant that she was still too shy of him to bear the thought of consummating their marriage.

It was all he could believe since it was certainly true that whenever he had ventured on the mildest of flirtations, testing the waters, so to speak, she had looked at him with such surprise he had always desisted . . . and there was the other side of the coin! Contemplating making love with Christian was leading Lance into exceedingly lustful daydreams, and he feared revealing his passion might very well frighten the young and innocent lass, who couldn't seem to see him as anything but the father of his daughters! So, because he feared putting his fate to the touch, he had agreed they should stay home and show his daughters the way of things.

But such thoughts were unprofitable. Lance turned back and reread what he had written and sighed. It was unavoidable, even under the happy situation of just wedding a woman he had unexpectedly begun to love, that his letter concerning that woman to his brother could not be illustrative of his happiness, but must tend toward his brother's *unhappiness*. If only his brother's wife were not ill! If only George were looking forward to the contentment and joy he believed would be his own lot! Eventually.

When he had sorted out his relationship with Christian! Ah well . . .

"My dear George," he added, "my thoughts are with my sister, your wife, my prayers that she suffer no pain as she continues along the path set for her. All my love to you both. . . ."

He read it through once more and sighed again. It was not what he liked, but it would have to do. He signed it with a flourish. As he settled his pen in the inkwell, Lance heard a welcome sound. He raised his head, a smile lightening his serious expression. Christian had suggested another picnic and fishing in her uncle's stream, and if his ears did not lie, then his womenfolk were coming to pry him from his study and haul him off on their little adventure!

And how willingly he would allow himself to be pried loose! How wonderful that, thanks to Christian, he had already become so well reacquainted with Elizabeth and Mary. Eleanor, with her skeptical and independent mind, was still a trifle stiff, but he was optimistic she would soon thaw.

Quickly, he folded his letter, scrawled the address and sealed it. An anticipatory smile crossed his features as he hurried to stand in one of the windows. There he waited, his back to the door, his hands folded behind him, as he pretended to contemplate the weather, which, come to look at it, was lovely, very obviously a perfect day for a picnic.

The door cracked open, and he heard whispers. He smiled more broadly, but wiped the grin from his face. He must pretend to be surprised when his girls tiptoed up behind him and hugged him. It had become a delightful game with them—and for him as well! When little Mary's arms came around his leg, he lifted his arms and looked down.

"Why, what is this? My darling Mary, is it not?"

The child nodded several times grinning up at him. She had most speedily adjusted to their new life, most promptly accepted her father was a nice gentleman who was willing, often, to give out treats of one sort or another. Even to be lifted into his arms, as he did then, seemed to please the chit. The others managed to stay behind him as he turned to Mary, and now he looked around, pretending bewilderment.

"But, Christian, my love, do I not have more than the one child?" He heard muffled giggles and smiled. "I am almost certain . . . is there not another? Even *two*, perhaps?"

Elizabeth and Eleanor burst around to stand in front of him. They curtsied, and Lance noted how much those curtsies had improved since Christian entered their lives.

She had told him the first week of their marriage how shocked she was at how ignorant the girls were. They could sew a fine seam, even little Mary, which was amazing at her age, and the older two were far advanced in the art of embroidery; but none of them knew their letters with any certainty, let alone how to read, and Elizabeth, at least, should be reading easily.

So Christian spent most of each morning in the small schoolroom beside the day nursery at the top of the house teaching his girls. Then she spent too much of the afternoon with his housekeeper and in the kitchen with his cook, or so *he* thought, and then, he had discovered, she would make the rounds of his few tenants or help the vicar with problems the villagers would bring to the poor man's haphazard attention. In other words, she did everything but spend time with her husband!

Which he regretted and worried about. Oh, he didn't regret the teaching. And he understood the importance of her work for the vicar because Christian had the knack of prying his parishioners' problems out of a mind that was preoccupied with much higher things than that the Widow Jones hadn't enough to eat or that Miss Selwyn was acting very strangely . . . This last Christian was describing at dinner that particular evening.

"She was very carefully cutting the top off each carrot and laying the fronds precisely east to west when Mrs. Rose looked over her fence. It is very odd, don't you think?"

"Poor lady. Has she enough money, do you know? Would worrying about where her living is coming from have turned her head? I could, perhaps, give her an annuity, if it is that?"

"How like you to think of something you might do to help!" exclaimed a glowing Christian. "Like when you ordered Cook to send the Widow Jones a basket each day for her dinner!"

Christian's heart filled with love and pride at her husband's thoughtfulness, and she rushed on before she should reveal her feelings which were *not* fading as she had hoped they would, but growing harder and harder to control.

"Dr. West thinks it is her age," she said. "I did not precisely understand all he said, and when I asked, he admitted he doesn't understand the why of it either; but evidently it is not unknown for unmarried women of a certain age to become a little . . . strange? He said it *sometimes* happens to married ladies as well, but not so often." Christian sighed. "He warned me there was nothing I could do, but one feels one should try . . . ?"

"If the doctor says there is nothing you can do, then, Christian, I fear you might only make things worse if you interfere."

"What I thought was that perhaps she'd like a puppy. The coachman's bitch had a litter some weeks back. They are nearly of an age to be weaned. I know Miss Selwyn had a dog which she loved perhaps too well! When one loses a pet, it is difficult to face replacing it, but I thought that maybe if I were to ask her, as a favor, to take one of them so it need not be destroyed . . . ?"

She stared at her plate, waiting to hear what Lance would say, unable to meet his eyes for fear she would reveal the longing she felt that he could love her if only a little bit. . . .

"Why don't you ask Dr. West, my dear? I frankly admit it is not a situation with which I've ever had to deal!"

Was there a touch of wry humor in that? Christian glanced at him quickly, quickly looking away. "Or I," she agreed, smiling slightly. "Ah! I believe I forgot to tell you that Mrs. Tempest's cousin has come to visit. She is rather younger than I'd thought, a very nice lady, although perhaps a trifle more quiet than one would have expected of someone related to the Tempests! And Colonel Wright has returned from Town. He was rather loudly complaining about how difficult it is to drive among the multitude of carriages which seem to have become more common in London than when he was young. He says he wishes he hadn't retired. It was much less dangerous being in the army!"

Lance chuckled as she had meant him to do and suggested they play chess. It was a game they both enjoyed not only for the intellectual stimulation, but for reasons neither would admit: the occasional brush of hand on hand as both reached across the board to straighten a piece, the touch of a foot under the table, the fact that they were—although again something neither admitted— sitting very near each other for upward to an hour, or, occasionally, even longer. . . .

Lance, in particular, found those evenings over the chess board difficult. It was, it seemed, next to impossible to get close to his wife, and the longer they lived under the same roof, the more Lance wished for that closeness! But, he reminded himself, he must be patient. He *would* be patient . . . even if it took his skittish wife a full year to feel comfortable with him!

"Speaking of the neighbors, my dear . . . ," he began one evening as they rose from the table, in response to a story she told of Sir Michael complaining that the smith had done a bad job of shoeing his team.

He guided her into the salon where he would drink a glass of port and Christian a cup of coffee as they talked. Discussions he dragged out for just as long as he could manage, since it seemed the only time of day she was his!

"Yes, speaking of the neighbors," he repeated when she was seated and had her coffee beside her, "I wonder if it is not the thing for us to hold an entertainment. A sort of introduction to the neighborhood? For both of us? I, after all, am something of a stranger to most, though I've lived here some time, and I think it is considered the thing for a young lady to be reintroduced once she becomes a married lady? I should like introducing my wife to all and sundry, I think . . ."

Christian's cheeks glowed. He couldn't tell if it was embarrassment or if it was trepidation or perhaps her flags flew from the pleasure of contemplating company . . . or if it was simply that she didn't know how to answer him. . . .

Christian might have told him. If she had dared. Simply put, it was that she didn't *feel* like a wife and, instead, felt strongly the hypocrisy of being introduced as such when, truly, she was not. It would be an ordeal, when what she felt herself was, despite the vows made in church, more a besotted servant or infatuated governess, ready and willing to do her best to fulfill her lord's least wish.

*Anything he wished!*

"Does the thought of organizing a party frighten you?" he asked, attempting to discover her problem.

"Oh, no!" She was well trained, she believed, and could do what must be done in preparation to welcome neighbors to their home. But her color didn't fade.

"My dear?" he asked, bemused. "Am I in error? Is it *not* proper for us to hold such a party?"

"It is entirely proper," she said and determinedly controlled her wayward thoughts, something which became more difficult with each passing day. "I will attend to it at once. Would you prefer a fete," she asked practically, "or a dinner or perhaps a soiree, my lord?"

"Which would you prefer?"

Thinking of the disastrous wardrobe her aunt had chosen for her when her uncle insisted one be provided, Christian responded as casually as possible, "Oh, something in the afternoon would be best because—"

Dare she ask Lance if she might order a new gown, a more mature-looking dress with a more matronly design? Merely from the local seamstress of course? Or would that be a terrible waste when she had more clothes in her closet than she had ever had before? No, she didn't dare. . . .

"—because then the tenant families and the villagers

may be invited as well. For games on the south lawn, you know, and races and perhaps"—she remembered a church fete her father had organized for which he had spent his own money on an exceedingly frivolous but happy notion—"you might contact that odd family in Stow-on-Wold, the one which does tricks and tumbling, and I've heard they even walk the slack wire. The children in particular would love such entertainment."

"An excellent suggestion."

Actually such an elaborate party was far more than he had had in mind, but wasn't that a good thing if she felt up to it? And, couldn't a good thing be made even better?

"Would it be too much," he asked a trifle diffidently, "if we provide fireworks just after dark? I know of a man who makes pinwheels and set pieces. They could be safely arranged in the pasture beyond the ha-ha, could they not?"

"That would be of all things delightful. And dancing . . . ?" she asked, glancing his way hesitantly, but for once meeting his gaze. She drew in a deep breath. "I believe it is rather costly to hire musicians, but we could clear the threshing floor if it would not be too much."

"Perhaps *two* sets of musicians," mused Lance, remembering fetes at Morningside when he was growing up. "The country people could dance their dances in the threshing yard in the afternoon and early evening and the quality after the fireworks and in the house." He recalled there was no ballroom as he had in his old home. "At least," he said quickly, "I believe there would be room if we clear the two salons, opening the one into the other."

"*Two* orchestras . . . Oh, yes, that would be excellent . . . but, so very costly?" Christian cast him a worried look.

"*Too* expensive, you fear?" Lance smiled, but sobered

when his wife of just a few weeks nodded. "My dear, did not your uncle explain to you my situation in life?"

"He said I was a very lucky young lady and that you would care for me very well indeed; but he didn't go into detail, and I've always had to worry about where the money for this or for that will come from, and well, I suppose it is habit?"

"I am glad you feel able to explain such things to me, my dear," said Lance softly. "You must never fear to ask about what you wish to know. And, my love"—he flashed a quick, mischievous smile—"just so you won't worry, allow me to tell you that unless you wish to purchase the king's crown jewels or perhaps buy up Windsor Castle for a winter residence, then you need not worry about spending my money! In fact, perhaps I should ask if there isn't something you need? I understand now why I've not noticed any bills related to *your* spending, although I told your aunt to explain that I've arranged for you to buy what you wish in Oxford, the bills to be sent directly to me."

Christian's eyes widened, and her mouth opened slightly.

"Ah. She did *not* tell you." Lance sighed. "My love," he asked with overly done politeness, "will you think me lacking in sensibility if I just mention to you that I think your aunt is a small-minded woman who enjoys setting all at odds?"

Christian giggled and turned fully toward him, meeting his eyes steadily for the first time in weeks. "Please, my lord, will *you* explain to me what I should know about money?"

Feeling that at last he was taking steps toward the closeness he longed for, Lance made the required explanations, and when he finished, Christian told him about her gowns which she felt improper to her new status.

The very next day, Christian, with her husband for escort, drove into Oxford. There they ransacked the mercers for a dozen dress lengths and the necessary trims, all of which were instantly carried to the most highly recommended modiste in town. With the woman's help and Lance's advice, Christian bespoke a brand-new wardrobe of just the sort of gowns a newly married young woman should wear, quite unlike those the small-minded Lady Merkham had chosen!

Feeling just a trifle small-minded herself, Christian went to bed that night wondering if she would confound her aunt when she appeared in church one day soon in one of her new outfits! The blue, with the darker blue pelisse, perhaps? Worn with the new bonnet with the feather which curled down around her cheek, dyed to match. And the lovely new gloves with the tiny buttons at the wrist and new shoes and . . .

. . . And best of all, although no one would know but herself, one of the new silk chemises next her skin! Lance had not stayed with her when she made those particular purchases; but he had had a word with the shop's owner before he went off to take care of an errand of his own, and oh, such lovely delicate intimate wear she had been shown. And had then *actually dared to purchase,* which was still more amazing!

What an orgy of wonderful surprises the day had held. Christian's heart filled with love for her wonderfully understanding husband. She wished for about the thousandth time that Lance was not so deeply in love with his first wife and that he would want more of her than as a mere companion of an evening and, most importantly of course, someone to care for his darling daughters. . . .

With the party to see to, Christian's already busy days were complicated by the extra work involved in such an entertainment. For the first time in a long time she felt the need for her mother, or for someone she could trust to give good advice. As much as she regretted it, she couldn't trust her aunt. And she wasn't well enough acquainted with her neighbors to go to one of them.

But, by good fortune and early on, the brand-new wife had discovered her husband's housekeeper was a surprisingly knowledgeable woman. Christian was far too sensible not to go to her when she needed help. The motherly woman was so delighted that the demanding Madame Beaumont had disappeared, something she laid, and rightly, at the bride's door, that she gave that help unstintingly.

Better yet, she did so with such tact Christian never once was made to feel she was a badly brought up young woman who had been thrust into a position far above what she should have expected. Which the woman might easily have done.

On the day of the fete Christian put on the very special new gown that was designed in such a startling way that by making a few adjustments to the bodice and with the addition of an overskirt, it would do very well for both the afternoon and the evening. A maid who had a light touch with hair had been assigned to help her, and when the girl finished, Christian looked at herself in the long mirror set on a stand near her windows and gasped softly.

"Is that truly me?" she asked.

The maid giggled. "You do look a treat, my lady."

"If I do, it is thanks to you, Libby. Thank you for your help. Oh, dear, I'd best hurry, had I not?"

Totally out of character, Christian rushed from the room, giving not one thought to the mess resulting from her preparations. She stopped at the top of the main stairs and looked down to where her husband stood consulting his fob watch. He glanced up, and slowly, a smile widened, his eyes lighting up.

"I look all right?" she asked anxiously, not certain how to take his good humor.

Did she, after all, look a *guy*, a little girl dressed up in her mother's clothes, perhaps?

Lance took the stairs two at a time, stopping just below her which put his face nearly on a level with hers. He grasped her upper arms gently. And then he kissed her. Not just a little peck, but a lingering gentle pressure against her willing mouth. . . .

A moment later his butler pushed open the servants' door and stepped into the hall. Her heart beating like a drum, Christian wondered where it might have ended if Frey had not come in and Lance lifted his mouth from hers. Oh, if only the butler had not intruded! Such tenderness was just what she wanted, what she needed . . . but, oh dear oh dear, she was so flustered she didn't know where to look!

A trifle sadly Lance smiled down at his obviously embarrassed wife, who looked anywhere but at him. It had been the impulse of the moment to kiss her. An impulse which had obviously left her upset, but . . .

His heart thundered under his white shirt and new vest at the thought.

. . . she hadn't *objected*, had she? Lance eyed the top of his wife's head a trifle thoughtfully. She *hadn't* objected. So? So he would try it again. But not now, he decided, albeit reluctantly.

Not when they must appear properly welcoming to their guests and deal, for the rest of the day, with the duties awaiting host and hostess at such a major celebration.

"Here comes the first carriage, my dear. Will you take my arm down the steps? You look good enough to eat, by the way. Don't stray too near the buffets or some hungry man might make the mistake of thinking you could be served up to him!"

Christian glanced sideways at her husband, her cheeks

so hot they must be as red as the carpet under her feet.
How dare he say a thing so . . . so . . .

"I shouldn't have said that," he apologized. "I have
embarrassed you. I merely wished you to know you are
beautiful in your new feathers and that I must be very
careful that some young man doesn't entice you into a
flirtation. I'd much prefer it if you were only to flirt with
me, you see!"

Was that, wondered Christian, a warning? An order?
She didn't know. "You needn't fear I'll flirt with anyone,"
she said, keeping her voice placid despite her raging emotions. "I don't know how."

Lance swallowed a chuckle. "I wasn't aware it was something one learned. I thought one was born knowing."

"Then it is a talent the fairies forgot to leave in my
cradle," said the still-flustered Christian a trifle tartly.
"Oh, it is my uncle," she said, turning the subject. She
looked beyond to where the carriage was pulling away.
"But . . . my aunt is not with him?"

"It would appear," said Lance, "that she is not. My
lord. Welcome to Redding Manor. I hope Lady Merkham
is not ill?"

"She didn't feel up to such a long day. And, as Christian knows, she isn't at all fond of the sun."

"Oh, dear!" Christian's eyes widened. "I didn't *think*.
She'll likely believe I chose such an entertainment to spite
her, and I did *not.*"

"Of course you did not," said her uncle quickly, "and,
although I did not wish to say so since it doesn't reflect
well on her character, she'd not have come *whatever* the
form of entertainment! . . . My dear child," he said in a
more kindly tone when Christian's frown did not fade,
"I'll not have you thinking you are at fault! You are aware
she didn't approve your marriage. She thinks that her
absence will make that clear to our neighbors without her
saying it, you see."

"She thinks me beneath her, I suppose," said Atterley, and decided then and there that if there was the least hint his wife was hurt by her aunt's attitude, he would reveal his connection to the earldom, since, given the woman's behavior, it must be that Merkham had not even told his *wife* the true situation! "She'll catch cold at that, I think."

"Yes, because I will be seen to approve a great deal." Merkham turned to his niece. "You look absolutely good enough to eat, my dear!"

Casting her husband a rueful look, Christian broke into laughter. "As you suggested," she said to Lance, carefully keeping her gaze pointed so it was not quite touching his, "I will be careful to stay far away from the buffets!"

Lord Merkham looked confused, and as Christian turned to welcome the Tempests, Atterley explained that using very much the same words a few moments earlier, he had embarrassed his wife no end. Then he, too, turned to welcome their guests, an occupation which went on for some time before they could remove from the front of the house onto the lawn where villagers and tenants were already organized under the careful eye of the eldest of Lance's tenant farmers, who had agreed to help with the games and races.

Lance's beloved daughters joined their father and Christian just before the races began, and as Christian had coached them, they offered up the prizes at the end of each race. The guests found it a delightful innovation, especially when it was little Mary's turn and she handed over the prizes to the boys winning the three-legged race. The little girl was careful not to drop the little bags of boiled sweets and said a softly spoken "congratulations," but no one missed how wistfully, hands tightly clasped behind her back, she stared at the hard candy as the lads each chose his first piece. One of the boys noticed, and grinning, he gave her one which Christian told Lance was likely to make the boy Mary's hero forever!

When the games ended the odd assortment of guests mingled on the lawns awaiting their turn at the long buffet tables. When the food had been served and everyone settled either on rugs or chairs or on benches under the trees with their meal, Christian began to feel the day might actually run smoothly after all.

As people ate, the acrobats from Stow wandered among them, juggling and doing tricks and occasionally forming a human pyramid which would then collapse in the most delightful of fashions, the acrobats tumbling off in all directions. Best of all was the daughter with her daringly short skirts who walked the slack wire set safely just beyond reach of even the tallest of the boys who might have tried jerking it just to see what would happen to her!

Many of the farm folk and some of the villagers were used to going to bed at an early hour, so the orchestra designated to play near the threshing floor tuned up as people finished eating the afternoon meal. A number of the more well-bred guests joined in a couple of the less boisterous country dances, and one of villagers actually enticed Christian onto the floor, much to the delight of the other dancers. That she had agreed only after looking to Lance for permission did her no disfavor among the watching matrons, either!

As the sun disappeared the musicians set aside their instruments, and everyone moved to the rising ground overlooking the ha-ha and meadow, where strange workmen had been busy keeping curious lads away from the dangers of the fireworks they had installed. Lance sent his head farmer and two of his footmen across the ha-ha to bring the lads away, telling them to say there would be no fireworks until everyone was safely on this side of the ditch which divided the meadow from the lawn.

Christian, primed by her dance on the threshing floor,

watched the splendid display with less interest than she had expected to feel. Instead, she wanted to dance. In particular, she wanted to dance with her husband! Just as the last few pieces were being readied, she remembered she was to change her day costume, and with a word to Mrs. Tempest, she moved up the hill toward the house. At the door, she turned and stared at a triple burst of light cascading above the last of the ground pieces.

As the burst of light faded, she hurried in and up to her room where, not wishing to interfere in Libby's enjoyment of such a treat, she removed the bodice insert, giving the gown a properly low evening décolletage. Then, fitting it carefully around just below her bust, she added the gauzy overskirt, which had been embroidered with huge sprays of flowers.

After a look in the mirror, she very nearly readjusted the neckline: she had never before shown so much chest and found it more than a trifle embarrassing; but she had been assured it was quite in the proper mode and not at all immodest, so she forced herself to go to her dressing table where she brushed her hair and was about to tie it at the top of her head when Libby scurried in and took over, scolding that Christian had not called her at once and, at the same time, apologizing for not being there when needed.

When Christian returned to the main floor and rejoined her guests, Lance instantly came to her side. "My dear, how lovely you look," he said, and again his eyes glowed with obvious appreciation of her looks. "Come now. One more touch will make you perfect!"

With gentle insistence, he removed her to his study where, telling her to turn her back, he lifted a lovely necklace over her head and settled it, his fingers warm at her nape where he struggled with the clasp.

He turned her, his hands on her shoulders. "Yes. I thought that would be just the thing."

Christian tried hard to see it, but when she dipped her chin, it covered the necklace. She fingered the jewels, trying to guess what it was like. "Lance?"

He grinned and, hands warm on her shoulders, pressed her toward one of the ornately framed gilt mirrors hanging either side of the fireplace.

When she saw what he had given her, a mixture of rubies and pearls set in a delicate filigree, she gasped. "Oh! Surely not for *me.*"

"And why not for you, my love? I neglected giving you a wedding gift, I think. Perhaps these will make up for it?" He held out a matching bracelet, the three rubies an incredible red, nested as they were within circles of rosy pearls. "Do you not like them?"

"How could one not like them?" she whispered, awed. "But surely it is too much!"

"It is next to nothing," he said carelessly. "Let me fasten this bracelet around your lovely wrist, my dear."

She stared at the top of his head when he bent to see the tiny clasp. He had called her his love! But, oh dear, he couldn't have meant it. Could he? Would he take her in his arms when he finished? Would he kiss her again? She forced her free hand to stay at her side, not rise to touch his hair. How she wished to be in his love, be in his arms. . . .

But she would, would she not? When they danced?

He finished, stood straight and smiled tenderly down at her, holding her gaze.

"Thank you," she whispered, very nearly overcome.

"I know another way you might thank me . . . ," he said suggestively, smiling at her.

Daringly, Christian rose on tiptoe and pressed a kiss to his cheek. Or she had meant it to be his cheek. Surely it wasn't her fault he moved. . . .

Lance's voice sounded a little raspy when he lifted his

head and stared down at her, his gaze very slightly somber. "Unfortunately, it is time we open our ball, my love."

"Open . . . !" The embarrassment she had expected was lost in the sudden worry his words raised. "Oh my, oh my. *Can* I?"

Lance chuckled. "Not only can you, but you must."

"No, no, you don't understand. I wonder if I know the steps!"

"You'll do just fine," he said, but wondered if she *did* know all the figures of the traditional cotillion. Perhaps he had best tell the musicians they would do only the first few measures before opening the dance up to everyone. . . .

Which worked very well. Christian managed the first movements beautifully, but then looked at him with just a touch of horror, obviously fearing the next combination. He smiled, made a motion to the orchestra and brought them to a graceful stop, bowing and smiling when she dipped into a quick but graceful curtsy.

The dancing became general then, and Christian, who had enjoyed the day so far, grew more and more unhappy. She had forgotten that as hostess, she would be obliged to dance with any and every guest who asked her . . . and it wasn't until just before supper that Lance managed to escape his own duties among the ladies to claim her.

Lord Merkham found them only a little after supper, complimented Christian on her planning and thanked the two of them for a delightful day. Many of the older guests followed his example and left then as well.

The younger ones, however, appeared set to dance away the night. Christian was just wondering how one gracefully made an end to such an evening when, with a flourish, the orchestra leader announced it was the last dance!

The Atterleys' lives changed after the party. Invitations arrived with regularity, and one evening a week, or even two, they found themselves entering their carriage and riding off to a dinner or a soiree or some other affair.

It was some time before Christian realized there was a bit of a competition going on among the local hostesses. Her delightful party had set them on their mettle, and not a one was about to let it be said the new bride had outdone her and that she had not invented some new and exciting form of entertainment as well!

But gradually, as the summer faded into early autumn and many of the local families left for the little season in London, life settled into a more placid existence. Lance found himself almost content. His darling daughters were once again the lively, loving, wonderful children he remembered. He had an attractive, intelligent wife who added much to his evenings and, when he could manage to think of an excuse, to his days.

So, all was right with his world, was it not?

Except that beyond the occasional stolen kiss, he had not yet managed to get any closer, physically or emotionally, to his attractive and intelligent wife! And, from his point of view, it was becoming more and more essential that he do so!

Then came the long-expected letter from his brother. It not only announced his sister-in-law's death but that the funeral, a private affair, was over and that after a few weeks rest, George meant to take his brother up on his invitation to visit. He now, he wrote, understood better why Lance insisted on moving to Redding Manor and away from scenes that only roused painful memories.

"My dear," Lance told Christian, after tracking her down where she talked with their housekeeper, "I've the sad duty to inform you, as I warned you must happen, that my sister-in-law has died. My brother will now visit us, coming sometime in the next few weeks. I don't know what must be done to prepare for him, but you will know.

I am sorry I can be no more specific as to the date of his arrival."

And then he went away to write his condolences and whatever he could find to say to a new widower at such a terrible time in his life. As he himself knew better than most, there was little enough one *could* say!

# AND EVER AFTER

George arrived. Subdued, but willing to be pleased, he was a pleasant addition to their little family. There was, of course, no entertaining since all of them were in mourning, but his lordship was content to enjoy Lance's little family—although he would, upon occasion, simply stare into space, lost to all around him. It wasn't until her uncle dropped by one day, as was his habit, that Christian felt free to ask, diffidently, for details concerning her brother-in-law and more about the man and his strange marriage, the end of which was in no doubt almost from the beginning.

"As I understand it, my child, he didn't leave her side the whole of the last few years," Lord Merkham said gently to Christian. "I suggest you go along with his desire for solitude and give him whatever you can in the way of a quietly happy experience of family life. I'm certain what he needs most is to feel that his brother and his brother's family are with him at this time."

So that was what Christian did.

The long autumn days with their morning mists and afternoon heat continued deep into the season. The poplars were heavy with their golden burden when Christian took the opportunity of a particularly fine day to organize what she feared might be their last picnic and fishing venture for the year. The girls were excited, and having arrived at their destination after a short drive, they tumbled from the carriage and pulled their father along with them toward the stream chosen for the day's outing.

George and Christian followed more slowly once Christian had given her orders to the footmen who would set up the picnic within a small grove a little downstream from the fishermen. "Lancelot wrote me, not long before your marriage," said George, "a long letter concerning his darling daughters and how worried he was about them. I believe he need worry no more!"

He smiled at her, and Christian smiled back. "They seem happy, do they not?" she asked.

"They *are* happy. You've done well with them, my dear," he continued as they strolled across the meadow lush with Queen Anne's Lace and wild poppy. He knocked at the head of one of the flat white flowers with his cane, looked at her, knocked at another, and finally, he said, "I'll admit I was a trifle *unhappy* when I discovered you were not yet carrying your *own* child, but since I've seen the love between you and my brother I'm assured the time will come when I'll see my heir teasing his older sisters." He cast her a quizzical glance accompanied by a rather impish smile. "Actually, half a dozen heirs would be better still . . . !" He smiled to see her reddening cheeks. "The Atterleys have not been a prolific family," he explained gently, "so it would be generous of you to provide us with a regiment of sons so that we never again find the family with no alternate line of heirs as we do just now."

Christian barely heard his last comments. His belief there was love between herself and Lance had caught her imagination to the point she couldn't care what else her brother-in-law said to her. Instead, her eyes settled on her husband, who helped little Mary set a line off the bank and settled her close beside him before he cast his own fly out over the stream.

"Yes, you love him very much, do you not?" asked George softly, smiling warmly. "I am so glad. My brother has been a very lucky man to find two such loving women."

"But," said Christian, startled from her exceedingly embarrassing thoughts, "*you* are not old. Surely you, too, will find another love?"

"I doubt it, my dear. There was always, from the first time I laid eyes on her, only the one woman for me. Elly was barely thirteen then, a bright imp of a girl just on the verge of womanhood. She was our nearest neighbor's daughter and I a fully grown man just taking up estate duties my father, who was involved in politics, was pleased to hand over to me. Elly had that odd grace one sees in a colt about to become a horse, that nervous energy and love of life you find in the young, almost-adult animal, of any species. I haven't a notion why I fell in love that day. Perhaps it was fated?"

The earl walked on silently for a ways, obviously remembering the past.

"From what I learned later," he said after a few minutes, "that nervous, coltish air was likely the earliest evidence of the sickness which became so obvious as she grew older."

He sighed more softly still, remembering those wonderful years before they knew of the illness, and then seeing Christian's commiserating look which he found painful, he added, "I'm sorry, my dear. I fear I'll be no company for some little time now, and if you do not mind, I will take myself off for a walk. Memories . . . ah, where would one be without memory? And yet, with it, we must endure the bad as well as find solace in the good." George stared into Christian's eyes. "Make many good memories, my dear sister. They are needful for when the bad times come . . . and they do come into every life, do they not?"

Remembering her own intense grief for her parents, Christian nodded.

"I knew you understood."

He turned away, walking off along the river, his hands clasped at his back and his head bowed. He looked so very sad, so lost, so . . . inwardly directed . . . that Christian hesitated, worrying about him, wondering if she should follow him or if he truly needed only a bit of time alone. She decided perhaps it would be best to ask her husband.

"George? Do himself a mischief? You mean . . . ?"

Christian, biting her lip, nodded.

"Oh, no, Christian, never would George do such a thing! He is unhappy as is any man who has lost a beloved wife, but he and Eleanor discussed what he'd do once she died, and he's determined to carry out their plan. He means to travel, you see. For many years he took her to Italy for the winter. They both enjoyed new experiences and new places, new people . . . but, fearing there'd be too many memories where they'd been together, he's going to Greece this time. The last few years they planned all the things they'd see there—all the while knowing she'd never go. But on such a lovely day we don't want to talk about such sad things. Can I not coax you into allowing me to teach you to cast a line, my dear?" he asked, teasing her, but hoping she would agree so he would have an excuse to put his arms around her.

Christian blushed, wanting very much to say yes, to feel him touching her, almost as if he were holding her . . . and very nearly she said yes. Then she wondered if George wasn't merely seeing what he wished to see when he said Lance loved her, that *wanting* to see a happy loving couple, he *did*.

"Maybe another time," she said, her eyes cast toward the ground.

"Well!"

She looked up quickly to discover Lance's brows arched high.

"You surprise me, my dear," he said. "Since, in the past, you've always given me a quite decided *no*, I'd concluded that perhaps you'd an aversion to fishing. But if you are willing to learn, it is not that?"

"I do not know if I'll like it, do I? But, in any case, not today. I'll just go see if Elizabeth and Eleanor are all right, shall I?"

She walked upstream to where the girls sat side by side, their faces a study revealing how very serious an occupation fishing had become to them. When Christian opened her mouth to ask if they were all right, Eleanor hissed that she was to hush. The child added a "Please?" as an obvious afterthought, and smiling, Christian strolled on up the path by the side of the placidly flowing water.

"What if . . . ," she muttered, but startled by her own voice she glanced around to see that no one was near enough to hear and closed her mouth tightly. *What if George is correct?* she thought. *What if Lance does . . . well . . . at least care for me a little? Enough he'd . . . that he'd be willing to give me a baby!*

There. The thought had finally been put into words. Christian wanted Lance's baby so badly. But what she wanted equally if not more was the closeness that she vaguely understood was required in order to achieve the much to be desired goal of having a child of her own. Not that she didn't love her darling adopted daughters, but she had not known them as infants, hadn't held their tiny bodies close or rocked them in their cradles or seen how they grew from babyhood to toddler to small child. And she wanted that.

But she also wanted to feel Lance's kisses, deeper kisses than those swiftly stolen when she never knew to expect them and was never properly ready to receive and respond to them. She *so* wanted to feel his lips warm on hers, both firm and soft as they had been the night of their ball—no matter how often her mind told her that was a contradiction!

And, although she didn't quite understand it, she wanted that long, lean body close, wanted him touching her in ways she couldn't even imagine—although she would wake from dreams in which she was almost certain she had dreamed of such things. Would he ever feel for her those necessary feelings so that he might want. . . . Christian drew in a deep breath and thought another formerly unformed thought: Would he ever want what she wanted?

Well, if he *did,* she concluded in that practical way she had, it would be a great change in their life, so perhaps it would be best if they were to wait until George left them alone again. It wouldn't be too much longer, she thought, not from something he had said only the other day at breakfast. Something about seeing his agent and making plans. . . .

Plans for the trip to Greece of which Lance spoke?

Christian turned and looked back toward where she had left her little family. The two older girls sat still as mice, their eyes on the water. Lance, farther on, drew back his arm and sent his line out in graceful curves over the water, or at least she assumed he did, since she was too far away to actually see the fly and the line attached to it. Little Mary wandered near by, pulling daisies from their stems and forming a ragged bouquet.

And, returning at a brisker pace from somewhere downstream, she could see George, still too far away to read his expression, but his renewed energy seemed a positive thing.

So. She would put aside all thought of her future with Lance until George removed from Redding Manor and she could have a quiet talk with her husband. He had once told her she must never fear to discuss anything whatsoever with him, so she would take him at his word and discuss the possibility of a baby for her to cuddle, a son, perhaps, for him, and an heir for George! Or even, as she vaguely recalled George suggesting, a whole clutch of heirs?

If, of course, that were not too much bother for a husband who had already been so very generous to her in so many ways. So very generous it seemed wrong somehow to admit she wanted more!

George departed, and the household settled back into the comfortable routine normal to it, when Christian decided it was time she take her courage in hand and followed Lance to his library which was where he went when she had gone up to bed that particular evening.

Actually, she had not gotten so far as her bed. As she unpinned her hair, she realized she had been making up excuses to avoid talking to her husband as she had promised herself she would do. She scolded herself as she brushed her hair. She brushed and brushed, trying to make up her mind to do it now, and not put it off any longer. And finally, catching her long hair in both hands, she wound it up anyhow and stuck a few pins in to hold it in place.

Lance glanced up from his book when she opened the library door and then just stood there. "Christian? Is something wrong?" He rose to his feet, closing his book and laying it aside. "My dear?"

Biting her lip, she came into the room and shut the door. And then found she couldn't make herself move nearer.

"Christian? You alarm me!"

"I . . . you . . ." Christian drew in a long breath. "You once said I should not fear to discuss anything with you."

"Nor should you." He bit off the words a bit shortly, saw that made her frown and drew closer. "My dear, I snapped, did I not? But it is only that you are acting strangely and you make me afraid. It is a man's tendency to snap and growl and otherwise become aggressive when he is afraid," he finished on a whimsical note and was pleased to see her relax slightly. "Come now. We will sit down and you will tell me all about it."

"I think I'd rather stand . . . if you do not mind?"

"I only mind that you hesitate to speak your mind!"

Once again Christian drew in a deep breath. "Something George said . . . it made me wonder. . . ." Again her words trailed off.

"Come, Christian. This is unlike you. George said. What did George say?"

"That-you-need-an-heir," she admitted, speaking in a rush.

"Well, that's true enough. Or it is if he holds to his determination not to rewed. But we will not let it concern us, my love. I will not have you made uncomfortable for such a reason."

"But . . ."

"No buts. I will never force you, if that is what you fear."

"But, it's that I fear you never will that bothers me!" she wailed.

Lance blinked at her words and almost laughed at her rising color and, at the same time, felt as if his head were in a whirl.

"My dear?" he asked cautiously.

Still again she drew in a deep breath, reminding herself she was a sensible person, a practical person. "I want children," she began. "But I don't want to make you do . . . something you don't want to do. I know you still love your first wife, and I would never wish to interfere in that; but I thought perhaps if it were not too much bother, then maybe, you . . . and I . . . could . . . well do whatever it is one does?"

Lance reached for his wife and pulled her into his embrace, holding her loosely, but allowing her to hide her blushes in his chest. He felt her hand tentatively climb up his chest to rest just over his heart and wondered if she felt how it slammed against his ribs at the thought of "doing what one does" to achieve the much to be desired heir.

When he was certain he could control his voice, he murmured, "I not only wouldn't mind, my dear, but it would please me very much to teach you what one does."

"It would? You can feel for me just a little affection, perhaps? Enough we can make a child together?"

"My dear, affection is such a *weak* word for what I've felt for you for such a very long time. I think I fell in love with you, just a little bit, that very first time we met, when you stood there, such a determined little Valkyrie, in defense of my darling daughters. That seed of love has grown, Christian. You are all my heart to me now, my dear." He touched her hair from which a faint scent of lemon wafted.

"You love me?" she whispered.

"Yes." He inserted a finger into the coil of hair she had loosely pinned up and wondered if it would come down as easily as it looked.

"But your wife . . ."

"*You* are my wife, Christian. I loved Beth with all my heart; but she is gone, and she would not grudge me a new love. In fact, she'd tease me dreadfully if I were to live my life a hermit only for her sake!"

"I was told . . ."

"Ah! That interfering aunt again? I really think," he said, when she nodded, "that I dislike that woman more each time we speak of her!"

"But it was not *only* her," admitted Christian, leaning back in his embrace and looking up at him earnestly. "It was well known in the neighborhood that you grieved deeply for your wife."

"I did when I first arrived, yes, but grief mellows and becomes comforting and warming memories when one allows it to do so." He moved his hands to her shoulders. "Christian, is it at all possible that you feel some affection for me?"

"Oh, I have," she said earnestly. "Forever, I think. But I feared my love might be a burden to you and that you would not want it, so"—she glanced up, away—"I hid it."

"And I assumed you were so shy of me that you did not wish for *my* love." He smiled. "How utterly absurdly we have behaved, have we not?"

"A silly misunderstanding," she agreed, nodding.

They smiled at each other. His smile faded. "Christian, before we proceed, do assure me this is what you want, because I do not think that I will manage to stop making love to you if we once begin . . ."

"I have wished that just once I knew you were going to kiss me so it wouldn't startle me and I could properly enjoy it!"

"Then, my dear, I warn you I am about to kiss you, and I promise you you will enjoy it very much!"


George William John Atterley was born ten months later.

His brother, Henry Lancelot Leo Atterley, was born eighteen months after that.

Their brother, Rufus Merrit Pelling Atterley, followed two years later.

And Louisa Christian Martha Atterley crowned all only a year after that.

After that, and it made no difference how deeply they loved each other, Lance and Christian had no more children.

Lady Merkham died when Rufus was fourteen, and Lord Merkham came to discuss the possibility of his adopting the lad. Christian and Lance discussed it, talked to Rufus about it, and finally agreed.

Henry was army mad almost from the time he first heard of the army, so his future was decided.

George was not told he was likely to become Earl of Morningside, because it was never impossible his uncle would fall in love again and remarry. Then word came from the Americas that on one of his rambling explorations, the earl had died of pneumonia, and forced to do so, Lance reluctantly stepped into his brother's shoes—just in time for his daughters by his first marriage to make their come outs as the daughters of an earl.

Elizabeth, Eleanor, Mary, George, Henry, Rufus and Louisa all had the great luck to have a happy childhood, and each grew to be a well-educated, affectionate, well-bred adult; so it was only just that eventually each achieved a marriage with his or her own true love and proceeded to provide the Atterleys with still another generation of happy children.

Occasionally, as her hair turned gray and her figure more matronly, Christian looked back on the first year of her marriage and shuddered at how close she had come to never knowing the great joys and the little sorrows of motherhood. If she and Lance *had* continued to misunderstand each other, would they have come to the point of a proper marriage? Ever?

Luckily they *hadn't* and they *did,* and Christian knew the joy of bearing affectionate children to go along with her darling adopted daughters, all seven of whom showered her with love all the years of her long life.

DANGEROUS GAMES        (0-7860-0270-0, $4.99)
by Amanda Scott

When Nicholas Barrington, eldest son of the Earl of Ul-combe, first met Melissa Seacort, the desperation he sensed beneath her well-bred beauty haunted him. He didn't realize how desperate Melissa really was . . . until he found her again at a Newmarket gambling club—being auctioned off by her father to the highest bidder. So, Nick bought himself a wife. With a villain hot on their heels, and a fortune and their lives at stake, they would gamble everything on the most dangerous game of all: love.

A TOUCH OF PARADISE        (0-7860-0271-9, $4.99)
by Alexa Smart

As a confidence man and scam runner in 1880s America, Malcolm Northrup has amassed a fortune. Now, posing as the eminent Sir John Abbot—scholar, and possible discoverer of the lost continent of Atlantis—he's taking his act on the road with a lecture tour, seeking funds for a scientific experiment he has no intention of making. But scholar Halia Davenport is determined to accompany Malcolm on his "expedition" . . . even if she must kidnap him!

## ROMANCE FROM JO BEVERLY

DANGEROUS JOY          (0-8217-5129-8, $5.99)

FORBIDDEN             (0-8217-4488-7, $4.99)

THE SHATTERED ROSE    (0-8217-5310-X, $5.99)

TEMPTING FORTUNE      (0-8217-4858-0, $4.99)

# LOOK FOR THESE REGENCY ROMANCES

SCANDAL'S DAUGHTER     (0-8217-5273-1, $4.50)
by Carola Dunn

A DANGEROUS AFFAIR     (0-8217-5294-4, $4.50)
by Mona Gedney

A SUMMER COURTSHIP     (0-8217-5358-4, $4.50)
by Valerie King

TIME'S TAPESTRY     (0-8217-5381-9, $4.99)
by Joan Overfield

LADY STEPHANIE     (0-8217-5341-X, $4.50)
by Jeanne Savery

*Available wherever paperbacks are sold, or order direct from the Publisher. Send cover price plus 50¢ per copy for mailing and handling Penguin USA, P.O. Box 999, c/o Dept. 17109, Bergenfield, NJ 07621. Residents of New York and Tennessee must include sales tax. DO NOT SEND CASH.*

## YOU WON'T WANT TO READ
## JUST ONE—KATHERINE STONE

**ROOMMATES** (0-8217-5206-5, $6.99/$7.99)
No one could have prepared Carrie for the monumental changes she would face when she met her new circle of friends at Stanford University. Once their lives intertwined and became woven into the tapestry of the times, they would never be the same.

**TWINS** (0-8217-5207-3, $6.99/$7.99)
Brook and Melanie Chandler were so different, it was hard to believe they were sisters. One was a dark, serious, ambitious New York attorney; the other, a golden, glamourous, sophisticated supermodel. But they were more than sisters—they were twins and more alike than even they knew . . .

**THE CARLTON CLUB** (0-8217-5204-9, $6.99/$7.99)
It was the place to see and be seen, the only place to be. And for those who frequented the playground of the very rich, it was a way of life. Mark, Kathleen, Leslie and Janet—they worked together, played together, and loved together, all behind exclusive gates of the *Carlton Club*.